GAME

BOOK 1 IN THE SILVER GILT TRILOGY

GAME

P.M. VANCE

First Paperback Edition
Cover art and design by *the*BookDesigners
Cover images © Shutterstock

The Library of Congress Cataloging-in-Publication Data is available upon request.

Paperback ISBN: 979-8-9905192-0-6
Hardcover ISBN: 979-8-9905192-3-7
eBook ISBN: 979-8-9905192-2-0

Published by PM Vance Lit, LLC

For additional book information and author inquires contact: email pmvauthor@pmvance.com or visit www.pmvance.com

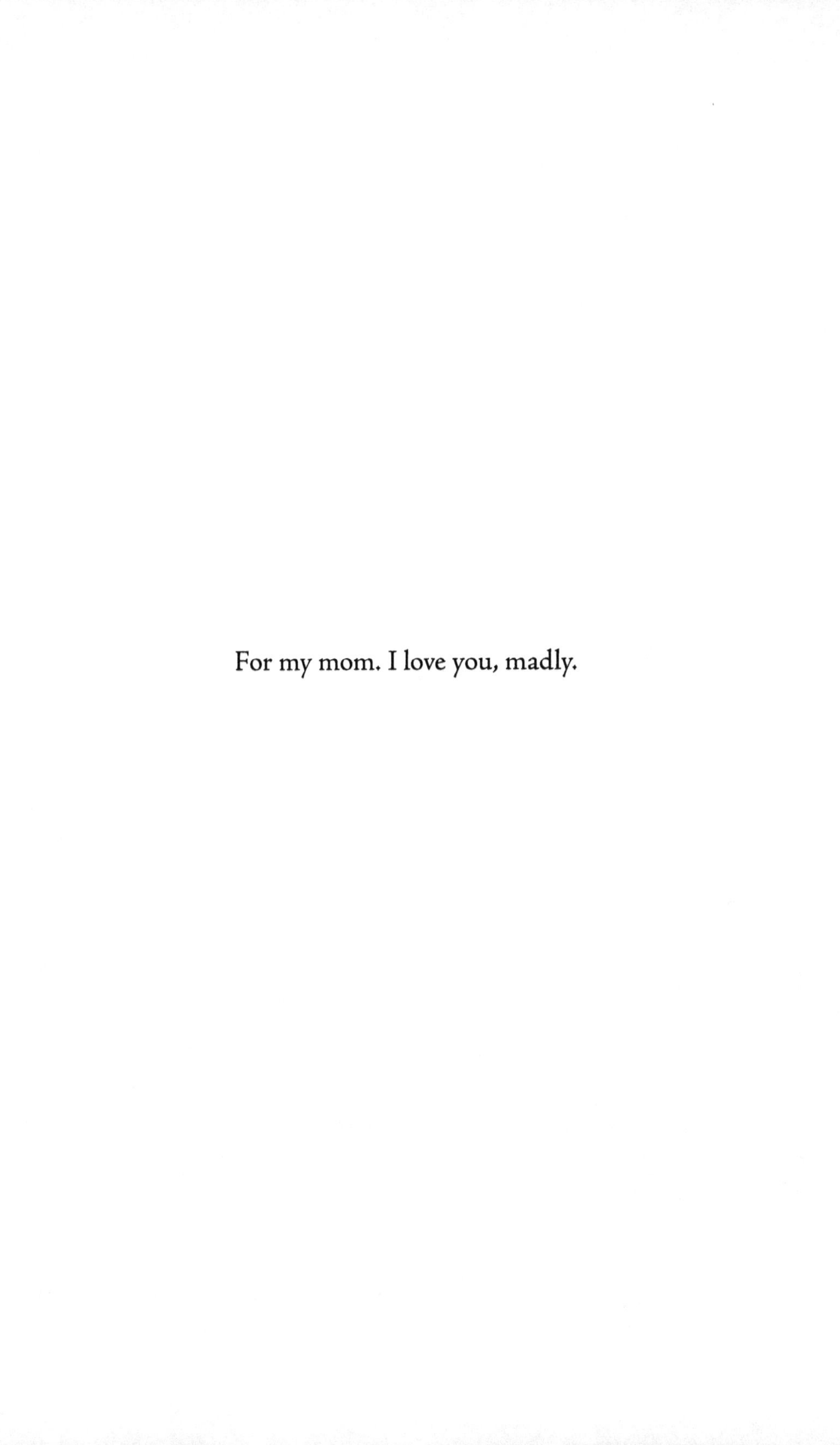

For my mom. I love you, madly.

PROLOGUE

The room is crowded. Even in such a big space it feels like too many people.

I'm staring straight ahead, past all the standing bodies, into the large, empty fireplace. All I want to do is get up from the couch, walk out the door, and go be alone in my room.

Someone just said something to me. They have a hand on my shoulder. I look at their hand and then up at them.

"I'm—I'm sorry, what?"

I'm staring at the person, and I know my expression is void and completely lifeless.

"I'm just so sorry," she repeats.

I don't know her, whoever this person is. Maybe she's a friend of my mom's or, more likely, some person desperate to be friends with my mother.

I'm being cynical. I know it. But my thoughts and assessment are probably true.

The woman has a perfectly empathetic expression. She's put together all in black, just like everyone else in the room, including me. Except I have white medical gauze wrapped around my right hand and the skin is still purple and puffy, which everyone seems to be sneaking a peek at.

I have a small porcelain plate held limply in my hands with some fancy hors d'oeuvres. I don't even know why I have it. I'm not hungry. I can't even think about eating. Not to mention, the meds I'm on have subdued my appetite. Either way, right now in this moment, I have a strong compulsion to throw it at this person with their hand on my shoulder who's telling me how sorry she is for me and my family.

I let out a long sigh. "Thank you," I say with a gentle smile.

I instantly feel my own tears, but when I see hers reflecting back at me, it causes my own to retract.

This scene repeats a dozen or more times. People come up, say how sorry they are, and I force myself to be polite. When I try to look at them, or at anything other than the fireplace, all I see is a blur. Colors and forms bleed together like a Picasso painting, only it's not pretty or even interesting. All of it feels ugly, unnatural, and grey.

The ritual ebbs and flows until I can't stand it anymore. All I want to do is curl up into the smallest ball possible and disappear.

Finally, I get up. I leave my plate on a table set with a banquet of food for all the guests and slip away upstairs to my room. I can feel the shadow of strange eyes following me. I feel my mother's also, but she's too busy being consoled to concern herself with me.

I lock my bedroom door behind me and drop face forward onto my bed. I stay still for a few moments with my face pressed into the fluffy down comforter until I turn my head and gaze up at the letter on the bedside table.

I maneuver so I'm sitting up. Moving feels laborious.

I grab the letter with my unbandaged hand and read it for the hundredth time. I could read it a thousand times, and it will never make sense to me.

Tears run down my face, and I wipe them away with the back of my good hand.

I sniffle, but the tears continue as I gingerly put the letter back into the envelope. Well, I put it back the best I can anyway, considering my slight handicap with my injured right hand. The letter is precious, as much as I hate it.

I press it against my chest, sitting in silence as the hot tears and snot continue to wreak havoc on my face.

I feel so numb. I've never felt this numb in my whole life. It's paralyzing, and I'm transfixed in this position, crying, and holding on tight.

Without thinking I put the letter down on the bedside table and go to my closet.

It's a big walk-in closet. It's filled with designer clothes, shoes, and bags—anything a girl my age would be expected to want. I close the door behind me and lock it. There's a small measure of comfort I find in being locked away behind so many doors, especially in this moment. If anything, it's an added barrier between me and the charade going on downstairs. It's my cocoon. My shield.

All my movements and actions are reactionary. I'm not really thinking about what it is I'm doing.

I drop to the floor and start searching the back of my closet as my frustration builds. It doesn't take long before I'm tearing through things, chucking all my nice clothes, shoes, and accessories over my shoulder and out of the way. I ignore the slight throb that has started in my right hand. I'm desperate to find what it is I'm looking for, and eventually I do.

I pull out a tattered old Nike shoe box. My vision is blurred, my face feels like a sponge and my hands are shaking. I take a moment to collect myself, then open it. Inside is a digital camera along with a bunch of other random trinkets and items from my adolescence. It's stuff that meant something once upon a time, even though once upon a time really wasn't that long ago.

I pull out the hot pink camera and feel myself choke back the tears that won't stop. I turn it on. The battery is low, but it has enough juice that I can flip through the digital load.

All I hear is the wheezing sound of my breathing through the mucus. The tears are a steady stream, and my soft moans are my grief.

I don't know how long I end up sitting there. But I take whatever time I need, reliving the moments captured by the pictures.

I miss him. I miss him so much.

CHAPTER 1

Not Just Another Smutty Romance

"BERRR-LINNN!"

The announcement over the train PA is loud and startles me awake. Meanwhile, the raunchy romance novel I picked up while on my travels slips from my hands and thuds against the floor. I'm left scrambling to collect it while I also pull out my passport from my bag.

I caught an earlier train out of Amsterdam than what I had originally planned, and I stayed up late packing to make sure I wasn't rushed in the morning.

"*Reisepass.*" Two German customs officials have made their way through the train car. One stops at my row and stares down at me with his hand stretched out. I hand over my passport, and he starts flipping through it, searching for an open spot to put a stamp. It's full—from cover to cover—and his look of irritation says it all.

I can imagine what he's thinking: She's just another spoiled American backpacking blogger traipsing through Europe for the umpteenth time on her family's dime.

The official lets out an exaggerated sigh and glances down at me as he finally comes to a suitable enough spot. I squirm uncomfortably in my seat and manage a courteous smile as I take back my passport while he moves on.

I want to tell him he's wrong. Mostly wrong, anyway. I only wish I were that kind of adventurous or that level of cool. But no, not me. Not Brooke Antoinette Neville. Nearly all those stamps are from me being dragged around the world by my endlessly boring and privileged family in a heavily guarded bubble. Poor me, I know—the very essence of spoiled and entitled. But appearances can be deceiving.

My giant Osprey pack on the ground leans to the side, knocking against my leg, just one of the lengths I've gone to play up the part of humble wanderer, trying to blend in, so-to-speak.

Jesus, I'm such a fake.

It's the first time I've ever really traveled on my own without family or some type of chaperone or bodyguard. Though this trip alone, I already have more than a handful of countries under my belt: England, France, Italy, Switzerland, Austria, and the Netherlands. Plus, I'm circling back and studying abroad for a year in London.

The experience of traveling solo is weird but thrilling. Weird because I'm mostly alone with my thoughts and experiences. But equally thrilling because I am utterly and completely alone. I get to make my own agenda, which I have—in great detail, I might add.

I look down at my wrist and check the time on my clunky but stylish analog watch and then check it against the arrival time on my train ticket. I still have an hour or so before we get to Berlin.

I stretch in my seat and let out a big yawn, then settle back in and stare out the window at the landscape rushing by. Some of the windows in the train car are down, and the early morning summer smells of the countryside fill the air.

My stomach flutters as I start to imagine what my adventure in Berlin will be like. My eyes gently shut as I take a deep breath and embrace the calm serenity of the moment, until my left hand moves over my right, and I feel them.

My smile disappears and is replaced by an uneasy tension as I open my eyes and glance down at my hand and the gnarled lines across my knuckles. Flashes of fragmented memories creep into my thoughts. My brother, my parents, my mom, my life, that day that the *something* happened.

I take another deep breath, but I don't feel the same feeling of serenity. Instead, I feel sadness, anger, regret, guilt, blame. It's an unforgiving kaleidoscope of emotions.

This is why you're doing this, Brooke.

That is, being on my grand adventure. Maybe it's an escape of sorts, but I certainly have a purpose. I always do. It's meaningful.

I feel the ache of a phantom pain in my right hand as I keep my eyes fixed on it. I imagine the damage all over again. The blood, the flesh, a frenzy. The things I didn't know and didn't understand at the time. I look away and stare back out the train window, pushing the vivid memories and emotions to the back of my mind.

"Entschuldigung? Excuse me?"

Someone is talking to me, a woman in a business suit carrying a briefcase. She motions at the seat next to me. I shake my head to indicate that no one is sitting there, and I scooch my bag closer to my side so she can take a seat and have plenty of leg room. She smiles and slides in.

"Ist etwas falsch?"

I don't know what she's saying until she motions to her own face. Then I put it together and pat at the warm moisture on my cheeks.

"Oh, um, allergies," I say sniffling, playing things off, and motioning to the open windows.

I hate when that happens. I'm not really a crier or the emotional type, either. At least I wasn't before the *something* happened.

"Ah! American?" the woman in the suit replies and proceeds to pull out a tissue to give to me.

The prompt segues into a chatty conversation in English about the United States, and I'm just relieved the woman doesn't ask anything else about the tears.

Sometime later, I'm in Berlin at the Hauptbahnhof, the Berlin Central Train Station. It's a massive transit hub with people everywhere, coming and going.

I find a spot out of the way to drop my big Osprey bag down on the ground and pull out my travel diary. I used to use it for journaling and other stuff. Not anymore.

In it, I have the name and address of where I'm staying, an itinerary mapped out of what I plan to see and do each day and cut-outs of small-scale maps I've pasted on to some of the pages to help me navigate the city. Sort of like my own Lonely Planet travel guidebook. I've done this for each of my destinations and added tabs so I can easily flip to each location. It's comprehensive and certainly the most arts-and-crafts-type thing I've done since kindergarten. The best part is it hasn't failed me yet. I also bought all the tickets I needed for each city I'm visiting ahead of my arrival.

This is all I have with me to keep from getting lost. I don't have a cell phone, tablet, or laptop. It may seem strange for a twenty-two-year-old American girl to be detached from her electronics, but it was a calculated decision. Like I said, I always have a purpose.

I do, however, have one electronic device with me, my small digital hot pink camera.

I make my way out to the street level and, in no time, I'm booking it on a local trolly car headed in the direction of the hostel I'm staying at.

Berlin is a major city, and I'm immediately immersed in people-watching, both on the trolly car and along the streets, with a silly little grin on my face. Even from an initial take, Berlin seems different from the other places I've visited. It feels electric, with palpable energy.

I get off at my stop and walk a couple of blocks till I see the sign for the hostel—Central Place.

My mother insisted on me only staying in single occupancy rooms with lockable doors, which was an easy compromise to make because I like my solitude. Plus, I didn't want to argue about it with her. It was enough of a fiasco convincing her that I should go on this trip to begin with. That being said, I'll admit that my solitude hasn't always been the healthiest thing for me.

I walk in, and the place is buzzing with people my age. The entry is a large open space, and right away I feel that the online pictures don't do it justice, with its edgy vibe.

I scan around until I spot the front desk. There's a bit of a line and as I stand by waiting, I take notice of a young couple, a guy and a girl walking hand-in-hand toward the front exit. The guy lifts the girl's hand, pulling it up to his lips. He places a gentle kiss on top and then lets both of their arms swing back down in unison.

The two exit the building, and I watch through the glass windows as the guy puts his arm around her shoulders, allowing her body to burrow into his side. Nestled up snuggly to one another, the pair passes from my line of sight and into lives having nothing to do with mine.

I can't help it, but I smile to myself even as desire tugs painfully at my insides.

I can't even remember the last time I hooked up with someone or was in a relationship. With everything that's happened over the last year, relationships haven't exactly been a top priority. Well, they never really were before that either.

I let out a deep sigh, snapping out of my wishful thinking.

Maybe I need to stop reading romance novels, but they're my guilty pleasure.

The line moves, and I move with it, inching closer to the front desk, until suddenly someone knocks into me, and I drop my passport.

"Oh shit, I'm so sorry," says a male voice with an Australian accent.

The guy picks up my passport to hand back to me but pauses. He squirrels his face and starts to thumb through my passport. He glances back and forth between me and the pages as he investigates.

"Um, it's okay," I say, shyly. If he wasn't so cute, I'd snatch my passport right back and give him a piece of my mind.

He has light brown hair with some length at the top, carefully styled to look like he just got out of bed. The lines and bones of his face remind me of a razor blade—sharp and menacing. A pair of serious blue eyes sends every hair on my neck standing at attention as my imagination starts to get the better of me.

He's standing so close I can almost *taste* him. I blink. Seriously, I need to stop reading those books.

"Quite the wanderer, aren't you?"

He's super tall with an athletic build and long torso, Caucasian with a light summer tan, and his easy smile has utterly and completely stunted my speech.

"Um, yeah . . . I guess."

If he thinks I'm some hip American backpacking blogger, that's fine with me. Fake it 'til you make it. No thoughts of correcting this time.

"I'm Patrick," he says, handing over my passport. I take it without saying anything but see on the inside of his outstretched right arm a tattoo that looks like the Olympic symbol. *Interesting.* "Nice to meet you, Brooke Neville," he adds, grinning through my awkward silence.

I flinch at his use of my name. When your family is worth more than a small country, you learn that a name can become a target, painted on your back.

He seems to pick up on my discomfort and nods at the passport. *Of course, idiot.* He just had my ID in his hands.

"Right," I say and feel myself instinctively roll my eyes at myself. *Oh God, I'm being weird.*

"So, you're staying here?"

"Yup. Just checking in."

"Cool."

I inhale deeply, trying to calm my nerves. I feel my chest rise as the clean fresh scent of his cologne penetrates my lungs. He smells so good, and he looks good too in his dark blue T-shirt, khaki shorts, and Puma sneakers.

"PATRICK!"

A female voice, also with an Australian accent, screeches from across the lobby. The girl is standing with a couple—a guy and girl—and I guess that they are a foursome traveling together.

Patrick turns from them back to me.

"Well, Brooke, it was nice to meet you. Or rather, bump into you. Maybe I'll see you around, then. You can tell me about all the places you've been to over a beer or something."

I feel myself blush because I'm certain he's flirting with me, even as his girlfriend stands a few feet away.

"Likewise. Nice to bump into you too, Patrick," I reply, and then immediately regret it because it sounds so goofy and oddly proper at the same time.

I force myself to smile, but internally I'm chiding myself. I run my hand through my hair self-consciously as Patrick walks off. He and the girl exchange a quick kiss. I drop my gaze from his direction and move with the line to an open spot at the front desk and finally start my check-in.

The attendant hands me a set of keycards for my room. Just as I'm about to leave and head toward the stairs, the attendant stops me.

"Oh! *Miss!* I almost forgot! You have a message!" he says in a German accent, with the "s" sound pronounced more like a "z".

I turn back toward the attendant and narrow my eyes at the slip of paper he's handing me.

"Thanks." I take the message and stuff it into my pocket.

As I head to my room, I've forgotten all about Patrick and the electric feeling of Berlin. Now all I can think about is the piece of paper burning a hole in my shorts pocket.

CHAPTER 2

Classic Prep

I look out the floor length windows, scanning the horizon. My single occupancy room is on the top floor of Central Place, which gives it a nice vantage point of the city. But as I plop myself down on the bed and close my eyes all I see are images of Patrick's magnetic eyes looking back at me. I start to visualize his lips on me, kissing me.

"Jesus Christ, I'm burning that stupid romance book, for real," I say out loud to myself, even though I know I wouldn't dare to because I love it.

I know I'm no different than anyone else my age. I'm not immune to my youthful hormones, even if emotionally I've got issues that I'm trying to work through.

I put a pin in my dreamy thoughts for the moment and start prepping to go knock out some of the stuff on my itinerary.

It's a hot summer day, so I change into a lightweight dress with a pair of casual walking shoes. It's not high fashion or a perfect match, but it works. It's utilitarian and I'm not really trying to impress anyone.

Or am I?

I kick myself. The guy has a girlfriend, for God's sake.

After getting changed and fussing with my hair, I look myself over in the floor-length mirror and explore the image staring back at me.

Considering how I feel inside most days, I scrub up okay. Travel has left my white skin sun-kissed, with some new freckles forming across my nose. My light blonde hair is all-natural, much to my mother's deep envy, though she likes to remind me that I missed out on inheriting her vivid green eyes. Mine are closer to hazel but appear brown in low light. Overall, I look the part of the classic preppy girl that I am, someone who's spent way too many hours on a tennis court.

Just the thought leaves me longing to pick up a racket. From the age of six I've been tennis obsessed. Maybe because it was something I was actually better at than my brother, which drove him nuts; nonetheless, growing up he was my biggest fan.

I find inspiration in my favorite men's tennis players—Vamos Rafa!—but I grew up admiring female players like Maria Sharapova, Sloane Stephens, Ash Barty, Li Na, Garbiñe Muguruza, Caroline Wozniacki, Petra Kvitová, Victoria Azarenka, Simona Halep, Karolína Plíšková, Angelique Kerber, Naomi Osaka, Venus and Serena Williams, and, of course the greatest of all time, Billie Jean King. The list could go on and on.

All that to say, tennis has made me so much of who I am today, and I can see that reflecting right back at me now in the mirror.

I hone in on my arms, where I feel—and can physically see— the muscle is looking a bit slack. As a top college tennis athlete, it's my job to scrutinize every muscle in my form. At least it *was* my job.

I'm still getting used to using past tense verbs for so many things that felt concrete in my life for so long.

I let out a lung-full of hot air and try to pacify the unconscious judgmental expression staring back at me. It's been exactly 251 days since I last picked up a tennis racket. I long to play again, but it's complicated.

"Remember why you're here, Brooke. Remember why you're doing all of this, and who you're doing it for," I remind myself out loud as I confront my own worst enemy in the mirror.

Yes, I'm talking to myself. It's not weird. It's a thing. Tennis players love to talk to themselves, both on and off the court.

My heart sinks. I can feel the weight of my sadness as I turn and shift my focus to the piece of paper in my pocket.

It's a message from my mother. I don't even have to open it or read it to know.

I reflexively curl my right hand into a fist. I can feel the scar tissue tighten along with my anger and resentment. I know I should respond to the message; my mom will keep calling the hostel until I do.

I breathe out a sigh and slowly release my fist.

Something feels different. The feeling manifests as I start to chew at the inside of my mouth, thinking.

Maybe it's Patrick and the little boost of confidence I felt with him flirting with me (I've totally convinced myself that he was for sure flirting with me, even if that makes him a two-timing jerk). Maybe it's Berlin, and that initial spark of electric, rebellious energy I felt from the city.

Whatever it is exactly, I don't know. But I take the piece of paper from my pocket, scrunch it into a ball, and toss it into the plastic trash bin.

I let another exasperated breath of hot air escape my lungs and feel the last of my anger and resentment pass with it.

I grab a few things to stuff in my day bag, along with my travel diary and my camera. I head out to explore, ignoring the ball of paper as I shut and lock the door behind me.

CHAPTER 3

Truce?

Of all the places I've traveled, my favorite place to be is New York City. More specifically, my favorite thing about being in New York City is going to the U.S. Open. I've been going every year since I started playing tennis and have, in fact, met a lot of the players I admire.

Imagine being in a stadium full of loud, crass New Yorkers, who cheer and yell and even boo at the players. Being there, sitting courtside, especially for a night match, always feels like a healthy dose of reality. Something outside the heavily guarded bubble I normally move about in my day-to-day existence.

As is my embarrassingly nerdy practice, I play out an internal conversation with the hot Aussie guy, where I can appear both wonderfully glamorous and intriguing, while also conveying the warm authenticity of a girl next door.

Patrick: New York City? U.S. Open? Is it really so amazing, Brooke?

Me: The City is just out of this world, Patrick, and during the U.S. Open, its pulse and energy is amplified. There's drama and excitement out on the courts. The U.S. Open is where the best tennis players make their mark on the world and in tennis history. To be there, to breathe it in . . .

Ugh. Even I want to slap my imaginary self.

I stop briefly on the street and pull out my travel diary to orient myself to my itinerary. I see that first on my list is the Berlin Cathedral, a.k.a. Berliner Dom on Museum Island, so I head in that direction. As I walk, I reflect on my imagined conversation with Patrick. So much of my life plays out inside my head, without ever eventuating.

Turns out being a billionaire heiress isn't enough to overcome my level of social awkwardness. My brother, Liam, never has that issue. He's the type of person that can breeze in and out of conversations and social circles with absolute ease and confidence.

As I get to Museum Island, I see the name is exactly what it implies: an island on the Danube River in the middle of the city with a bunch of museums. At the center of Museum Island is the Lustgarden, a wide-open grassy quad. People are out everywhere sprawled across the soft inviting grass. Sunbathers, picnicking families and friends, people reading, sleeping, and others simply soaking in the pleasant summer day.

There is a part of me that is tempted to join in the relaxation and chill vibe, but I stick to my itinerary and head toward the massive domed cathedral.

"One ticket, please."

The lady at the front kiosk hands me my ticket, and I join the group inside waiting for the guided tour to begin.

There are some people around my age clumped together who are giggling and being a bit rambunctious. Their commotion garners a few head turns from others, but they settle themselves.

The tour begins and I'm immediately immersed in the history. The church is massive and was apparently built to rival St. Peter's Basilica in Rome. Inside, it's a mix of gothic and classical style architecture with a huge dome stretching some three-hundred feet up in the air and the biggest organ I've ever seen in my life looming above the arcade.

Some people have FOMO: fear of missing out. I have FOMOOI: fear of missing out on information. I hang on to each nugget of information and detail on the tour and get annoyed when the group of young people starts laughing and joking with one another, as if totally ignorant of the somber splendor around them.

This time it's me that turns a head. I stare in their direction with my iciest expression.

"Varun, shut the fuck up. You're going to get us kicked out," I hear one of them say in a low voice.

A girl sees me looking and mouths a sincere looking "sorry."

Satisfied that the ruckus has ended, I turn back to absorbing everything I can from the tour. Eventually we end up walking through the infamous Hohenzollern Crypt located underneath the ground level of the cathedral. It holds nearly a hundred entombments of the Brandenburg-Prussians that ruled from the sixteenth century to the twentieth century, and I can't help but reflect on my own family's deeply rooted legacy.

I'm all too familiar with the feeling of growing up in the shadow of extravagant legacies.

"It is a bit cold and creepy down here, don't you think?" says an erudite voice from over my shoulder.

I briefly turn my gaze without any effort to hide my annoyance.

"Excuse me?"

"Ah! American, right?"

It's one of the guys from the group that's been acting up throughout the tour. He looks to be southeast Asian and has a drawling Eton accent that exudes money and confidence.

I don't answer, but I give him a look that politely confirms his guess, then start to walk off as the tour continues.

"What are your plans after the tour ends?" he asks, sticking to my heels.

His voice is as smooth as his sleek jet-black hair, and I almost have to look away from his dazzling smile. No doubt it's snared many unsuspecting hearts.

"I'm not sure," I lie. My entire day is scheduled down to bedtime.

"Well, I can certainly help you with that," he says, fluttering his eyes at me.

"You're kind, but . . ." I demur, thanks to the etiquette classes I suffered through growing up, that subconsciously force me to be agreeable to others—to a point, anyway.

My unspoken refusal is interpreted as an invitation. He folds his arms, and an assortment of bracelets slide and rattle against his warm copper skin. "I'm called many things, but kind is rarely one of them. Most know me as Varun. And your name, darling?"

Again, my manners force me to relent even though I'm irritated by the "darling." His interest in me seems to be growing the more I try to evade him, which is weird and annoying. Maybe if I'm nice he'll lose interest.

"Brooke," I say, moving along with the tour as it winds down.

Varun is Velcroed to my hip as we both listen quietly to the ending remarks from the guide. He's got his hand on his chin, rubbing it gently, and is staring off in no particular direction. "Brooke . . ." he says, like he's tasting something for the first time and contemplating its effects on the palate. "Nice to meet you, *Brooke*," he says, bowing his head slightly as if he were a proper gentleman.

With the tour over and the group dispersing, the other young people from Varun's group walk up to where he and I are standing.

"Is this bowsie bothering you?" one of them says with a distinctively Irish accent, slapping Varun on the arm, all buddy-buddy.

"We were just introducing ourselves is all," Varun objects.

Bowsie? What's a bowsie?

"Do you two nerd bots ever stop? Seriously, don't listen to either of those two idiots. I'm Lauren."

The girl extends her hand, and I shake it. She's clearly also American from her accent, and possibly Latinx from the looks of her long dark hair and striking features.

My politeness is on autopilot as I give her my first name and try to find a way out of the situation.

"You're American? Where are you from?"

"Connecticut."

I don't ask in kind, but she offers anyway, explaining that she's from Sacramento on the West Coast. I don't want to be rude, but I'm eager to get to the next destination on my itinerary.

"I'm Grady," says the Irishman, who also extends his hand.

Grady's short with shaggy dark blond hair, burnt freckled skin from too much sun, and his front teeth slightly overlap. He gives me a big warm welcoming smile as we shake.

"And that's Olivier," says Lauren. "Don't mind him, he's a pretentious snob."

Olivier rolls his eyes at Lauren and gives me a languid expression. He's dressed like a hipster and has a clean groomed look, even with his man bun and facial hair set against his medium tan. He and I shake hands as well, but he doesn't come across nearly as inviting as the others in the group. As he pulls his hand away from mine, he gives me a curious look.

"Hello," he says, and I think I catch a French accent.

"So, you backpacking on your own or something?" Lauren asks pointedly in a no-nonsense manner, in contrast to the girly octave she was just speaking in. "I think I saw you at our accom, Central Place."

Great.

I confirm her assertion is correct, as my skin itches to get away.

"Yeah, actually I think I might have seen you in there this morning checking in. Were you talking with Patrick?" she asks, scrunching her nose curiously.

Just like that, the itching stops. But before I can answer, Varun starts talking.

"Never mind that. So, now that we've made introductions, and we're all one big happy family staying at Central Place, what do you say, Brooke? We were going to go picnic out on the Lustgarden. It's a lovely day for it. Don't you think?"

"Well, I—"

"Before you make some excuse, just know that I'm buying. It's the least I can do for interrupting your tour experience."

"You mean, you're buying for *all of us*, right?" Lauren interjects in a teasing voice.

"Everyone except for you, darling."

"Fuck you, too," she responds, maintaining her sweet cheerful tone.

I don't know what to say so I just smile.

"So, darling, what do you say, truce?"

They're all looking at me, smiling, except Olivier who eyes me distrustfully, as if he suspects me of hiding something. I guess in many ways I am.

I can feel my face turning hot. "No, thank you. I really do appreciate the offer though," I say with all the sincerity I can muster.

"Oh, come on. Are you sure? I promise we're harmless. And—"

"No."

My voice is resolute, and my irritation is clear. No more of the politeness. I've already wasted enough time getting mixed up in the encounter, and I'm getting antsy to move on.

"Wow," Lauren says with her eyes popped wide open. "That's gratitude for you. We'll know to steer clear of you at the hostel."

Lauren turns and walks off without missing a beat. I can see Varun doesn't look exactly offended by my response, but clearly he's taken aback.

He pumps his hands trying to settle the dust-up. "Sorry, didn't mean to ruffle any feathers or make you uncomfortable. It's just—well, it looked like you were sort of lonely and could use some company," he says. "I always do this. Push too much, miss the hint, and—"

His friends start to pull him away as he continues to babble, and my stomach twists. This is a new level of mortification, even for me. And he isn't wrong. With a jolt, I realize this is the most I've talked to anyone my own age in months.

I've welcomed and embraced the solitude as a means of cleansing myself, a way of repairing the damage. But I was just given an easy opportunity to change that (for the better?), and I blew it—royally.

I can feel the unease and shame color my face as Varun and Grady turn and catch up to Lauren. But Olivier lingers a moment longer. His eyes narrow in on me, and we stare at each other. I can see something is turning in his thoughts, but I'm not sure what.

With a curt nod of dismissal, he turns and walks away.

CHAPTER 4

The Way, Way Back

I spend thirty minutes loitering around the crypts, too ashamed to unearth myself from the bowels of the cathedral, both literally and figuratively. If the group is hanging out at the Lustgarden, then I'll have to pass them and their judgment in a horrifying walk of shame. Surviving that, I'll definitely run into them back at the hostel.

Why do you have to be like this, Brooke? So . . . difficult.

I collapse into a pew at the back of the cathedral. My mind slips back in time as I stare ahead at the ornate altar.

"I'm just so frustrated, Liam. I don't know what to do," I said, sighing into the receiver, my voice whiny.

"Well, you sort of make things hard for yourself, sis," he replied in his cool and casual way that is only him.

"If you weren't all the way out in California being a Stanford snot, I would strangle you right now," I said, pacing my dorm room.

He laughed. "Who's the snot? Ms. Yale-y."

"Gross, don't call me that. You know I'm only here because it's what Mom and Dad wanted—not me. Well, mostly what Mom wanted."

"Don't blame Mom. You gave in."

I scoffed. "Yeah, getting to play tennis tournaments, *only* if I promised to go to their alma mater—I'd say that's a highly manipulative and weird bargain to make with a fourteen-year-old whose only focus is tennis."

"Nonetheless, you gave in. Also, you're still *only* focused on tennis."

"Liam, I didn't 'give in.' It was never going to be a choice, even setting aside the bargain. Mom never lets me have a choice. Unlike you, Mr. Golden Boy, King of Perfection."

He ignored the jest, and I ignored the fact that he had called me out for my drug of choice—tennis.

"Just tell her what it is you want. You deserve it. Nothing will change unless you stand up for yourself."

I groaned. "I can't. It's a waste of breath. We both know the trajectory of my life . . . I'm a Neville, *and* I'm a girl."

"So?"

"So? You're Franklin Lee 'Liam' Neville the Fourth. . ." I said, pausing momentarily. "Everyone loves you, and you can do no wrong."

I sensed him rolling his eyes on the other side of the country at the inference to the sexism that runs in our family. In truth, it runs in a lot of families like ours. The men are the masters of the universe, and the women are trophies. Nothing has changed in New York's high society since The Four Hundred of the Gilded Age. If anything, it's been reinforced. But no one openly talks about that; it's implicit.

"You know I text with Alex, on your team, right?" he said, changing the subject, or at least I think he had.

"I know . . . You don't have a crush on her, do you?"

"No. And even if I did it wouldn't matter. You know Alex is a lesbian, right?"

"Yeah. I know. I've met Kim. She's okay."

I started to gnaw at the inside of my mouth. Alex and I hadn't exactly been on the best of terms at that point in time. I kept my lips sealed, expecting Liam's rebuke.

"She says you never go out with the team anymore."

And there it was. "I've been busy," I clipped. I hated when he poked at me for not being as extroverted as him.

"She also said . . ." he cut off and cleared his throat. I could tell he was stalling to tell me.

"She also said what, Liam?"

"Don't get mad, but she also said you've been kinda bitchy to her and the other girls."

I huffed. Funny how competitive, assertive guys are celebrated, but the same laser focus and ambition in women is seen as a flaw.

"Don't isolate yourself from everyone. People can be helpful. People can be friends. Friends are a good thing."

"You're my friend," I said cheerfully and stopped my frenetic walking to lean against the window that looked down onto the quad below.

"Yeah, but I'm your younger brother, and I'm going to school a thousand-something miles away."

"I know, but—"

"But nothing. Having friends and a support system is good. We all need one. Besides, Alex is a nice person. You don't want to alienate someone who's on your side *and* on your team."

I fell silent from the other end of the line, feeling every atom that stretched in between the distance that separated us. I wished for him to be there with me in that moment.

My eyes shifted to look outside. The trees were a brilliant blend of fall colors. Other students walked carefree, laughing and joking with one another across the grassy quad. Pumpkin spice latte season was in full swing. Meanwhile, I felt like the walls were closing in on me with no escape. Nothing sweet or comforting about that.

"Hey, cheer up. I can tell you're pouting," he said.

I smiled to myself, full of love for the one person on this planet who truly sees me.

"Look, I gotta go. I have a bit of a headache and need to rest up before football practice."

In addition to being funny, smart, and wise, my brother is one of the best up-and-coming quarterbacks in the country. Athletic genes run in the family.

"That's what you can expect from getting beat up out on the football field. Barbarian."

How my brother convinced our family to let their precious heir play a contact sport is beyond me. I told him I love him.

"Love you too, sis."

As I continue to hide out in the crypt, my thoughts back in the present, I wonder how Alex is doing. We haven't talked since the *something*. Subconsciously my left hand glides over my right. I wince at the scars.

Get over yourself, Brooke. I can almost hear Liam in my ear. A determined burst of air rushes out of my chest.

With my back straight and head up, I stride out of the Berlin Cathedral. Outside the weather is still beautiful, and the Lustgarden is packed with small clusters of people. I scan the horizon looking for Varun and the others as I walk along the pathway that circles the large green field.

I finally spot them, and my stomach somersaults a few times. They're having fun as they lie out on the lawn, eating, drinking, laughing, and bantering with one another. Lauren is posing for selfies and snapping pictures of the group with her phone, relaxed and confident.

I walk toward them.

I can do this. I got this. I think, channeling my inner Liam.

I feel like I can hear him cheering me on.

But just as I'm within shouting distance, my body wrenches in the other direction. My nerves fray. Before I know it, I'm walking away, too embarrassed to face them.

Liam loves people, but I don't need to hang out with a bunch of random strangers to have fun. Safer to just stick with my plan.

CHAPTER 5

We're at an Impasse

In my travel diary, under Berlin, I've now ticked off: Berlin Cathedral, the Brandenburg Gate, and the Pergamonmuseum. All in one day, I might add. I feel accomplished as I unlock the door to my room and collapse on my bed.

I'm kicking off my shoes when I notice something on the ground. It's a note. It looks like it must have gotten pushed under the door while I was out.

I slide off the bed, pick it up, and open it. It's another message from the front desk letting me know that my mother called. An exasperated breath unfurls from my nostrils, and instinctively my eyes roll.

Without much further thought, I crumple the message and toss it toward the trash bin, not caring if it makes it in. Outside, I can hear the faint sound of some people in the hall chatting and joking around as I fall limply back onto the bed.

This is precisely why I don't have a cell phone, tablet, or laptop with me. My mother's need to invade my life makes me feel like a twelve-year-old that's late for curfew. It's worse now. Ever since.

I let out a deep sigh and keep my eyes trained on the ceiling above as the hallway falls silent, and the youthful bantering vanishes.

It's weird how my mom and I are in this place where we can barely function communicating with one another, yet she's been following my every move. She calls every hostel before I even arrive, making sure to leave a message for me to pick up upon my arrival.

Why can't you just give me the space I need?

Of course, I could never say that to her in real-life. It wouldn't help or change anything. I'm convinced of it.

I consciously turn my thoughts away from my mother and the constant reminders of the *something*. I think of the high I felt from my exploring, trying to refocus on that instead, despite the initial failure with Varun and his friends. This leads me to reevaluating that whole situation once more.

Maybe I should try again?

In the back of my mind, I can hear Liam: "Yes, you definitely should." Besides, I need to get out of the funk that the messages have put me in.

But I feel like I totally blew it.

I close my eyes and groan out loud, feeling split. "I know, I know, 'Get over myself...'"

How hard is it to say sorry and buy some people a round of drinks? Though it could raise flags if my mom looks at the charges on my credit card. It wouldn't surprise me if she's paying closer attention while I'm away.

My eyes flutter back open. "Who cares," I say to myself.

I feel that little spark of defiance again.

I pull myself off the bed, take a shower, and get cleaned up before heading downstairs to see if Varun and his friends are at the bar.

It's my first time in the space since checking in, even though I pored over the pictures online. Again, the pictures don't do the place justice, and the vibe is grungy but cool. I dig it. It's different.

The lounge area has some pool tables, a dartboard, a few TVs, and clean-lined furniture, including couches and chairs set up in various seating arrangements. On the wall are some framed pictures of graffiti. The pictures are curious looking and pique my interest enough that I walk up to one to look at it closer.

Banksy. 2015.

That's what the small index next to one of the framed photos reads. I've never heard of them. The artwork is of a man dressed in coveralls and a driver hat carrying a bucket and paint brushes. On a wall is written FOLLOW YOUR DREAMS with CANCELLED written over it.

Sad, yet ironic.

I turn and head toward the bar. The smell of burning pinewood wafts in from a fire pit outside, along with sandalwood, beer and wine, and the building's centuries-old damp masonry stone. The closeness of life hugs the air around me; it's warm and inviting.

The space is mildly crowded. It's still too early for the hordes of young people that I assume will eventually consume the space before hitting up the bars and clubs that Berlin is known for, and as I scan the horizon, I don't see Varun or anyone from his troupe. But my stomach does start to grumble as I smell the delicious food coming out of the kitchen.

I order some food and a sparkling flavored water at the bar, then settle into a spot by myself that gives me a vantage point looking out into the courtyard. It's quite beautiful with its mature trees and bouncing squirrels.

I'm dipping my fries into a big helping of ketchup *and* mayonnaise—because dipping fries in both is apparently a thing in Germany—when I hear his voice.

"Hey . . . Brooke," says the familiar Australian accent.

I freeze.

It's Patrick, and he's got a beer in hand and motions toward the empty seat at my table. "Can I join you?"

"Sure, of course," I say, as the concoction of sauces drips from my fries onto the currywurst on my plate.

Patrick slides into the seat, and I proceed to stuff the fatty fries into my mouth, trying to chew quickly and swallow inconspicuously. Not something my mother would approve of—neither the food choice nor me inhaling food in public.

"What did you get up to today?" he asks all cool and casual, like we've known each other for ages and we're catching up in our usual way. Also, apparently not caring a hoot about the grease platter I've put a healthy dent in.

I tell him all the places I went to and things I found interesting but leave out the whole encounter with Varun and his friends.

"Wow. That's impressive for day one. But from the looks of your passport, seems like being on the move is not really a new thing for you, eh?" he says smirking and raising his brows, a curious twinkle in his eyes.

"No," I reply, and I can feel myself blush because I know the truth is far less glamorous, at least to me it isn't.

Patrick takes a swig of his drink, sets it down on the table, and cups it between his hands. "So, you were supposed to tell me about all those stamps over a beer. You want one? Unless you're good?" He nods his head at my sparkling flavored water.

"I'm good, thanks. It's important to hydrate."

Nerd. Nerd. Nerd.

"Hey, beer is like 99% water." He laughs before his face grows serious. "I think it's cool that you're traveling on your own, by the way. I almost came alone on this trip but chickened out at the last minute."

As I start to relax, the conversation flows, and when Patrick asks about some of my favorite travel destinations, I find myself launching into my prepared script about New York City. Before I get to anything related to tennis, Patrick stops me.

"Wait, *wait*," he says abruptly and scrunches his face curiously. "You call it 'The City?'" he says, making air quotes with his fingers.

"Yeah, most people call it that," I retort in a slightly petulant tone, returning the mock air quotes.

"Most *people* or most *Americans?*" he presses. This is not at all how I imagined this conversation going. This seems like a silly thing to be hung up on, too. "You know there's more than one city in the world, right?"

He's obviously being ironic, and I can tell from the sly grin he's giving me that this might actually be his version of flirting.

My mouth goes thin, and I roll my eyes. But inevitably the contours of my face ease and I'm smiling. I can't help it.

"Yeah, I know it's silly," I say, poking at my food, grinning and avoiding eye contact. "If you think that's bad, you should hear the Americans who refer to the US as 'the world.'"

He almost spits out his beer. "Seriously?"

I shrug. "Don't you Aussies say, 'going *to* hospital' instead of saying, 'going to *the* hospital?'"

"That's right," Patrick returns, proudly. "*We* do that. Because true English speakers know that there's *more* than just one hospital in the world. Ya know, proper use of a definite article in a sentence. No big deal."

I scoff at Patrick's smug explanation and roll my eyes again. I admit, I roll my eyes a lot, but Patrick hardly seems offended.

The whites of his teeth are sparkling at me, as is the touch of violet in his eyes.

Definitely flirting.

As we continue to spar back and forth, his grin seems to have inched up a little higher into the left side of his cheek, and the sparkle in his eyes has intensified.

"So where in the states are you from?"

I hesitate, like I always do when people ask.

"Connecticut."

I avoid saying exactly where—Greenwich, Connecticut, to be exact. Patrick might be from Australia and may not know of the reputation of my hometown, but I don't want to chance opening that can of worms. I just want to be anonymous in this moment. Just a girl flirting with a boy.

I can't help but cringe slightly thinking of the inflated and overgrown bubble I come from. With its who's-who societies and members-only leisure establishments, like the various sailing and yacht clubs, tennis clubs, golf clubs, polo clubs, etcetera. Greenwich is sublime in its appearance but impenetrable in form. My family has been there for generations, and so has their wealth.

"The Constitution State or something, right?"

I am totally caught off-guard and snap to.

"Yeah . . ." I say, scrunching my face at him. "How do you know that? Seems like a random fact for someone from Australia to know."

"I was planning a trip to 'The City' last year and was looking at some of the surrounding states. I read some stuff about Connecticut."

"What about you? Where are you from?" I ask, purposely changing the topic.

"Well . . . I'm from *Australia*. Obviously." He's beaming, and I'm giving him an unamused look. "I'm from Adelaide."

"Sounds kind of familiar," I return, trying my own hand at recalling world geography.

Australia is one of those many stamps in my passport. However, the placement of Adelaide escapes me.

"It's all right," he goes on. "It's a decent-sized city in South Australia. There's maybe, like, just a bit over a million people that live there, I reckon."

"I guess that's pretty decent."

Patrick snickers. "Well, it's no New York City, *but* it's plenty big for my taste. What do they have, like a *billion* people in your precious city?"

I laugh at the ribbing comment. "Not even close. It's more like eight-and-a-half million people. But there are five boroughs, so it's pretty spread out."

"*Boroughs?*" Patrick shoots back confused. "Sounds like a place a hobbit would live."

I chuckle.

"No, no hobbits. At least none that I know of. Besides, isn't that an Australian thing, anyway?"

"Nah, that's the Kiwis. New Zealand."

"Right. My brother—" I break off, and my throat suddenly closes up at the mention of Liam. I'm quiet for a few seconds, trying to find my voice.

"Your brother . . ." Patrick assists, giving me a probing and expectant look.

"Oh—um," I begin again, gulping down, trying to moisten the dry spell that's coated my throat. "He's a—he's a Lord of the Rings fan."

It's a slightly awkward blip in the conversation and I quickly switch things up—again—as I lower my eyes and eat a few more bites of my food. If I were by myself, I would scarf it all down, but I'm trying not to scare Patrick off like I'm a pig at a trough. Not that I think there's anything wrong with wolfing down a meal, even if my mother would be repulsed by it. To her, proper young ladies should never finish a meal.

The conversation turns to his itinerary or lack of one. I tell him I could never travel without a firm plan. "Ha," he says and laughs, genuinely. "You should try it sometime. You might like it."

"Doubtful," I say, giving him a skeptical look.

Patrick lets another swig of his beer glide down his throat. His bottle is almost empty, and I really don't want him to leave. I wonder if I should ask about the group he's traveling with, in particular, the girl who called out his name and kissed him. But as is usually the case, I avoid the possible awkwardness and keep quiet. Then I notice the mark on his arm.

"So, I have to ask." I muster up my courage because it feels like the question is slightly more intimate. "What's up with the tattoo of the Olympic symbol?"

I can visibly see Patrick tighten up from his comfortable slouch. His eyes narrow on his beer bottle, and he starts to fidget with peeling off the label.

"I was a competitive swimmer growing up and swam in the Junior Olympics for Australia," he replies, absent of any emotion, as if he's talking about the weather.

"*What? That's crazy!*" I'm totally impressed and feel an immediate kinship, athlete-to-athlete.

"Yeah, yeah," he says passively, tempering my clear enthusiasm. "I don't swim competitively anymore, though. I haven't for a while . . ."

"That is super impressive, Patrick," I go on, hung up on the fact that he swam at that level. Wow, just wow. I happen to know Australia has one of the strongest swim teams in the world, despite being a relatively small country.

"Thanks," he replies with zero emotion, eyes glued to the bottle.

I can't help my own curiosity. "What happened? I mean, why did you stop?" I gently probe.

Patrick's demeanor tells me that it's a topic he's not too keen to talk about, much like me not wanting to talk about home or the *something*. But I'm intrigued.

His eyes flit up at me, and he stops pulling at the label to take a small sip.

"It's a long story," he replies, avoiding the conversation all together. "What about you? What sport do you play?"

"How do you know I'm an athlete?"

"Just a lucky guess looking at that sock tan."

He points to my feet, and I look off the side of the table to where my legs are stretched out.

I have on a pair of flip-flops and look as if I have my own tattoo. Even though I haven't played in some time, I have yet to rid myself of the unavoidable tan and mark of a white girl tennis player: tan legs and milky white feet. It's annoying, and if I'm being honest, sort of gross, especially after a long match when you've been sweating a lot and pull your shoes and socks off to discover your wrinkly, pruned feet, and sometimes a toenail that's fallen off because of too much sliding on the court. Thank goodness, I have all of my toenails intact.

Patrick is easy to talk to and before I can really think about it, I'm telling him I'm a tennis player and gushing about how much I love the game. But then I pause.

"Well, I *played* tennis . . ." I correct.

"Past tense?"

"Yeah."

Now it's me with my eyes lowered, avoiding eye contact and a further explanation. I stab a few fries with my fork and dip them in the sauce, chewing slowly.

"Well, now, I can't help but ask," he prefaces, and I can feel the reciprocal question coming. "How come you don't play tennis anymore?"

I swallow the mashed-up potatoes with the tangy sauce that are sitting in my mouth and take a sip of my fizzy water to wash it all down. I look Patrick in the eyes. "It's a long story." I shrug, throwing his words back at him.

His eyebrows shoot up and he looks at me skeptically, then downs the last of his beer.

We smile politely at one another, at an impasse. The air between us seems to sizzle with intensity. But then Patrick checks his watch and looks slightly stressed.

"Got somewhere to be?"

"Yeah, actually I do."

He's probably meeting up with the girl, and once more I'm tempted to ask, but I'm way too shy to be that forward.

Patrick gets up and grabs the empty bottle. His hands look strong yet tender, and I wonder what it would be like to have him touching me.

"It was really nice talking to you, Brooke."

"You too, Patrick."

"Hope I see you around," he says, seemingly dangling the hope for another chance encounter between the two of us.

"Me too."

He pauses for a beat. "Hey, and if you need anything, ya know, since you're on your own and everything, don't be afraid to ask. Me and my mate, we're pretty big guys."

My lips press firmly together, trying to quell the smile that wants to spread across my face. "Thanks," I demure.

Just before he's out of sight, Patrick turns and waves in my direction.

He might be taken, but he's definitely a flirt.

CHAPTER 6

Finding an Equal

I'm in the hostel computer lounge, staring at the words on the screen, reading back over what I've typed out to my mother. It is a perfect summary of my day, minus the failure with Varun and his friends, and there is definitely no mention of Patrick. Zero. Zip. None. Nada.

I read it a couple of times, proofing both for spelling and grammar and also that it won't raise any questions or prompt further intrusion into my grand adventure. It must be both sterling and sanitized.

While she would have preferred a phone call, the email is exactly what my mother would want to hear. That is, that I followed my itinerary and that I'm safe. But, if truth be told, it's not necessarily what I want to say. There's a lot I would like to say to my mother. There are a lot of questions I have for her, too.

One of the last—and only—times I confronted my mother was at our family's annual holiday extravaganza, catered for New York City and Greenwich's ultra-elite. My mother didn't like what I had on and wanted me to change into something more "appropriate for the occasion," as she put it. What my mother really meant was an outfit that would make me look rich and attractive since Jarrod Callaghan was going to be there and she'd been trying to fix me up with him for ages. He came from the right type of family and had just as much money as my own. It didn't matter that he was as dumb as a bucket of lobsters. To my mother, he and I were equals in the most important sense of the word.

My mother kept fussing at me about my dress, but all I wanted to do was talk to her about what I had decided I wanted to do after graduating from Yale. I had been practicing my speech for weeks with Liam, who had been encouraging me to just go for it. My brother. My confidant. My best friend.

But my mother was completely dismissive of me, especially since, as she kept saying, "people would be arriving soon." Two and a half hours later those people had arrived, and I forced my way through the party, faking congenial small talk and peppering my interactions with prim laughter and fake cheer.

Liam had some football thing and couldn't make it back home for the holiday party in time, so I was stuck on my own.

At some point, I was roped into a conversation with a group of people, in which my mother was the ringleader. Someone asked me what my plans were after graduation. They asked *me*. Not my mother. ME.

In the split second before I could answer or even open my mouth, my mother jumped all over the question. With a coy glance at Jarrod, she explained that I would work for my father until "a decision has been made about what the next step for Brooke will be."

I remember looking straight at my mother, my eyes searing with agitation, knowing full well that her words were coded. She didn't care about my education or career. She only wanted me to be in the right kind of place to nab a suitable husband.

Back in Berlin, my hand directs the cursor across the computer screen. It hovers over the little paper airplane icon ready to send. But I stop. I hesitate, then move the cursor. DELETE.

Again, I feel something unwind in my chest, as well as a new heat begin to grow.

I breathe out a sigh of relief even though I know it means that the poor people at the check-in counter are going to keep getting calls.

Sorry, not sorry . . .

I close out of my email, but I stay seated. I look over both my shoulders, as if what I'm about to do is secret and I don't want to get caught. I guess in a way it is.

With a slight breathlessness, I go to the internet search feature and look up the Yale women's tennis team.

I scan the roster and see that my picture and bio have been taken down for the upcoming season. My face turns hot in response even though I know it's been like this for a little while.

I check the rest of the roster and see Alex. There's also a news feature of her with a few pictures of her in action out on the court and a cheerful one of her with the rest of the team.

A wave of guilt and embarrassment hits me because she is unfortunately mixed up and tied to the *something*, and I wish she wasn't.

On that horrible day, our coach had been pumping us all up before our big match, the outcome of which would determine if we made it to the national championships. I hadn't felt pumped up at all, though. I'd felt numb. In fact, I had been feeling numb all season, ever since my mom and I had finally had it out in a huge blowout.

As my coach was talking to the team in a huddle, all I could think about was the fact that I'd been doing what I'd been told my entire life—without question or complaint—and yet I had no say in deciding what I would do once I graduated.

The same questions kept circulating in my mind: When do I become an adult? When do I finally get to make choices for myself? I knew exactly *what* I wanted to do and exactly *who* I wanted to be. But I might as well have been planning to open a nightclub on the moon.

My coach could tell that there was something off with me, more so than usual. She took me aside before the match started and asked me if I was okay.

Maybe I should have said something different. But I didn't. I was compliant and assured her that I was going to do exactly what was expected of me as the number one player on the team—win. I could still see her face, just a few hours after that fateful conversation, cast in a mask of terror as she looked upon what I'd done.

I sign off from the computer and decide to have a drink. A *real* drink. Again, I feel the simmer of defiance stir in me because I rarely have alcohol, but I need something to take the edge off.

It's a Friday night and the bar area is full of milling twenty-somethings.

I go to the bar, order a drink, and find a spot to sit by myself. It's not long after that when I see Varun and company. They are loud and gregarious as they mingle with other people and don't seem to notice me at all. But eventually, Lauren and I make eye contact. I can feel my heart start to pound, from both my nerves and hopefulness. I smile and give a little wave, but Lauren flicks her eyes away from me, and I lose my nerve all over again.

I feel stupid and realize that the whole idea is a disaster. The thing is though, I don't blame Lauren. I blame me.

I've only taken a few sips of my drink, but I feel an urgent need to get out of the space, and I start to collect my things and go. Always polite, I place my half-empty drink on the bar, so the bartender doesn't have to walk around to collect it.

"Hey there, you did not like your drink?" he asks, in near perfect English.

"Oh, no. It was fine. I—I just realized how tired I am, is all. I was going to head to my room and go to bed early."

"Understood. Berlin can be exhausting."

He asks if he can get me anything else, and I order a bottle of water. As he fetches it, I nod my head toward Varun's table. "You see that group over there?" I say and try as inconspicuously as possible to point them out.

"Yes, Varun and his friends."

"Yeah, exactly. Can you put their tab for the night on my credit card?"

The bartender gives me a questionable look. "You're sure about this? Those guys are some of our thirstiest customers."

Classic Brooke. Take the coward's way out, then over-compensate and go way overboard.

"I'm sure."

I grab my bottled water and head out, giving a last glance in the direction of Varun and the others, but they don't notice me at all.

It's probably for the best.

@milgirlbratluv

Slowly, I peek up from my squatting position to look around. The grass around me undulates. There's a waning fall sunset, and I'm somewhere in a country setting.

I walk in slow motion and go several paces when suddenly I'm eclipsed by an instinctive feeling—I am alone here. Not just in this place but in the world.

I take several more steps, then break out into a run with my arms extended, no longer trapped by the feeling of moving through gelatin. Suddenly, I take flight.

I feel free. As if I were born to be a bird and my human body is merely a shell disguising my true self. I swoop playfully downward over the tall grass. There's a feeling—a rush and exhilaration—as if I'm on a swing-set reaching higher and higher with the sway of the pendulum.

Just like that, it's over. Everything abruptly ends.

I'm on a road. There's a canopy of trees creating a tunnel down both directions of the road. Something's hidden. I'm being watched.

I walk down the road, one foot in front of the other, back to moving in slow motion.

The end of the road leads me to the edge of a clearing, and at a short distance is a hill. At the top is the house I grew up in. It's grand and extravagant.

From behind, I feel the watcher in the trees. The watcher wants me to go to the house.

I'm standing in front of the oversized front doors, hand gripping the handle to open it and walk through. Inside, the interior of the house looks familiar. Nothing out of place. Modern and sophisticated. Picture perfect.

I'm wearing a gown with a long flowing train. I search the house as if I'm looking for something.

I'm back at the front door. The handle is gone. There's nothing to open the door with. I don't panic, but I have another instinctive feeling that hits me—there is no way out.

I'm in the living room. On the mantle there is a single empty frame.

I reel the train of the dress in toward me and wrap the silk gown around me like a cocoon. I hug my knees tightly to my chest and start to rock in place.

I wake up to the sound of my analog watch. It's 6:00 a.m. Even though I'm on my backpacking adventure and not playing tennis, I keep up with a watered-down version of my training routine. It's too hard to go cold-turkey and let it go completely. I need to do enough to fill the void. Get my fix.

Maybe void isn't the best description, but it's a lingering feeling of things left unfinished.

I uncurl my body from the fetal position I've woken up in, stretch my right arm out, grab my watch, and turn off the buzzing sound.

You again . . .

I've been having the same dream—or some version of it—ever since the *something* happened and wake in the same coiled position.

The dream always feels so real, as if the distinction between reality and sleep is indistinguishable. Like I'm Alice coming back from Wonderland.

I'm sure the dream is related to the contentious relationship I have with my mother—she's my watcher in the woods. But also, I'm sure it's related to Liam.

I push the covers off me and pull myself out of bed. I get dressed in my running gear, do a light stretch in my room, and head out for an hour-long run in the direction of the Tiergarten.

The Tiergarten is a huge inner-city park in Berlin, similar to Central Park in New York City, though not as big.

As I run, I see that a festival is being set up. There are vendor trucks, a stage, and other equipment that is being staged. It's then that I notice someone ahead of me, also running, that I'm sure is the American girl, Lauren.

No way. Impossible. She looked like she was already pretty wasted last night when I saw her and the others.

I think of Lauren rolling her eyes at me and feel the stab of guilt again. But it fades quickly.

She is running really fast!

I pick up speed because now I need to know. I sneak a look out of the corner of my eyes as I pass her to see if I'm right.

"HEY!"

I stop running and so does Lauren. She hunches over to catch her breath and takes out her earbuds. She's sweating profusely, and I can smell the stench of booze coming off her.

She puts up a hand. "Hey—thanks—" she says, gulping in air. "The drinks—our tab. You didn't have to. That was nice of you," she manages.

She drops her hand and stands up straight, seeming to have recovered somewhat.

I feel a little shy about her thanking me.

"I felt bad about what happened at the—"

She shakes her head, coughs, hocks a loogie, and dismisses what I'm about to say with her hands.

"I'm sorry. I was being a jerk. I shouldn't have rolled my eyes at you last night. Varun can be pushy. I get it. Besides, I've watched that *Hostel* movie enough times to sometimes think twice about who I hang out with when I'm traveling."

I give her an ironic smile at the horror film reference. "How did you know it was me that paid?"

"The bar tender. I asked. FYI, it was *expensive*." Lauren raises a brow at me, I'm assuming looking for a reaction.

"Oh. That's okay," I say, playing cool. "I er—saved a long time for this trip."

She shrugs.

Neither of us feel the need to keep running, so we slowly walk back to the hostel and Lauren tells me a bit about herself, that she is a self-proclaimed military brat.

"Growing up I survived six PCS moves, eight different schools in five different countries since I was born, and I never miss PT in the morning—even if I am hungover as fuck, which I definitely am right now BTW," she explains, wiping the sweat from her face with the back of her hand.

All the acronyms, I have no idea what she is talking about. It sounds like a foreign language to me.

I don't personally know anyone in the military, let alone someone who has served in combat. Nor have I ever interacted with someone that grew up in a military family.

"Was it hard picking up and moving every couple of years and being in a new place?"

"It was exhausting at times. I mean, don't get me wrong, I've met a ton of cool people along the way. But it can be a lot, especially as a teen when, ya know, people are already awkward as fuck." We exchange a look because of course everyone knows the universal feeling of teenage angst. "It definitely made for some contentious moments between me and my parents. Well, mostly my dad."

"You and your dad don't get along?"

"Oh no. We have a super tight bond. But we are *complete fucking opposites*."

Just like yesterday, I notice her pitch undulates up and down in a girly way, but when Lauren speaks, she's very direct and pointed, which I'm now assuming has something to do with growing up in a military family. She also uses the f-bomb more than anyone else I've ever met.

"How so?" I ask.

She glances at me, her perfectly manicured brown brows peaked. "Well, he's like this high-up conservative ranking officer in the military, and I'm his feminist-liberal daughter that's always causing a scene." She's wiping the sweat from her face again, this time using the excess of her fitted shirt that's drenched and reeks of day-old booze. I can see that she has a heart tattoo under her rib cage and a jeweled belly button ring. "I'm totally for common sense gun control, voter rights, etcetera. I've gone to—I don't know how many BLM marches. And, of course, fuck the one percent of uber wealthy people in the world. Especially, that nut that occupied the White House."

When I was at Yale, I would sometimes see people on campus rallying or handing out leaflets advocating for positions like what Lauren is talking about. Often, I might get asked to join, or a fellow student would start explaining to me the importance of various issues. But I admittedly was always way too focused on school and tennis to get involved. Politics is not really my thing.

Lauren's on a soap box now.

"I mean don't get me wrong, my dad's not some sort of war hawk or right-wing conspiracy theorist or anything like that—believe me, he wouldn't be where he is today in the military if that were the case," she says, giving me a confidential look. "But when you flip off his commander-in-chief whose political party has been trying to dismantle women's fundamental rights for decades, it causes some friction in the whole, ya know, father-daughter relationship."

"You gave the president the finger?"

Lauren scrunches her face. "You mean the Occupier? Yes . . . Well—okay, sort of. I flipped off his motorcade. But still."

I laugh. Not that I find it funny. It's more like a nervous chuckle because I could never do something like that. Plus, the "Occupier" is unfortunately the sort of ilk I grew up around, scandals and all.

"Anyway, so, what's your story, Brooke? Where ya from? What's your travel status? Etcetera."

I give Lauren a brief overview and tell her a little about myself and my travels. Again, I avoid mentioning that I'm from Greenwich and tell her only that I'm from Connecticut. I also mention I play tennis. But nothing about not playing currently.

By the time we get back to the hostel, Lauren and I are joking and getting on. I feel like she's softened toward me enough that I slyly ask what she and her group are up to for the day.

"Oh, I see. Now that you and I are cool, you wanna come hang out with our group? But, *Brooke*, you were *so* adamant about not wanting to join us yesterday," she jests with a big teasing grin, using her sing-song voice and pawing at me all sappy.

I can tell she's enjoying razzing me, especially since I know I'm visibly clamming up. But I nod anyway.

"Are you sure? We are sort of an obnoxious group, as you know. I don't want to disrupt any planned brooding you might have scheduled today."

"The brooding can be rescheduled," I say, only half joking. Lord knows I will probably need a 12-hour sulk-fest once this ordeal is over.

"I *guess* you did pick up the tab last night, so how could I say no? Money can buy everything, as they say."

If only you knew.

For all the teasing, I still feel a sense of pride blossom in myself. I can be spontaneous. I can make friends. I can be social. I can even make decisions for myself and live my own life. Even if it did take a few hundred euros to cross that line.

Liam would be proud. I know it.

"Well, welcome to the crew!"

Before I can say anything else, Lauren is wrapping her arm around my shoulders and positioning her phone in front of us.

"One-two-three girl power!"

I blink, mouth slightly ajar.

Lauren unwraps her arm and starts maneuvering her thumbs over the screen.

"There. Posted. My handle is milgirlbratluv. FYI, I'm an 'influencer'—well, trying to be anyway," she says, her eyes fluttering up from her screen momentarily. "I'm still working on the content, but for the most part I have a fairly legit following. Look. It's already getting likes."

She shows me her phone, staring at me with an eager smile.

"I snap a picture after every morning run and post it," she explains. "We look good, don't we? You're cool with it, right?"

Her big pearly whites and her almond-colored eyes are narrowed on me, and I feel the pressure, especially with her pitchy squeal that I'm sure could crack windows.

"I mean, you look good. I look pretty sweaty and gross. I'm not sure it's a good idea—" I start.

"Oh, Brooke! Come on! You're starting to sound like you did yesterday, all uptight and shit. You look fine!" She waves off the beginnings of my excuse.

My hesitation is not really about how I look. I sort of groan, on the fence, but she ignores me.

"Now don't forget to find and follow me."

"Okay," I say relenting, even though I barely use social media and obviously don't have a phone with me.

"What's your handle?"

"Uh," I stall, trying to recall. "I think it's tennisfan_1234."

Lauren gives me a disturbed look. "Yikes. That's pretty sad. Not the creative type, huh?"

She quickly starts typing away again.

"One picture. You, on a tennis court. Looks like I'm not the only one who needs to work on their content."

I feel my face flush. My mom wouldn't allow Liam and me to create any social media accounts till we turned sixteen. By then it had lost the allure—at least for me it did. I had a one-track mind by that point, which is aptly reflected by the one picture I did actually post.

Lauren and I make arrangements for meeting up later that day and go our separate ways. I take the stairs up to my room and as I do, I again feel a sense of pride, but also relief for how things seemed to work out. There's only one small thing that my mind latches onto.

Brooke, chill. It was just one picture.

CHAPTER 8

Portrait of a Young Girl

I'm cleaned up. My hair is dried and styled. I put on something cute and even added a dash of makeup to my face.

As I'm packing my little day bag, I glance across the room and freeze.

There, lying quietly on the floor, is yet another message. It must have been slipped under the door while I was getting ready in my ensuite bathroom.

I pause and unconsciously start to gnaw at the inside of my mouth. Third time is not a charm, Mom.

She knows I'm here and that I'm checked in. *Why can't she just take a hint and leave me the fuck alone?*

Clearly, Lauren's foul mouth from the morning's encounter is rubbing off on me because I rarely curse, let alone think to myself using profanity.

"Fuck it."

I grab my bag and throw it over my shoulders and have a last look in the floor-length mirror. I pause before my travel diary, with all of its helpful maps and bucket list items, but decide to leave it. I appear nerdy enough, without added help.

The journal is laid out on the bed open to today's agenda. I close it, running my fingers tenderly over the words crossed out on the front proclaiming its original purpose, and feel a touch of self-torture.

I then step out of my room, while unceremoniously ignoring the message by leaving it on the ground, untouched.

You are not going to spoil my day, Helena Rose Neville.

I imagine how angry she must be that I won't respond to any of her attempts at contacting me. Normally I would worry about not obeying. I would also feel guilty.

But this time, I'm not bothered in the least. In fact, I feel a sense of pure gratification as I make my way to meet up with my new friends.

"Where are we off to *now*, darling?" Varun says in an exasperated tone.

"We're going to the Gemäldegalerie Museum next, *darling*," Lauren replies in a sarcastic tone as she stares frustratedly down at her cell phone at a map of Berlin.

It's only been a handful of hours, but it feels like we've zigzagged across Berlin at least three dozen times, trudging past fountains and through gardens, somber memorials, and cavernous museums. There's so much history here. So rich in culture. Plus, an innate feeling of defiance wrapped around the soul of the city.

I'm exhausted, but it's the most fun I've had so far on my travels. The group is great, although I'm still a little leery of Olivier and sense that the feeling is mutual. The sentiment seemed to become amplified by the fact that one of the receptionists tried to flag me down as we left, telling me I needed to call my mother. Beyond embarrassing. That definitely elicited a healthy bout of teasing from the group that took about an hour or so to die down.

Also, everyone thanked me for picking up the tab, and only Lauren has continued to give me crap about the cathedral incident.

Mostly friendly jabs. Nothing I can't handle, and in a way, it's comforting because it reminds me of bantering with Liam.

Varun hunches over, looking weary. "Are you planning on carrying me there, darling?"

"No, stud. Let's go."

And just like that, we're booking it to the next stop, speed-walking through a free-flow of pedestrians, surrounded by all of the typical city sounds and obstacles.

"So, you said that you three were roommates?" I ask Lauren as we dart around a few people headed in the opposite direction as us.

"*Flatmates,*" Varun corrects me from behind.

"Oh," I reply.

"Urgh, stop being a know-it-all, Varun. And stop creeping in on our convo!" Lauren glances over her shoulder at Varun and sticks out her tongue.

"Oh, ye two love birds, always at it," Grady pipes in.

I chuckle at the remark because Lauren and Varun have been flirting-slash-bashing each other like two middle schoolers all morning.

"Anyway, yeah. The three of us are flatmates in London," Lauren answers, focused back on me as we dart around more foot traffic. "Varun and I are students at Kings College, and Grady's at London School of Economics."

"Really? I'm going to be studying abroad for a year in London at LSE," I say, genuinely excited that I'll know people before even starting school.

"What?! No freaking way! We're totally going to have to hang out when we're all back!" Lauren squeals, grabbing excitedly onto my arm as we walk.

"For sure," I say with a broad smile, feeling a similar level of enthusiasm. "So, you said the three of you live together? That's sort of . . ."

"*Interesting?* Yeah, I know. How'd I end up with those two goons?" she says still clutching my arm, with a pep in her step.

Again, Varun interjects. "*Goons?* Who are you calling a goon, darling?"

Lauren ignores him completely.

"Well, that's not exactly how I was going to phrase it, but I was curious how you three ended up as roommates—I mean *flatmates*."

Lauren smiles at my quick correction then launches into a story about two nightmarish-sounding girls she lived with—one an apparent klepto, the other who stopped paying rent—until she kicked them out, and how Varun and Grady became their replacements.

"Now we're one big exuberantly happy family," Varun remarks with a healthy dose of sarcasm.

"Aye, we most certainly are!" Grady declares sincerely, contradicting Varun's jaded tone.

I chortle, charmed by how the threesome's energy seems to circulate and bounce from one to the other like a pinball machine.

"Did things work out with the klepto?" I ask Grady, who apparently went on a few dates with her.

"Oh, no. Nice enough girl, but a bit too clingy, if ye know what I mean," he replies, laughing at his own joke, which he seems to do often.

Varun is shaking his head unamused as we start to move again, making our way across a busy intersection. "Clever devil."

We stop once we reach the other side of the street so Lauren can check her phone to make sure we're headed in the right direction. Not wanting to be rude, I include Olivier. "What about you, Olivier? How do you know everyone?"

At my question, Lauren glances up and she and Olivier exchange a look.

"2019. Paris Climate Agreement protest," she answers ominously, dropping her gaze back to her phone.

"Be careful with those two. They'll start recruiting you before too long," Varun warns.

"Shut up, Varun," Lauren hisses, her eyes remaining focused on her cell screen.

"It's true. You've dragged Grady and me to—I don't even know how many rallies. Like hostages, I might add."

"That's not how I remember it, friend. You seemed pretty willing to put the pink pussy hat on, Varun," Grady tells.

The two exchange a look, and I'm confident that Varun has a secret—or maybe not-so-secret—crush on Lauren.

"Okay, two more blocks that way and we'll be there," Lauren announces, pointing straight ahead.

"You looked cute with the pink pussy hat. It's a good color for you," Olivier pipes up, smirking at Varun, who rolls his eyes.

"Thanks, *Olive*," Varun pings back.

"Oh, hey, I just got a text from Max."

"Who's Max?" I ask as Lauren puts her phone in her back pocket.

"He's one of the Australians. There's like a group of four of them—Max and Abigail, and then Patrick and Lizzie. Wait, weren't you talking with Patrick yesterday? I might have already asked. I think before you shooed us away at the cathedral." She gives me a teasing grin.

"Uh-yeah," I sort of moan-slash-answer. But before I can really respond, Lauren is jabbering away again.

"Anyway, seems like they're coupled up. I don't really know. They're all staying at the same hostel as us. They're cool. We hung out with them last night."

I immediately want to ask questions but am unsure of how to broach the subject without being obvious. I'm tongue-tied.

"'We hung out with them'?" Varun laughs. "More like you drank Max under the table. All on Brooke's tab, I might mention."

Lauren turns and glares at Varun and then turns to me.

"Sorry, not sorry," she remarks, batting her eyes and shrugging her shoulders innocently. "Max was boasting that he could handle more tequila shots than me. Couldn't let that happen."

I don't respond because I'm still trying to work out how I can slyly ask about Patrick and maybe get some details on who the other Aussies are, specifically the two girls.

"Well, you certainly beat out Max on the tequila tolerance, darling," Varun remarks. "Lucky for him, Patrick seemed sober enough to get him back to their room. I assume Max was out like a log by that point."

"I would hope so. From what I could hear when I walked by their room, someone—or *someones*—were having their own little after-party. I think maybe Patrick and Lizzie were taking advantage of the quasi-alone time," she says, giving me a racy look. "I know I would. Hot Aussie—yes, please."

My mouth starts to open to say something, but I don't. There's no point. What I figured is confirmed. Patrick and Lizzie are a thing.

"Okay! C'mon! We're almost there!" Lauren commands, corralling her troops.

We're off once more, and I've chalked up the interactions with Patrick as either me misinterpreting or him being a giant flirt. Whatever.

A few minutes later, we make it to the Gemäldegalerie. I grab one of the audio tour headsets so I can learn about some of the art. I'm the only one in the group that does.

We all start to wander collectively, until the audio tour leads me into a large room adjacent to where the others have stopped, and Varun and Lauren are debating several pieces of early Renaissance artwork.

In the other room, I walk directly toward one painting and am completely mesmerized. I look at the information card next to the painting—*Portrait of a Young Girl* by Petrus Christus—and start to listen to the audio about it.

Like so many classical pieces it looks completely ordinary. There is nothing special about it. No wild splashes of color or fantastical designs. No elaborate background or landscape, nor any religious messaging or connotation—none that is apparent, anyway. It is simply a young girl who sat for a portrait painting. Yet this image is haunting.

As I scrutinize the piece, I guess that the girl looks to be about twelve or thirteen, maybe younger. The painting depicts her from the bust up, and she's wearing what looks like a plain navy-blue dress. But as I look closer, there are subtle details in the fabric and design, indicating she was probably someone of a higher station in her society. She has a long slender neck and milky, translucent skin, and she's wearing an elegant gold necklace, while fastened to her head is a traditional Flemish headdress—according to the audio commentary. But it's unmistakable under the stark lighting of the picture: Her eyes are dead. Empty and blank. She's numb.

I know you.

I do. All at once, I feel as though I'm looking in a mirror. The miserable expression is all too familiar to me. She's trapped.

I wonder about the girl as I stare intently at the painting and imagine what her life was like. *Did kids get bullied when you were in school? Were girls even allowed to go to school when you were alive?*

I was called all kinds of names growing up. Kids can be mean, no matter who you are or where you come from or how much money you have.

"Hmmm, yes, I wonder what it is this young girl, she is thinking?"

I can hear someone talking in the background of the audio tour, but I don't realize that the person is speaking to me.

"There is a certain kind of sadness in her eyes, no?" I follow the words but am still lost in thought. "Even as she glitters in jewels, while the common way starves in the streets."

I finally take the headset off and glance to my right. It's Olivier.

Immediately, I get that sense of unspoken mutual skepticism between us.

"Maybe the jewels are a heavy burden," I say.

He raises a brow at me but doesn't respond. We stay with our eyes locked on one another for a moment until I glance back toward the girl in the painting.

There is something about Olivier that reminds me of all the snobs I grew up with. Growing up around money means, more often than not, you can smell it a mile away. He confirms as much when he finally speaks again. "My father, he is a businessman. He's dealing with petrol—oil and gas—and such things. I do not think he is a happy person. This is the same for many men in my family, this status."

Nailed it. But I don't say anything and let him keep talking.

"My mother, on the other hand, she is an artist. She is a very *good* artist, in fact. She does both, it is this sculpting and jewelry-making as her profession. She is happy, I think. She is *free.* I mean her—how do you say? *Esprit* is *free?*"

"You mean free-spirited?"

"Ah, yes, *oui,*" Olivier responds with the same smirk as before.

There is a twinkle in his eyes. It feels like even though he's telling me about himself, he's really probing me. Like he's dangling information about himself to get me to bite at the worm and talk about myself.

"Are your parents still together?" I ask.

Olivier scoffs, and I assume it's a sore spot for him.

"They divorced when I was young—maybe five or six? I don't know, something like this. My father has a whole other family. A new, young wife. Children."

"Oh."

Heard that story a million times.

"My father is . . . hmmm . . . I think he likes things a certain way, no?"

"Controlling?"

He nods. "I think this is an easier life with the partner he has now. His wife is a child. On top of this, they have children. Like I say."

Same thing happened to three of my mother's closet friends. It didn't change their lifestyle very much, of course. Mostly, because alimony and prenuptials can be bittersweet.

"I know this look well." He points at the painting, and I realize as Olivier speaks that we probably are not much different, and it softens me a little toward him. But only a little because my spidey senses warn me not to divulge details about myself.

We're both still staring straight ahead at the portrait when he says something that causes all the fine little hairs on my neck to stand up straight.

"You know, Brooke, you look *familière . . .*"

I'm frozen, not sure how to respond.

"Your last name? What did you say it was again?"

"I didn't say," I reflexively respond and immediately I know that I sound defensive.

He turns and looks at me, his head and man bun cocked to the side, waiting for a clear answer.

"Smith."

Not true. Obviously.

"Hmmm . . . and where did you say you were from? *Exactly?* Connecticut . . . What city?" His words sound slippery but with a venomous sting at the end.

"New London."

False.

"And your parents? What do they do?"

I swallow and can feel the lump in my throat go nowhere. Nonetheless I keep my eyes trained straight ahead, playing cool. If I look at Olivier, I'm sure he'll see the deception written all over my face.

"My father is a high school teacher, and my mother is an office manager for a law firm."

It's what Alex's parents do for a living.

"Interesting. And you say you are studying abroad? What is this, for a year, yes? At LSE? This is quite impressive. LSE is a very prestigious school, very expensive too . . ."

I temper my breathing and turn to face him. I feel like if I don't confront him head-on by looking at him eye-to-eye that the questioning will continue, and I'm going to run out of responses.

"Thank you," I say politely. "I'm on scholarship."

"*Très magnifique!*" Olivier cheerfully declares in response, giving me a satisfied look, though I can tell he's still skeptical. "Well, I guess I have you mistaken for someone else, maybe. Congratulations on your scholarship."

"Thanks."

Before I can think too deeply about the lies I've told and the details I've stolen from Alex's life, Lauren rushes up with Varun and Grady in tow.

"HEY!" she says in hushed but still loud voice.

"Shhh!" someone says off to the side.

Lauren mouths the word "sorry" at the person and continues

on in a whisper-shout. "Hey, so this is fun and all, but I'm done with the educational stuff. Let's go to that music festival in the Tiergarten. You two down?" she poses to both me and Olivier.

I don't hesitate to respond.

"I'm in."

"*Oui.*"

"Fuck yeah! Brooke, you don't have to ask your mom for permission, do you?" she jokes, giving me a wink. I give her a flat look, lips pressed tight together.

Again, Lauren's attempt at a hushed voice carries, and a few museum patrons turn in our direction with an offended look.

Grady is laughing, and Varun is shaking his head disapprovingly as we drag Lauren toward the exit.

I'm relieved to leave the conversation with Olivier behind and more than happy to be the butt of Lauren's amusement in order to do so. Though I can't help but wonder to myself about the girl in the portrait and whether she ever had to lie to protect herself.

What am I thinking? Of course she did.

CHAPTER 9

Watch Yourself

"Come on, Brooke!" Lauren shouts, grabbing both of my hands like we're playing the children's game of London Bridge, prompting me to get into the rhythm of the music along with everyone else. The festival is packed. The music is loud. We've fought hard to work our way through the throngs of people to the front of the stage, and for the past ten minutes, I've stood frozen off to the side, watching as everyone else bops and gyrates.

I've gone to exactly one concert in my whole life. The girls on my college tennis team convinced me to go see Florence and the Machine freshman year. For three hours straight, Florence belted out her songs, pitch perfect and jumped all over the stage. It looked like the best kind of therapy. Better than sitting in a chair for an hour, week after week.

With Lauren tugging me closer, I reluctantly start to move. I'm slow at first and then give way a little more. I try my best at dancing and letting go, but it's hard, and I'm sure I look as uncomfortable as I feel.

"That's it!" Lauren encourages me as she twirls us into the orbit of the crowd.

Every man around us has their eyes glued to Lauren, including Varun. Not only is she beautiful but her energy radiates.

"Don't give a fuck, girl! Just have fun!"

I smile back at Lauren as I try to absorb some of her carefree vibes.

Yeah, Brooke! Let go! Don't give a fuck!

Even if I'm awful at dancing, I'm smiling. I'm having fun. I'm laughing. I can feel a touch of perspiration from being jammed together with a sea of young people in the hot afternoon sun.

I'm a free spirit!

"YAAASSSS GIRL!" Lauren screeches.

I shout and howl along with the rest of the crowd as the song hits the chorus, and the stage lights explode in a tsunami of flashes. I'm not sure how much time passes before Lauren grabs me, drenched in sweat, saying she needs to catch her breath.

We all wind our way back through the thickest part of the crowd and find a place to settle down in the open grass out of the fray. I pull out my camera from my backpack. I realize I've not taken one picture all day.

"Whoa! What is that thing, a dinosaur?" Lauren remarks, lurching forward and snatching the camera.

"Seriously, I can't remember the last time I saw an actual camera, can you?" Varun poses to Grady and Olivier, with a mild gobsmacked face.

Everyone seems to marvel at my camera as if it's an artifact from ancient times.

"Aye, and it's hot pink," Grady comments.

"Do you not have a phone *with a camera*, darling?"

"Yeah, but I left it in London."

"Where is this place you are staying in London?" Olivier asks casually even though I can hear the underlying cynicism in his voice.

I pause. This is something I can't lie about, as I'm hoping to hang out with these guys when I'm there.

"Mayfair."

I cringe, knowing it is the most expensive area of London. It's just a stone's throw away from Buckingham Palace, made up of luxury Georgian brick townhomes—one of which I'm renting for the year—and it's home to some of the most exclusive hotels, restaurants, and premier shopping outlets from top designers around the world.

I can already see from their expressions that Lauren, Varun, and Grady are familiar with Mayfair and are trying to process my response.

"You said you are on *scholarship?*" Olivier smirks, all-knowingly.

Before I can respond, Lauren interjects.

"Who's the hottie in the picture? Looks a little young, but he's super cute."

"Let me see that," Varun says, turning the back of the camera toward him so he can see the display screen from over her shoulder.

I don't have to see the screen to know.

"Liam. My younger brother."

"Oh, yeah, I can see the resemblance. How much younger are we talking?" Lauren says playfully.

"Too young for you, darling."

Lauren jabs Varun and pushes him back from spying at the picture, to which he feigns an offended look.

"Two years younger than me."

"Single?"

I pause and shrug.

"These pictures are so cute! You two seem really close." I'm lost for words as I wonder just how scandalous it might be for me to launch myself across the grass and rip the camera out of her hand. "Is this a birthday party?" Her eyebrows shoot up. "Looks super fancy."

I know exactly which pictures Lauren is looking at. I didn't want a big party for my thirteenth birthday, but my mother planned an extravaganza anyway. The parties were mostly for the parents anyway, a sort of subtle—or, maybe not so subtle—way of flaunting her extravagance under the cover of being an indulgent parent. I could still remember her ordering me to pose beside two zebras, while loudly complaining to her friends about how spoiled I was.

"Earth to Brooke. HELLO!"

Lauren hands me the camera back. "Well, hopefully your brother comes over to visit you in London and you can introduce me."

"And you call yourself a feminist," Varun teases.

I don't remark on the suggestion, and the conversation segues in a few different directions until I suggest getting something to drink. I need some space and wave down their offers to come with me, promising to return with waters and beers, and some snacks. Varun tells Lauren she could learn a thing or two from me about being a good hostess, and she almost punches him.

"I think Grady is right," I say. "You two are love birds." It feels good to joke with the crew—minus the lingering cold vibes I keep getting from Olivier.

Grady claps his hands together and bursts out laughing. Even Olivier is amused.

"Hey! You're my new friend, Brooke. You're not supposed to be taking up the side of either of these two clowns!"

"So, you don't deny it," I smile, tapping my chin.

I'm pretty sure Varun is blushing as he moves his shades back in place. Meanwhile, Grady is still roaring with laughter, and Olivier looks just as entertained.

"I'll be back in a minute," I say with a little wave.

I make my way through the crowd to a bunch of vendors. I see one that looks like it has a good beer selection and head toward it. As I do, I see a sweep of soft brown hair atop a broad, strong back and prickle with instant recognition.

Get a grip, Brooke. Remember he's taken.

Patrick's standing alone. I pause.

Deep breath. I can't help it. I don't have anything to lose.

I head in his direction, but before I get to him, I see the Australian girl—Lizzie—rush up and embrace him, leaning up to kiss him on the cheek. As she does, her eyes turn in my direction. I immediately freeze. She and I are looking directly at one another. Her dark eyes give me an unquestionably challenging look.

Well, that's a twist. Possessive, much?

Patrick doesn't notice me at all, but I certainly take note of the fact that he seems neutral in response to her affection. He doesn't seem like the type to go for a girl who is super clingy.

I finally steer away and head toward a different vendor. Not only do I feel confused, but I feel hurt, even though I know I shouldn't.

I can't help it. My brain is spinning in circles with all manner of thought and hypothetical scenarios to explain away our interactions, trying to make sense of the situation, combined with Lauren's insights from the night before, as I stand in line to order. It's a bit obsessive but totally me.

Once I get everything, I throw the bottled waters and snacks in my pack and carry two giant beers, one in each hand as I make my way back toward the group. As I'm gingerly cutting through bodies, trying not to spill, the thing I'm trying to avoid happens as someone crosses right in front of me, and I dump the beers all over myself and the ground.

"Oh no! That's terrible. You should really watch yourself."

I stand, soaking wet, the two cups completely empty and on the ground. Lizzie stands in front of me with her lips pursed and snakish eyes glaring. A few people pass us and notice that I'm drenched but don't say anything. It's just me and Lizzie, with her contemptuous look up in my face.

Lizzie doesn't say anything else for a solid minute as I shake off as much of the dampness from the beer as I can. In the flick of a switch, her eyes light up with warmth and happiness, and she brushes past me as if I were nothing more than an annoying figment of her imagination.

I feel defeated and, even worse, disgusted with myself. I can only imagine the satisfaction she must feel as she thinks of my wide-open eyes, stunted mouth, and dumb expression.

Coward.

Like a wounded animal I stalk off, abandoning my new friends and what had otherwise been one of the best days on my grand adventure.

CHAPTER 10

Special and Finite

BEEP-BEEP-BEEP.

It's 6:00 a.m. I reach out from under the covers and snatch my watch from off the bedside table, pulling it under the covers and hitting the snooze button.

I don't really fall back asleep so much as squirm around under the warm comforter with my eyes closed. I still feel sort of paralyzed from the whole incident yesterday with Lizzie. Behind my eyelids I keep replaying everything that happened, which is basically how I fell asleep last night. My brain won't stop analyzing the whole disastrous episode.

That's what happens when you get off-track.

I blame myself. Yeah, the group thing was fun, but once I got back from the music festival, stripped myself down from the beer-soaked clothes, and took a hot shower, that's when I started to reevaluate.

Don't try to be something you're not.

These are the thoughts that keep running through my head as I lie awake in bed repeatedly running through the reel from the day before.

I also feel bloated and sluggish, because after the whole incident I stayed locked up in my room vegging out on potato chips, cookies, crackers, and cheese, and reading my romance novel like some sort of doomsday prepper. Not exactly how I anticipated spending the rest of my day, but it felt like a suitable punishment for failing to stick to my plan and looking the fool, once again.

BEEP-BEEP-BEEP.

This time I turn the alarm off and slowly emerge from under the covers.

I throw on my workout gear, do my stretching, and head out. I sneak through the lobby, even though it's basically empty, and decide to avoid the Tiergarten park this time.

I finish my run and again sneak through the hostel lobby back to my room to get ready for the day. I'm headed out and almost at the bottom of the stairs leading into the lobby, when a voice booms across the space.

"Brooke!"

I don't need to turn to know it's Patrick. *That voice.*

I pretend I don't hear and keep walking toward the front exit, but he calls my name again and rushes up, grabbing my arm to catch my attention.

"Brooke! Hey, are you okay?"

I stop and turn to face him. It's the first time he's touched me since we met, and I'm looking down at his hand cupped around my arm.

He loosens his grasp and lets his hand slide down the length of my arm. I flinch away. I'm not interested in being touched by someone else's boyfriend, even if she is a psycho.

"I heard you were at the music festival yesterday," he says, and I'm not sure if he's asking or making a statement. When I don't say anything, he furrows his brows, clearly confused. He's taller than me, and I stare up into his eyes. They're so warm and inviting with that touch of blue-violet beneath the light brown. I'm definitely attracted to him, even as I shrink from the thought.

He clears his throat. "I heard you took off early though. After you spilled beer on yourself, or something," he says lightly.

He's trying to break the ice, but I'm sure it's also obvious to him that I've put up a wall, since I've just folded my arms in response to the suggestion.

Spilled beer on MYSELF? No big surprise in guessing who told him that.

"Been there, done that before," he remarks. Meanwhile, I've yet to respond to anything he's said.

He cocks his head, as if I'm a puzzle he can't work out. Suddenly I feel tired. Why is he trying so hard with me, anyway? I get that we have good banter, and there is a stirring of attraction even as we stand there in awkward silence. But from the very beginning it's like he's singled me out and made an effort to push past my defenses. I can't work out why.

"By the way, how is Berlin comparing to The City?" he continues.

I look down at my watch that I had left off the day before but am back to wearing so I stay on my schedule.

"It's great, Patrick. Listen, I have to go. I have somewhere to be. Bye." I wave.

I break my gaze from looking up into his eyes and turn to walk off. I can palpably feel the confusion from him.

"Did I do something, Brooke?" I hear him say from behind me.

My eyes wince and again all I see is Lizzie with her hands all over him, kissing his face and her warning me to "watch yourself."

"Nope. Bye, Patrick."

He doesn't say anything else as I walk out the door. There's a small part of me that wishes he would rush up and press me against the wall, kissing me stupid like the hero in my romance novel.

I let the door slam behind me.

I've been following my itinerary all morning and mostly exploring West Berlin. I ate breakfast at a café that I previously researched, famous for its brunch menu, and located near the Zoologischer Garten, which is one of the oldest zoos in Germany. I visit the zoo after eating and then head farther west to the Schloss Charlottenburg palace.

The palace was built over several centuries, with a beautiful expansive garden spread over eighty or so acres. Originally called the Schloss Lietzenburg, it was later renamed in honor of King Friedrich I's wife, Queen Sophie Charlotte. It was her summer retreat but over time and under different rulers, was built up, encompassing thousands of square feet of ornate and splendid estate rooms, ball rooms, halls with frescos and gilded plaster designs, libraries, and sitting rooms, all lavishly decorated in a Baroque and Rococo style.

I wander the long sprawling corridors from one room to the next listening and absorbing the history while on my pre-booked English tour I reserved months before my trip. The tour ends in the gardens, and when it's over, everyone disperses.

I continue winding my way through the gardens alone. The grounds were inspired by Versailles and are just as immaculately manicured.

I stop at a park bench to sit. My thoughts and emotions drift, as they have all day. I find myself staring down at the scars on my right hand, reflecting, realizing that I didn't even notice them yesterday. The poignancy of this is not lost on me. My mind drifts some more as I trace the lines with my other hand and stare out at the wide-open countryside, with the perfectly trimmed hedges and rose bushes and sprawling fountain leading up to the palace.

———

"Why is Mom doing another holiday party this year?" Liam huffed. "I mean one is already enough, but *two*? Seems like overkill . . ." He drew back the sheer curtain and looked out one of my bedroom windows.

"Duh, because you weren't here for the first one, and you know Mom wants to parade her favorite child around," I answered snottily.

I was sitting in the lounge chair in the hangout area of my over-sized room, flipping through *Tennis* magazine. My eyes didn't leave the article I was reading as Liam walked over and plopped down on the couch adjacent to me, snatching the magazine from my hands as he settled in.

"HEY!"

"I'm definitely not her favorite child," he responded, fanning through the magazine. "Why do you read this junk?"

"The same reason you watch football documentaries, and read football stats, and watch the Football Network all the time."

"Except that *I* have a life." Liam stopped turning the pages to look at me and laughed. He knew me well enough, and I'm sure he could tell something was up. He set the magazine on the coffee table and ran his hands through his shoulder-length blond hair. Apparently, growing long hair was the thing to do as a football player, even though our mother hated it. Dad had no opinion, per usual.

I couldn't help but wonder that if I were a male too, would I be perceived differently and more like my brother, where people championed his drive and persistence?

"You still haven't talked to them, have you?" he sighed.

"I tried to talk to Mom at the annual party, but she didn't want to listen."

"Don't try. Do."

"And be more like you? Mr. Perfect," I teased.

This time it was Liam who rolled his eyes. "You need to be more like yourself and who you want to be. Stop being who everyone thinks you ought to be," he replied before pausing. "You know what you need?"

"What's that?" I asked, genuinely curious as to what my brother thought I needed—even as he just finished saying I needed to think for myself.

"A boyfriend. You need to get laid. Seriously, I think that might help you chill out."

"So a guy is going to solve all my problems, is that it?" I responded in a snarky tone.

"Your crush, Jarrod Callaghan, is going to be at the New Year's party."

"Don't make me gag. I had to stomach a solid thirty minutes of him at the last party. I think he thinks we're going to end up together, too."

Liam knitted his eyebrows at me. "I'm going to take a nap," he said, yawning and ignoring my additional commentary. He rubbed his fingers into his temples. "I need some aspirin."

"You always have headaches lately. Now that you're a West Coast guy, it's like you're allergic to coming home."

Liam dismissed the joke. "Wake me up for dinner if I'm not up by then," he said, as he walked out and shut the door.

"I'm not your keeper!" I hollered over my shoulder.

"Yes, you are, sis!" he shouted from outside my bedroom, down the hall somewhere.

As I sat with the magazine in my lap, all I could think was that at least I had Liam to support me. He might have terrible advice in terms of dating, but he was the one person who was really on my side. In that way at least, I felt truly wealthy.

I'm still sitting on the bench in the gardens at the Schloss Charlottenburg palace and every part of me hurts, thinking back over that conversation, over so many conversations just like it. All of them special and finite.

If Liam was here, I know he would tell me to just go with the flow. Who cares about the guy and the spilled beer. Just have fun and enjoy being free with my new friends, because that's what I really want to do, that's who I really want to be. That's what I want for myself.

But he doesn't get a say anymore.

That's the price you pay when you leave everyone you love behind.

The War of Attrition

"MISS! MISS!"

The lobby is packed, but one of the front desk workers rushes out from behind the desk and makes a beeline straight for me, shouting to get my attention.

I stop as the check-in guy pauses in front of me, waving a handful of scribbled notes. A few people are staring at us, but the guy talks privately, and their attention immediately goes elsewhere.

"Miss, your mother. She keeps calling and asking that you please contact her. I don't—We don't know what else to tell her," he says in his thick German accent, pausing with pleading eyes. "She's threatened to call the *authorities*."

He hands me the notes, and I stand there mortified and . . . something else.

My mom isn't worried. This is a war of attrition, and she won't give up till I do what she wants, which is call or email or communicate in some fashion.

"I'll take care of it," I assure him between tight lips.

I don't mean to be, but I know I sound cold and ungrateful. At this point, I no longer care. Or maybe I do, a little. Either way, I'm angry at my mom. I'm angry at Liam. I'm just angry.

I turn and head straight toward the public computers. I sign on to my email, type out a message, and press send. "I AM FINE."

I hate myself as I send it, but sometimes you have to pick your battles, and this is not the hill I'm going to die on.

No doubt, that time will come sooner rather than later.

CHAPTER 12

Mental Toughness

My travel diary hasn't failed me yet, but there was one time in Italy that I got turned around because of some restoration work and had to get directions from some slick-looking James Bond guy with a weird accent. Today, I'm having a bit of a repeat, only worse.

It's early morning. It's hot and humid, and I'm surrounded by loud jackhammers and bulldozing equipment doing construction work nearby. I can't for the life of me figure out the street signs in German. I'm usually good at navigating, but today my internal compass has lost its magnetism, and I'm spinning precariously in circles like a spindle top.

A bead of sweat rolls down the nape of my neck as I squint down at my travel diary and bobble my head from side to side trying to make sense of my surroundings. The walkway is crowded, and people are brushing by me dismissively.

I walk a block or two, my focus split between the pages of my journal and trying to get my bearings. My irritation is splintered, and stubbornness is preventing me from doing the most basic thing, which is to ask for help. No doubt, my emotions from yesterday are being compounded today.

Then I hear it—a clear, crisp popping sound. The familiar sound that makes me stop dead in my tracks as I'm about to pass a pub. They have Wimbledon playing on the various outdoor televisions. The familiar, rhythmic beat of the ball pinging back and forth is deafening and pierces my nerves.

I suck in a deep breath and watch. It's a big match—men's semi-finals—and it's close too. The stands are full at the All England Club, and each player is donned in full white attire. I, of course, recognize both players and know everything about their careers, one of whom is the new "bad boy" of tennis, Landon Simon, a former college tennis sensation who dropped out of school to go pro.

It's meditative watching the match. For a minute I forget the heat of the day and that I'm lost. I'm completely absorbed and even feel a stir in my muscles aching to be on a tennis court again.

"Silver Gilt, Volume Two."

My travel diary slips out from my hands and lands on the ground half-open.

Patrick bends over and scoops up the journal. He runs his fingers down the torn-out pages that it's fallen open to and flips through the pages still intact.

"Coloring book?" he says wryly as he hands it back to me.

I eye him warily. "Thanks. No. Travel diary." Just like before, I'm definitely not in the mood for flirtatious banter with him. Also, I'm wondering where the hell he turned up from and why he's not with his girl, Lizzie.

"What does that mean? The 'Silver Gilt' thing," he asks in a friendly tone.

I shake my head. "Nothing."

There's a pregnant silence that looms till he gets straight to the point, switching to a more cautious tone. "Are you mad at me? Did I do something?"

Another long pause. I can tell that he feels unsure of me, after my curt response to him during our last encounter.

My face folds a little. "No, it's just—" I start. "Never mind." I realize I'm caught up in my own head and personal complications that have nothing to do with him. There's no reason for me to take out my frustrations on him. Bottom line, he's super cute, but he has a girlfriend. Time to let that train roll out of the station. *Don't be a jerk, Brooke.* "We're cool. Sorry for being short with you yesterday." I give him an olive-branch smile.

"No worries. We can start over," he says reassuringly. "*So?*" He nods at the book, clasped between my hands.

I point to the television, where a giant roar erupts from the crowd.

"It's what the trophy is made of. Silver gilt."

Patrick's brows turn inward, clearly probing for more of an explanation.

I exhale a deep breath. "I used to use it as a tennis diary. To track opponents and my own progress and stuff," I tell him. "But since I don't play anymore, I decided to use it as my travel diary. I upcycled it, sort of thing."

"Uh-huh. What happened to the pages?"

I shake my head again. "I told you. I don't play anymore. No point in having them."

"Yeah, but you clearly love the sport."

His words linger between us, and I feel knots turn in my stomach, like I'm totally exposed. I default to chewing at the inside of my mouth as I analyze what to say next.

"It's complicated. Long story, remember?"

"For both of us, right?" He smirks, rehashing the sentiment from our previous conversation. "Where's volume one?"

I snort ironically. "Ask my mother."

Patrick straightens up and looks at me, his eyes drained momentarily of their calm and collected nature.

"I was being sarcastic," I assure him and see the edginess slip from his gaze.

"Oh. I didn't know what you meant," he says, a bit quick. "Does she have it or something?"

"I don't know. I think so. I lost it my senior year of high school before I was getting ready to leave for college. I'm pretty sure she took it as some sort of deterrence."

"Your mum doesn't like you playing or something?" he asks, casually leaning against the low gate framing the outdoor pub space.

My eyes are back to being trained on the screen. "Not really. She'd rather me follow in her footsteps and be a country club trophy wife, rather than want to win a trophy."

"That's rough. Pretty well-off, then?"

Shoot. This is what this guy does to me. Talking to him is easy and disarming. And those eyes.

I don't look at him. My eyes are searching as I try to come up with a plausible response. "No, that's not what I meant. I'm just talking. That didn't come out the way I meant. It's just—" But as my eyes momentarily dart in his direction, I can tell he's not buying it. My shoulders slump as I huff out another breath of hot, humid air. "Can you keep that to yourself?"

"Sure. Secret's safe with me," he answers gently. The thing is, I believe him.

There's suddenly a big burst of noise from the television. Landon Simon has lost in a fifth set tiebreaker and is smashing his rackets on the court, causing an uproar from the crowd and commentators, who he's mocking in return.

"Wow! Look at that guy! He's insane," Patrick remarks. We both watch as Landon takes another racket from his bag and smashes it to smithereens.

I snicker. "Yeah, he's got a bit of a reputation on the tour. Definitely not something you do at a Grand Slam tournament, let alone the most prestigious of all. He is a good player, though."

"You like that guy?"

I shrug. "Yeah," I say dully, even though I'm a big fan, minus the over the top behavioral issues. Who doesn't like a bad boy?

"You were never like that out on the court, were you? I couldn't imagine you losing your stuff like that."

I feel my face go hot. "No. Not on the court."

Things go quiet for a minute before Patrick starts talking again.

"I imagine you have to be pretty mentally tough to play a sport like tennis, eh? Out there on the court, all on your own . . ."

His words make me think of what my college coach used to say. That tennis is 90 percent mental, 10 percent skill. It's true. The best players get beat when they lose control inside their head.

"For sure," I reply. "What about you? Ever lose your 'stuff' after getting beat in the pool?"

Patrick points at himself incredulously. "*Me?* No. But I've seen people lose their stuff because of swimming."

There's another extended silence between us. My fingers are tapping the front of my journal like I'm on the brink and want to let myself fall. I feel vulnerable, and I yield to the sentiment. "I had this thing—a mantra—I used to say to myself when I was play-ing, to stay focused and get in the zone. It helped me stay mentally tough, to not lose my stuff. It made me feel like I could stare down my fear or self-doubt and defy all obstacles, sort of thing."

Patrick looks at me genuinely interested. "Oh yeah? What was it?"

"Don't think, just do," I answer, immediately feeling self-con-scious. "I know it sounds weird—"

"No, that doesn't sound weird," he interrupts me. "I had my own mantra for swimming: all now, all at once."

"That's a good one. I like it."

"Thanks." His eyes drift. "Yeah, I don't know. It always made me feel like I could pour every bit of myself into that sprint in the pool. Like it wasn't about my opponents, it was me against myself and the clock. I just had to be hyper-focused. Push my body to the limit, and that's *all* that mattered. Nothing else."

I give him an ironic look.

"What?"

"Nothing," I say shaking my head. "Just being overly focused. Sometimes it can backfire. Mess things up. That's been my experience, anyway."

I turn back to the TV but take stock of the fact that I can see from Patrick's mannerisms that I'm not the only one feeling vulnerable.

"You're different, aren't you?" he says, rhetorically.

I'm watching the next match that's started, but I can feel his eyes on me. He lets out a big yawn and stretches.

"Man, I'm knackered."

My mind jumps to what Lauren said about late-night liaisons, and I have to ask. "Something keep you up late?" I slyly probe, though I can hear my own jealousy poking through.

"Yeah but not by choice. Max, my mate, has had a couple of late nights. I think one was thanks to you," he points out with a laugh. "I got him to bed, but he had company. I wasn't about to stick around for that." We exchange a knowing look, just like Lauren and I did previously. "Let's just say I went for a long walk till I figured it was safe to return."

My heart is pounding. So it wasn't Patrick and Lizzie that Lauren heard. "Oh."

"Not super happy with Max at the moment, to be honest," he huffs. "I need some space."

"Oh," I repeat. I'm assuming he's saying that to explain why he's alone.

He shakes his head dismissively. "Sorry, you don't need to know any of that. A bit of guy drama. Anyway, I was headed back to the hostel. You headed that way? I can walk you back."

"Yeah, sure," I answer, decidedly ditching my plans.

We meander back to the hostel, talking more. It feels candid and easy, and when we cross the street, Patrick gently puts his hand on the small of my back. I don't know what's happening, but there's something equally different about him to me and my heart is back to fluttering at the thought of him.

We're about to walk into the hostel when Patrick's cell rings. I'm laughing at something he's just said and before I can say something smart or flirtatious in response, he brushes my elbow with the tips of his fingers and rushes off.

"Have to take this! I'll catch you later!" he shouts over his shoulder, nearly halfway down the block.

"Okay," I say to myself.

Patrick is a mystery, and I'm left in his wake with an overwhelming feeling of wanting to figure him out.

CHAPTER 13

Rodeo Drive

Time to make things right. I'm on a mission to find Lauren and the group, headed in the direction of the bar-slash-restaurant-slash-lounge area of the hostel, when the front desk guy from earlier comes rushing out from behind the check-in area to flag me down. This is mortifying.

"MISS, MISS!"

Are you serious?!?!

I guess the one saving grace is that none of the staff know who I really am, or how truly insane my family is.

Or do they?

They're not supposed to. All my reservations are under a pseudonym.

I have a moment of paranoia, wondering if my mother has told the hostel staff exactly who I am, which would defeat the whole purpose of me traveling anonymously.

I can hear her now: "Do you know who *I am* and who my *daughter* is?" I feel the knots in my stomach grow tight even thinking about it.

The guy reaches me with a smile. His stress from earlier seems to have subsided.

"I was just going to go up and slide this under your door," he says, handing me yet another note that I take. "You are very popular."

He's trying to be lighthearted about things, but I feel myself blush. It's embarrassing to be the adult backpacker whose mother won't stop calling. But then I read what's scribbled on the front of the folded piece of paper.

TO: Brooke / FROM: Lauren

I look back up at the front desk guy and muster a smile to try to make up for being such a grouch. "Thanks," I reply, sincerely.

"*Bitte.*"

He walks off and I flip open the note and read.

> *Dude, WTF? What happened to you at the concert??? And where have you been??? I heard something about you getting clumsy and spilling beers on yourself . . . Anyway, we met someone at the concert who has an in at . . . Brücke! If you're down to go, meet us at the hostel bar around 9 tonight and all will be forgiven. See ya – L*

Huh. Apparently, Lizzie is going around telling everyone—not just Patrick—that I spilled the beer on myself.

What a be-otch.

I'm flattered though that Lauren would go out of her way to invite me to join the group even though I abandoned them the other day at the concert.

I wonder what Brücke is . . . Club? Bar? Restaurant?

I look up at the time on the big wall clock behind the reception desk. I have plenty of time till nine, but I start to get a little anxious thinking about the logistics.

What do I wear? I don't even know what this place is . . . Is it fancy? Does it have a dress code? I definitely didn't pack anything super nice.

I flip open the note again.

"Brücke," I say to no one except myself.

I bite my lower lip thinking. I sneak a look in the direction of the computer lounge. All the computers are taken up. I look back at the check-in. The front desk is busy. I'm too excited to wait around to research or ask about Brücke.

I've already made up my mind and head straight to my room, grab my wallet with the motherload of my credit and debit cards, and head out. I'm going shopping.

I've got a good idea where some of the designer shops are because I remember seeing them near the zoo, on the west side of Berlin, when I was walking there yesterday.

Since I don't have a phone to set up an Uber or Lyft drive, I grab a taxi.

It doesn't take long before I'm walking along the Kurfürsten-damm, the Rodeo Drive shopping drag of Berlin. There's Gucci, Valentino, Louis Vuitton, Chanel, Yves Saint Laurent—all names I'm familiar with but am having reservations about going into to look around.

Is it too much? Am I overthinking this? We're probably going to some grungy speakeasy, and I'm going to show up looking like *Pretty Woman*. Though, that wouldn't be so bad, especially if I ended up with the guy at the end of the night. Patrick, of course.

I shake my head as if erasing my frenetic thoughts away like an Etch-A-Sketch and just pick a store. I start in the direction of Chanel but just as the security guy at the front is about to open the door for me, I pause. This is my mother's preferred store for dressing me up like her little doll. *No.* I back away, turn, and head across the street to Dior instead.

Inside I start looking around, combing the displays. I see a pretty floral dress I like and look for my size. I find one, pull it off the display, and hold it out in front of me. It's beautiful and I really love it, but as I hold it out in front of me, I'm struck by a similar thought as to the one I just had standing in front of Chanel.

It's an off-putting feeling. A sense that, aside from buying basics and active wear, the clothes I've worn have never really been my choice.

I look at the price tag on the dress. Fancy clothes mark you as different in our society, supposedly in a good way. But you are marked, and I'm still not sure if I want to be.

"*Hallo. Kann ich Ihnen helfen?*" says one of the sales associates, who's come up to me.

"Oh, sorry, I don't speak German."

"You are American?" she replies, skeptically. I see her comb me over in my grubby backpacker attire that's meant to be camouflage so I blend in with the masses. There's a sizable detergent stain on my shorts from my attempts at doing my own laundry.

"Yes," I start.

"This is *very* expensive," she remarks rather impatiently, her penciled brows raised, looking chic and sophisticated in her pin-stripe pantsuit. This is certainly not how I'm used to being treated at a store like this.

I hang the dress up and walk out. I try another store and have a similar experience. My patience is thinning. I march into Valentino. *Screw this noise. This is not happening again.*

I find a couple of dresses in my size I want to try on, but when the sales associate comes over, I can already see she's wary of me. It's like a WANTED poster of me has circulated among the various stores, or a cruel game of telephone is being played by the sales associates. "Don't let the pant-stained American riffraff in your store!"

"I want to try these on," I demand in a tone that I don't like.

"*Sich beruhigen.* Madam, please calm," she says in a wispy German accent.

My patience snaps in two. All politeness goes hurtling out the window. Before I know it, the store manager and security guard have walked over.

"This is complete B-S. I can pay. Why am I being treated like this?" I start to unshoulder my bag, ready to flash my various black and platinum cards, and the wad of cash I have stashed.

"Madam, you are causing a scene," says the manager with an unamused look, as her sidekick security guard shuffles closer, hinting toward the exit.

"Is everything okay?"

I turn around. At first I don't recognize the person, but then a vague recognition hits me from when I checked in.

"Hey girly. Brooke, right? Max. Everything cool?" he says, in a distinctive Australian accent. He's a pretty big guy, tall, built, tanned skin, with longish blond hair flipped out from under a ball cap. He winks at me, gives me a cheesy smile, and steps a little too close for comfort into my personal space.

"No," I reply indignantly, then wield back around to look at my accusers. "These people are treating me like a common criminal, and I have no idea why!" I sling my bag back over my shoulder. "Forget it. Whatever. I'm out."

I briskly walk past Max, shoving the dresses at the sales associate, and storm out of the store.

"Hey! Brooke, wait up," Max calls after me.

Then I feel his hand on my shoulder, and I stop to face him. "*What?*"

"Whoa. Chill, woman."

Suddenly Patrick is not the only one not happy with Max.

"I am chill. I didn't ask for your help back there." I narrow my eyes at him. "What do you want? Why were you in there anyway—*alone?*"

I don't really analyze my question, it just pops out. Either way, he's giving me a patronizing look like I'm being an unreasonable, overly dramatic twenty-something girl, which is making me go from not happy to wanting to slug him. Hard. This woman is ready to fight.

"Whoa, whoa, lady," he repeats as if I'm a horse without a bridle, and I can feel my arm start to draw back, ready to lay one on him. I am not in the mood. "I don't want anything. I was shopping for *errr*—shopping for Abby. Look, I'm sure it's nothing personal. I bet they get their fair share of backpackers who come in and try to nick things, is all. They're just trying to be cautious. It's a totally reasonable thing, ya know? You can understand, right?" He flashes another of his cheeseball smiles, winks, and is staring at me as if he's solved all the world's problems.

"Okay, but *all* the stores I went into treated me like that. It doesn't make any sense," I say, exasperated, arms flailing. He doesn't say anything in response but cocks his head, raises his brows, and gazes off to the side like he's growing tired of me and my need to know. Apparently, he has no further follow-up to his mansplaining. I turn and start to walk again, with not so much as a nod or a wave of goodbye.

"You headed back to the hostel? I can walk you back. No need for a pretty girl like you to be on her own," he calls after me, sounding desperate.

Weird. "No," I say and keep my pace. "I need to clear my head—and be *alone.*"

Suddenly, I can understand exactly why Patrick would need space from Max—total chauvinistic vibes. Gross.

CHAPTER 14

Eccentricity

I look at my watch. I've gone from having plenty of time to feeling like maybe I should throw in the towel.

"MISS, MISS!" calls out someone new from the check-in area. Their accent is so intense, it sounds as if a bee is buzzing in the lobby.

Between me and the front desk girl who's just yelled in my direction, I'm not sure who's got the winning irascible look. She might have a stinger for sure.

The girl is petite with a bleach blonde bob, but the left side is shaved down to the scalp, where a long sterling silver cross earing is haphazardly dangling in the wake of her agitated movements. The front desk guy, who I've mostly been dealing with, is behind her shaking like a leaf.

I walk over as she slides out from the counter, antsy to confront me.

"Miss, we keep getting calls from your mother! You *need* to call her," she instructs forcefully. "This is very *serious*. She is making threats to my staff. Otherwise, I am going to have to ask you to leave."

Shit.

My features soften. "I'm sorry. It's my fault. I emailed. I thought that was good enough. But I will call her."

"Now. Or you go."

The girl is dressed head-to-toe in black and has shiny dark-coated fingernails sharply filed that look like a set of cat claws ready to strike. She's giving me a hard stare, as if daring me to say no.

I nod submissively. "Do you have a phone? I don't have a cell."

She rolls her eyes, fuming, but turns on her heels and motions for me to follow. I walk with her past the reception desk, where the rest of her staff glare at me in disgust. *So embarrassing . . .*

We go into a back office, and the girl points at a landline for me to use. "Keep it short."

"Okay. Can I have a little privacy? Me and my mom are going through—um. Things are a little rocky."

Another eyeroll. She steps out, but I can see her linger, apparently wanting to make sure I follow through.

I nervously punch in the numbers. Country code, area code, phone number.

"Hi. It's me."

"Yeah, I'm fine. I know. I'm sorry I haven't called."

I turn away from the half-cracked door and talk softly into the receiver. Five minutes later I wrap things up.

"Done."

The woman nods, satisfied, as I scooch by her and make my way out past the front desk, but then I stop in my tracks. The manager looks like the very essence of Berlin—grungy, sleek, cool— surely, she has to know. "Hey, can I ask you something?"

If looks could kill. She has her arms folded, standing out in front of her staff like a warrior shielding them from my wickedness.

"Do you know a place called Brücke?"

"Of course," she scoffs. "Every young person in Berlin—perhaps all of Germany, Europe even—knows this place," she says matter-a-factly, pursing her dark, maroon-colored lips at me.

"Oh. What is it?"

She laughs in amusement, her rocker-girl goth exterior seeming to crack at my complete naivety. "It is only one of the most exclusive clubs to get into in all Germany. It is world famous," she answers, sort of gushing at the fact.

"Oh," I say again and feel completely daft.

"*You* are going there?" She looks amused as her eyes sweep me up and down.

"I think so, yeah."

She shakes her head and brushes her hand through her hair. "This is not what you wear to Brücke," she advises.

"Well, I wasn't planning on wearing this. I went to the Kurfürstendamm, but—" I start, about to explain the whole *Pretty Woman* experience but think better of it, not wanting her to think further ill of me as some type of shoplifter, especially since she is being somewhat nice to me now. "I was going to wear like a cute summer dress or something . . ."

She's glaring at me, shaking her head again. "No. Not the place to shop. And you don't wear this 'summer dress' to Brücke, either."

"Oh. Well, is there a place you would recommend going to shop?" I ask meekly, testing the waters.

There's a labored pause. I can see from her expression that she might be trying to work out whether to take pity on me or not. "You want to stand out at Brücke," she starts to explain, "but you also need to look like you belong."

I give her a confused look.

Deep sigh. I can see her face fold. "You will find out about this when you go—more fun that way. For now, I will write down the name and address of a shop that has what you need."

I'm so relieved I could hug her, but I keep my gratitude under wraps so she doesn't change her mind.

"Here you go," she says, handing me a piece of paper.

"Thanks, and sorry again about my mom," I say, taking the paper. I look at it and try to pronounce the name of the place but end up butchering it worse than any of my other attempts at German words.

"No, no. You say, Exzentrizität. In English, the word is 'Eccentricity.'"

I raise my brows at her, thinking of the time I once tried to wear a silk shift in March, and my mother had a meltdown.

This should be fun.

As the taxi cuts through various side streets, we pass small dive bars and cafes, some restaurants with outdoor picnic bench seating with a variety of ethnic food options, and graffiti murals galore, as well as spray-painted writing on walls and buildings. It's a far cry from Charlottenburg and all the fancy shops.

I'm intrigued and truly spellbound by the graffiti that is large, colorful, vibrant and seems to be everywhere in Kreuzberg, where the hostel manager's directions have taken me. I hadn't even planned an excursion into this area of Berlin—only to the top tourist spots, for art and culture, i.e., all the stuffy museums—and would have completely missed it had I not strayed from my itinerary.

Good riddance. Let go!

I put down the backseat window and breathe in deeply as the passing air lifts and swirls my hair into a tussled mess. I am exactly where I need to be, and it feels good.

We start to slow, and the taxi slides up against the curb.

"*Hier*," the cab driver says, and points.

"*Danka*," I reply and pay.

I get out of the cab and walk up to the shop listed on the piece of paper.

Exzentrizität is cast in bold brass letters above the door and the display windows are . . . quite something.

"Here goes nothing," I say to myself and walk in.

It's huge inside, bigger than what I could have imagined from looking at it from outside. It's also busy.

I wander at first, combing the racks that are filled with wild looks that are dark, alternative, leather, grungy and avant-garde. I don't know where to start or what to try on. For a split second I wonder if I shouldn't just walk straight out because I'm starting to feel a little intimidated. But then I feel a tap on my shoulder.

I turn around, and looking at me is a trans woman, suctioned in a leather bodice and twirling a feather boa.

"You're the lost American girl going to Brücke?"

"Yes." *Lord, is it that obvious?*

"I'm Violet," she says with a muted accent, extending her hand, and we shake. "Mara called me. I've already pulled some stuff that should work at the club." She huffs, looking me up and down, something that has happened about a dozen or more times to me today. "In fact, I think you will be eaten alive."

Her eyes flare excitedly. I gulp, hoping her words are intended as a compliment more than a warning, and follow her bouncing brown locks to the changing rooms.

CHAPTER 15

Something to Remember the Moment

"Brooke, it's the end of the offseason! Come out with us at least *once* before we start training again. Please!"

Alex was putting her lipstick on in front of her dresser mirror and looking at me in the reflection. I lifted my eyes from the economics book I was reading at my desk and glanced in her direction.

"I never stopped training. I'm getting up early to do weights and some footwork exercises tomorrow," I said, going back to my book.

"It's a Friday night. When are you ever going to be college age again? Don't you want to be young and have fun?" She turned around, and I lifted my head from the book again, so we were looking at each other. "What about hanging out with me and the rest of the team? Remember team bonding? It was a thing we *used* to do."

But that was before. There were things I was trying to accomplish by that point in time.

"No one is forcing you to drink. Just come and hang out. Come and *relax*."

Alex was pretty. Really everyone on the team was beautiful, but Alex was strikingly different. She's mixed race with light brown skin and green eyes. Plus, besides her looks, everyone who met her loved her. Her personality was gravitative. She was kind, always looking out for others and being the attentive and nurturing one, like the team mom, in a way.

She probably didn't really care if I came or not. She was just being nice.

"I can't," I said, dropping my gaze back to the pages in my economics book.

I could feel her exasperated look without even having to lift my eyes back up.

"I give up. I can't do this anymore. I've tried."

"What's that supposed to mean?"

I glanced back up at her as she stuffed her little shoulder purse with cash and her ID. She paused. "Do you *not* get it, Brooke? Why do you think I agreed to room with you? You've changed so much since our first year here."

There was a long pause. We both knew that my efforts to be part of the team started to wane last year, and since the start of our senior year I'd mostly kept to myself. I knew and she knew that it was off-putting to everyone, but I was still by far the best player on the team.

I continued to give her a blank stare as I twirled the highlighter between my fingers nervously, thinking about how we'd known each other the last couple of years, and this was the most serious conversation we'd ever had together.

"Because we're friends?" I finally replied, as if it was a question.

She dropped her head and huffed out a big breath before looking back in my direction.

"We are, Brooke," she said, with a bit of an ironic smile and reluctant undertone, and I could feel the caveat, the "but," to her reply, even though she didn't say anything else. In my head, I finished her broken thought: *But you've become an anti-social, hyper-focused recluse, and no one wants to be around you.*

Alex put her shoulder bag on and headed toward the door. I went back to reading and highlighting.

"Bye, Alex."

She didn't say anything in response, locking the door behind her. I stared at my textbook for a solid minute, closed it, pushed it away, and pulled out my tennis diary and started writing feverishly.

Alex and I hardly spoke again after that, and we definitely haven't spoken since the *something* happened. Or rather, she hadn't responded to anything I'd said.

I can't help but wonder what Alex would think of me now if she saw me dressed the way I am, about to go out to some world famous nightclub. I can feel my nerves as I walk into the hostel bar. I'm about three inches taller than what I normally am with the chunky black platforms I have on, and I can feel the air on my butt underneath the tight leather miniskirt.

I'm still thinking of Alex and that ordinary Friday night. Sometimes I do that. I wonder about Alex and reflect on that evening as if there was something pivotal about it. What if I had just gone with her and the rest of the team? Could it have changed the course of everything after it? Probably not. I was a ticking time-bomb and so was everything else.

I practiced walking while I was at Exzentrizität and Violet kept barking at me to "own the look." I try my best to at least appear as though I "own the look" as I walk into the crowded space.

Immediately, I can feel and see a number of people look in my direction as I walk toward the bar. This outfit couldn't be further removed from the Connecticut world that I come from.

Mom, eat your WASPy heart out.

"Shit! Brooke? Is that you?" Lauren breaks away from the bar and stands before me as if she's viewing the second coming of Christ. "Holy fuck, girl! I *love* your hair and makeup, and your outfit is so on point! Have you been to Brücke before? You look like a pro!"

I would describe my makeup as glamour grunge. It's dark and

foreboding but not so over-the-top that I feel the compulsion to wash it right off. But for sure, I would never in a million years think to ask for my makeup to be done like this. When I was paying for my clothes, I tipped generously, and Violet seemed to decide it was her moral imperative to take full responsibility for my look, hair and makeup included. I did have to temper some of Violet's ideas, though. She was prepared to put little hearts under my eyes and add other designs, which I rejected, caving instead to the Viking punk braids that now sweep back from my temples.

I also have a fancy-looking bralette on, in place of the diamante nipple pasties Violet wanted me to wear under a sheer top. Even though everything is technically covered, I still feel like I'm walking around in my underwear.

"Come on. I want to introduce you to our new friends. FYI, Lars and Erik are spoken for tonight—if you catch my drift," she says, winking at me, with a greedy smile.

"Got it," I say with a knowing smirk.

"Brooke, I'm so glad you decided to come out. I was worried for a minute you'd be a no-show . . ."

We exchange tentative smiles as Lauren loops her arm through mine and drags me in the direction of the group, who are all sitting around a table with a slew of empty beer and wine bottles cluttered on top like a chess board.

Varun almost spits his drink out. "Well, hello. That's quite the transformation."

All eyes turn to look in my direction, including the newbies to the group—a girl and two smoking hot dudes. Everyone else, including Lauren, is dressed in a gothic glam style, but I have definitely pushed it to another level. For a moment, I feel the same satisfying rush as when I take a reckless shot on the court and pull it off. I haven't always enjoyed being invisible. Sometimes it's fun to be seen.

Lauren introduces me to the newbies—Lars and Erik, both Scandinavians, and the girl, Alda, who is from Germany.

"Well, now that we have everyone here and we're all acquainted, how about a round of shots to kick things off?" Varun suggests.

Before I can respond, Varun grabs some empty cups and shot glasses that are already spread out across the table, and everyone is shuffling so I can take a seat.

I'm not really into taking shots, but as the glasses get filled and I settle into my seat with the commotion of the group sucking me in, I'm struck by a thought.

I don't look like me tonight, and I don't feel like me. So, I get to be someone new. I'm breaking from the siege.

Varun hands me a shot glass with clear liquid, and I can smell the pungent scent of liquor.

"What are we drinking to?" Grady asks.

There's a short pause.

"New friends," Lauren responds definitively with a big grin to the group.

"Ah, darling, how sentimental." Varun tucks her into his side, and I feel a pang of longing for that kind of closeness with someone. Something I've never really felt before, other than Liam, and my mind automatically drifts to him.

"Works for me. Cheers, friends," Grady says, raising his glass and rolling into a speech. "May your pockets be heavy, and your heart be light. May good luck pursue ye each morning and, definitely *please*—for the love of God—find me tonight!"

Grady lets out a roaring laugh at himself as he clinks his glass on the table and throws back the shot, followed by the rest of us.

"I like your look," Alda says to me, her German accent heavy but understandable.

Alda is pretty edgy herself in leather pants matched with an oversized, ripped-up black T-shirt and boots. She has a vibrant red bob and dark eyes and seems perfectly at ease sitting squished between the two hulking Scandinavians who look like Asgard warriors.

"Thanks. I had a little help," I explain. I'm about to tell her about Violet's magic styling powers when Lauren cuts in.

"So, after you spilled beer on yourself at the concert and ditched us—" Lauren starts, all chummy.

"That's not exactly what happened," I interrupt, turning from Alda to Lauren.

Lauren gives me a curious look. "Okay, well whatever happened, you left, and we never saw you again." She pouts. I shrug. I'm not going to trash Lizzie in front of a group of people, so I try to give Lauren a look that promises a private explanation later. "*Anyway*," Lauren continues, "that's when we met Alda. She's the one I said had the in at Brücke."

"Cool. Sorry I missed you at the concert, Alda. Sounds like you guys had a good time."

Lauren and Alda exchange mischievous smiles.

"Yeah, we may or may not have bonded over doing Molly at the concert together."

I narrow my eyes in surprise at the two, even though I barely know Alda.

"Hey, don't judge," Lauren starts. "Besides, I only do it recreationally every once in a while," she continues, still defensive but ignoring my admonishing look.

"I do it all the time," adds Alda with a laugh, like *so what*.

I feel the new me take hold and push my judgment to the side.

"I guess, to each their own," I say with an easy smile.

"Cheers to that," Lauren replies and hands me a beer from a pack on the table that I readily take.

"Cheers."

I find myself scanning the room occasionally, but I've yet to see the one man I keep telling myself I'm not interested in. There's also no sign of Lizzie or the other two Australians. I feel a little disheartened, but I'm still having a good time. Eventually though the group is ready to head out, and we start clearing our table of the battlefield debris of empty bottles.

"Okay, so remember, there are rules at Brücke," Lauren says to everyone in her usual way of rallying the group.

Alda is nodding her head. "Correct," she adds and takes over listing them out. "Everyone understood the dress code, though Brooke puts us a little to shame." She smiles, showing that she's only teasing. "Second rule. No phones."

"I feel so naked!" Lauren pretends to sob, and everyone laughs.

"Third and last rule. No cameras."

I feel my face flush again as Lauren's eyes stop at me. I have my digital camera in my waist purse that I bought at Exzentrizität.

Violet told me all about Brücke but didn't mention anything about no cameras. She said no phones but probably didn't think someone would *actually* bring a camera that was not already part of a phone.

"Let me guess. The hot pink digital?"

I slowly pull out the contraband for everyone to scrutinize.

"No cameras," Alda repeats, wagging her index finger.

While the group finishes the last of the drinks and clean up, I make my way through the crowded lobby to return the camera to my room. That's when I see Patrick.

I should go up to him.

The little voice I refuse to acknowledge is the one pushing me to show off my hot outfit, while Lizzie the Lizard Witch is nowhere to be seen. But as I walk up to him, he turns around and walks straight past me.

I stand there, dumbstruck.

He didn't even recognize me. Feeling like the biggest dork in the room, I pause to consider if I should run after him like a lost puppy or continue on to my room as planned. Even though earlier it felt like the spark was real between us, I'm still not sure since he rushed off to take a call and totally ditched me.

"Brooke?"

I grin and turn.

He's looking at me as if I just slapped him.

"I didn't even know it was you. Then I smelled your perfume and . . ." My heart squeezes. He knows my perfume? We stand in a sort of awkward silence at this admission, until he finally croaks, "You look amazing."

"Same."

He's in a black tee, dark jeans, and lace-up boots—a pretty standard outfit by any measure. But on Patrick, it looks sculpted, and slightly dangerous. My fingers itch to test the softness of his shirt against his abs. I tuck my hands under my arms and tell myself to stop acting like some lovelorn spinster. *You are a lovelorn spinster.*

Neither of us says anything for a moment. The lobby is swarming with people, but I feel like we've been swept away to our own dimension where it's just the two of us.

The new me decides to cut to the chase, as I let out a deep breath that feels like it has been trapped in my chest since I stepped in front of him.

"I like you," I say, shocked by my own audacity.

His eyes widen with surprise, and if I'm reading him right, a touch of pleasure. "Brooke, I—"

"Wait." I put up my hand. "Let me get this out." I need to tell him that I would like to get to know him more but not if he has a girlfriend who's going to murder me in my bed the moment my eyes are closed. I'm about to say as much when a familiar screech fills the room.

"Brooke, what the hell. You still have the camera!"

Lauren strides over with a bossiness that would be terrifying coming from anyone else.

"Sorry, we're going to some weird club that doesn't allow cameras," I explain to Patrick, deflating with the realization that my moment has passed.

"We're leaving!" she declares, before turning to Patrick. "You look hot. Wanna come?"

Patrick darts a glance at me, shy suddenly. "Would you like me to?" We stare into each other's eyes, and again I feel the compulsion to throw myself into his arms, but I don't.

"Sure."

I gulp and lick my lips because my throat has gone dry.

"Lucky me."

I smile and give him a flustered look because it's clear he's not holding back at this point. Now I know for certain the attraction between us is real and has been the entire time. But is this a giant mistake? Will Lizzie be joining us too?

I turn and run up to my room to finally get rid of the camera, only to hear a set of heavy footsteps behind me.

"Hey, you were about to say something before," Patrick ventures, but I wave my hand as he catches up to me.

"Now's not the time."

"All we have is time." He smiles, then his eyes light up. "We should take a picture," he suggests. "Something to remember the moment by . . . I mean since you can't bring the camera with you and all."

We both stop. I sigh and pull out my camera, hoping Lauren doesn't leave without us. As I mess around with the settings, Patrick puts his hand on my side. Just as he knows my perfume, I instantly recognize his scent as well. It's deep and woodsy, and something else I can't quite put my finger on. Perhaps it's just him. A swirl of heat rushes through my body as my fingers fumble before finally succeeding in their task.

I extend the camera in front of the two of us and he pulls me even closer.

"1 . . . 2 . . . 3," I count, just a little breathlessly.

I snap the picture and drop my arm wrapped around him so that I can check the picture.

"Looks good," I comment.

"Better than good," he adds, his arm burning against my bare back.

I'm not me tonight. I'm the new me, and the new me wants to pull his face to mine and kiss him. I can feel my eyes flicker back and forth from his gaze to his soft lips, anticipating what they would taste like. He followed me up here, away from the others, and he's looking at me now with an intensity I don't think I've ever experienced. I can feel temptation gripping tightly on every fiber of my being, and the only thing I can hear is my measured breathing.

"Come on," he says, pulling us both out of our trance. "Your friend is waiting."

Way to play it cool, Brooke.

It only takes a few minutes to drop off the camera, but since I'm in my room, I use the bathroom and double-check my makeup and hair. Looking at my reflection in the mirror, I see the new me and feel my confidence surge wondering what the night will bring.

As I leave the room, I'm surprised to find him waiting for me, and we make our way down the stairs with a new awareness of one another. With his tall form at my back, I allow myself to imagine what it would feel like if he was mine. If we went together, as a pair.

Everything feels surreal—where I am, who I'm with, what I'm doing. I could never have imagined that I would be in this present moment a year ago, so far from home, with my life completely different and turned upside down but somehow finding my own happiness.

We find the others at the entrance, and when I wobble in my chunky platforms, Patrick shifts forward and takes my hand. I can't help the smile that slips across my face, until I turn, and my eyes find Lauren. Instead of her usual grinning optimism, she frowns at me, then Patrick, and lightly shakes her head.

My stomach drops.

I pull my hand from Patrick's, determined to have a good time and not get involved in any drama that isn't mine to own.

CHAPTER 16

'90s Teen Movies

We head to the subway but decide to take a short detour and do some night-time sightseeing on the way. We've only made it a short way from the hostel when Lauren declares she needs to stop and use one of Berlin's questionable public toilets. With an overt side-eye and flick of her head, she signals that my presence is also required, so I stand in the dingy fluorescent lighting, waiting and wondering what it is she must share with me so urgently.

"Whoa! Sweet relief! My seal has officially been broken for the night," Lauren howls as the flush of her toilet echoes and she emerges from her stall, as does Alda.

I'm quiet as I wonder if I imagined the funny look Lauren gave me earlier, but I don't want to be the one to ask, because whatever warning she might have for me about Patrick will become real. I'll play along, I'm just not initiating.

The three of us primp in front of the mirror for a moment, pinching, pulling and fussing with our hair and makeup. But still Lauren says nothing, and the suspense is starting to kill me. Scratch that, I'll initiate.

"Can I ask you something, Lauren?"

She drops her eyes from mine since we're looking at one another through the mirror. She caps her lipstick and puts it in her little shoulder purse. Her movements and mannerisms remind me of a dog with its tail between its legs.

"You know what I'm going to ask about then?"

"Yeah. I don't exactly have a poker face."

"What are you two talking about?" Alda wonders out loud about the mysterious, coded conversation we're having.

Lauren huffs out a heavy breath.

"Patrick. Brooke's date," she says, turning so that the three of us are now facing each other with our backs to the sink and mirrors.

"Oh, he's very handsome, and Australian, yah?"

"He's not my date," I say to Alda.

"What about him?" she returns, ignoring my clarification.

"I don't know. I'm waiting for Lauren here to figure out the best way to tell me."

There's a smidge of impatience in my voice as I wait for her to cough up whatever information she has on him.

"Look, I know we just met, but I'm the type of person who is *fiercely* loyal to my friends—new, old, whatever," she begins.

My stomach starts to twist in knots, even though I can tell she is being sincere and probably trying to soften the blow to whatever she has to say. I just want to tell her to get on with it and tell me.

"Well, we did just drink to new friends," pipes in Alda cheerfully.

"Right," Lauren agrees with a sad smile in Alda's direction, still looking uneasy about the nugget of information she's yet to reveal to me. As I shift with impatience, she raises her hands. "Look, I'm just trying to look out for you and give you some information to consider. Do what you want with it, but—"

"I *can't* do anything with it until I know what it is," I interrupt.

Alda laughs at my insolent remark. "Yah, Lauren, tell us. We are in suspense, now!"

"Okay, okay," Lauren says, dropping her hands. "I'll tell you.

But, honestly, Brooke, I just don't want to see you get hurt or mixed up with some asshole pretending to be Prince Charming."

"Thanks, Lauren," I say, tempering my tetchiness, realizing it's doing me no favors when Lauren is honestly trying to help.

Alda makes a cooing noise at the touching moment, which lightens the intensity of the mood.

"When we were hanging out with the Australians a few nights ago—the night you paid for all the drinks—I heard Lizzie talking about a wedding . . ." Her words trail off at the end.

I feel my heart pounding. The sound reverberates in my chest like symphony drums. I can hear the timpani thud rhythmically in my head as Lauren goes on.

". . . and something about blowing off steam before life gets too serious." I catch a little more of what she says, but I've become completely catatonic.

I don't say anything. I just take it like rubber bullets spraying against a Teflon vest. It hurts. I know it's going to leave an impression, but it's not going to kill me.

"Also, you know *we*—I mean, Varun, me, Grady, and Olivier—we've hung out with them since we've been here. The Australians. And Lizzie is always hanging all over Patrick. Like, every time we've seen them. Touching him. Getting close to him. Kissing on him."

"Ah! Yah! That's right! The concert! I see them together too! I forget about this," Alda adds. "Wow, now I put two and two together."

Alda glances at me and is now giving me a wary look herself.

"Actually, Lizzie is the one who told us that you spilled the beer on yourself and took off," Lauren says matter-of-factly.

"That's not what happened. Lizzie spilled the beer on me and told me to 'watch myself.'"

Both Lauren and Alda's mouths drop open.

"That bitch! What the fuck?"

"Oh, yah, for sure . . . what a bitch," Alda agrees.

Lauren continues to curse up a storm as a group of older women, who appear to be Chinese tourists, come into the bathroom and frown at the amenities. Meanwhile, we step away from the sinks and huddle together, speculating as to what the truth of it all is—in other words, what the relationship really is between Patrick and Lizzie.

"Well, I never asked if they were a couple. I mean, I just sort of assumed," Lauren offers. "Although, I will say, Patrick didn't, or hasn't, seemed as *into* the exchange of affections like Lizzie . . ."

At this point, the pounding in my head has turned to a dull throbbing in my left temple. Part of me thinks it might just be the alcohol I've had.

"Either way, when I saw you two holding hands, alarm bells started going off in my head, and I thought you should know what you were getting into." She puts a soft hand on my arm. "You reek of innocence, Brooke. No offense. But that energy can really attract dirtbags. Also, I feel a little guilty since I blurted out for him to come with us. I think I'm already a little tipsy. Things start to get really unfiltered when I drink."

Lauren lets out a deep breath, as if relieved to get the bit of gossipy dirt off her conscience.

"Thanks, Lauren."

"You know, I could ask him what the deal is. I can be sly about it and try and get the facts," she volunteers.

"Yah, I can help too," Alda chimes in eagerly.

"No. It's okay. I'll handle it."

I can see the concern on Lauren's face and suddenly feel like a gawky thirteen-year-old trying to play dress-up with the big girls. The leather, the makeup. It's probably clear to everyone that I'm desperately trying to be someone I'm not.

Before I can deflate further, Alda makes another one of her cooing sounds and brings the three of us together for a hug.

It's funny how quickly people become bonded—especially young people—when traveling and getting lost in these microcosmic hostel worlds. I've seen enough campy '90s teen movies to know it happens. Here I am living it.

As I embrace Lauren and Alda, I try to feel flattered that Lauren is looking out for me and thinks of me as a friend. Alda too, even though we just met.

We pull away from each other, and right away Alda starts in.

"You should just have fun and go with it, especially if you like him. He is not with this girl, Lizzie. He is with *you*."

I could tell from our conversation earlier when we first met that Alda was a bit of her own free spirit—sexually permissive, that is. She had recanted some stories about multiple hook-ups—with guys and girls—during the gap year she is on. Lars, one of the Scandinavians and her apparent date for the evening, hadn't been bothered by her divulging this information. Rather, it seemed to excite him. Bearing that in mind, I find myself looking at Alda not feeling altogether confident in her advice. Still no judgement, of course.

"Alda's right," Lauren says.

I'm hurt and feel a little disappointed but also determined to ask Patrick about who Lizzie is to him. Besides, it's nice to know I have some girl power and back-up if I need it. Also, Lauren was wrong before about Patrick and the noises coming from his room (according to Patrick). She could be wrong again, though it feels doubtful.

I nod without saying anything.

"Come on, we better go. I'm sure Varun is pitching a fit at this point wondering what is taking us so long. We're probably going to have to listen to him complain for a good five minutes, *darlings*," Lauren says, mocking her flatmate.

"Yah, I don't understand this. Why is he always saying this 'darlings'?"

Lauren and Alda walk out ahead of me dissecting Varun's use of the word darling while I walk behind them doing my own dissecting of the information Lauren's just given me about Patrick.

We can start over. I hear Patrick's words from earlier in the day come back to me.

Where did we start from to begin with, and where are we starting from now?

CHAPTER 17

Falling Unequivocally

I'm doing the thing again. I'm imagining a theoretical conversation. This time I'm bold, and I confront Patrick about Lizzie.

Me: So, I need to ask you something.

Patrick: Of course. Ask me anything.

Me: Who is Lizzie, and what does she mean to you?

The imagined answer splinters in a thousand different directions after that.

Me: This is Brooke Neville, investigative reporter, signing off from CNN: Breaking News.

I roll my eyes at myself.

Maybe Alda is right. Maybe I should just go with it. Whatever "it" is . . .

My platform shoes continue to be a life-threatening—or at the very least ankle-breaking—obstacle and Patrick holds my hand as our group heads toward the Brandenburg Gate. It's supposed to be spectacular at night, and I can see it is as we walk up to it.

"Wow . . ." both Lauren and I say in awe.

The large marble columns tower above us, as does the chariot that carries Victoria, the Roman goddess of victory who sits above centered on the structure. The gate is lit up and casts ominous shadows that make it look twice as big. I know from reading about it that the gate had originally been built under the orders of the Prussian king Fredrick William II as the city gate leading from Berlin to Brandenburg an der Havel, but that it had transformed over time to become a symbol of freedom and democracy. In my enthusiasm, I share this with the group, only to clam up when I realize how much I sound like a nerdy know-it-all and total vibe-killer. Patrick squeezes my hand, and I try not to melt into the ground in embarrassment.

"Yah, when the Berlin Wall came down, this is where the Hoff sang. My mother was there," Alda says, with an air of pride.

Lauren is still looking up toward the tops of the columns. "Who's the Hoff, Alda?" she asks.

"You never watch *Knight Rider*? The eighties show with the talking car," Erik offers. "Or *Baywatch*, maybe?"

Everyone looks at Erik with a questionable look. "What? I watched old reruns with my dad growing up."

"Fucking weird-ass Swedes," I hear Varun mutter, grimacing at Erik's fingers that are hanging off Lauren's back pocket.

"The Hoff is only one of the *greatest* pop icons in all Germany. He sang 'Looking for Freedom' when the wall came down. This does not ring a bell?" Alda asks, then proceeds to break out into song.

I listen to Alda unabashedly belt out the lyrics. Even with her strong accent there is no mistaking the words. It's a story of being born rich and having everything, except the one thing all humanity wants: freedom. Strange coincidence.

The song echoes against the columns of the Brandenburg Gate under the stillness of the night. Alda has a pretty decent voice, and the sound ripples into the night as if the universe is a dark pool of water. As I listen, I feel the notes reverberate back and reach toward the core of my very existence.

I shudder, feeling naked and exposed, even though no one around me is the wiser.

Just like the muse of the song, I've left home too, strapped with my own burdens; my emotional baggage and physical scars prove it. These have been my twin companions over the last almost year, pain inside and out. Now here I am, in search of my own path and a way to find peace of mind. Is that too much to ask for?

About halfway through, Lars, Erik, and Grady join her in the chorus, apparently familiar with the song. They start singing at the top of their lungs, which gives the rest of us a good laugh and some interesting looks from passersby.

My hand tightens around Patrick's, and he squeezes back, then loosens his grip and starts to draw slow-moving figure eights with his thumb against my palm. Meanwhile, the song and its lyrics hang in the air all around us. I feel a chill run down my spine, and I'm not sure if it's the song lyrics or my desire for Patrick.

I'm thinking of the recurring dream. The road with the watchers. My home on the hill. Being trapped with all of my bottled-up emotions.

My eyes shift to Patrick. He's oblivious, having a laugh at Alda's horrendous backup vocals. Again, there is that feeling that it's just the two of us who exist, and everything else around us melts away. I'm not thinking about asking him anything or, for that matter, about some girl named Lizzie. Then suddenly there's some shuffling around us, and I'm pulled up from the haze.

"TAG! You're it!" Lauren says, as she rushes up to me.

"What?" I say confused, standing frozen with Patrick at my side.

"YOU'RE IT!" Lauren yells out from over her shoulder.

Apparently, unbeknownst to me, a spontaneous game of tag has broken out. I see the others making circles, chasing after one another around the columns, with Olivier looking the least enthusiastic of all.

I look to my side. Patrick gives me a playful look and quickly loosens his hand from mine.

"Bet you can't catch me," he says challengingly and jets off in an instant, ducking behind one of the columns ahead of us.

"Challenge accepted!" I return friskily, slipping off my platforms and sprinting forward in his direction.

"Hey, you two! You're supposed to play with the whole group!" I hear Lauren yell in our direction. But I'm laser-focused on catching Patrick, and the two of us go back to the place where it's only him and me, and everything else in the world is just white noise.

"You're quick," he says, only slightly breathless after a few circles and close calls, where I'm almost able to tag him.

I'm panting lightly too and feel only slightly jelly from all the alcohol.

"You should see my serve," I huff. "I can send a ball across the court at a hundred miles an hour—almost too fast to see." The thought of Patrick watching me on the court sends a new burst of desire rushing through me.

He's hiding, and the competitor in me feels like I finally got him this time, but the minute I start for him he reaches out and grabs me, pulling me in close to him.

"Gotcha."

I giggle like a schoolgirl and try to catch my breath. "I've heard of fight and flight, but never *hug*."

"Maybe I'm the one chasing you . . ."

I don't respond, but I'm sure he's not talking about tag anymore.

I maneuver in his arms, so I'm facing him. He is gorgeous. Funny. Strangely sincere, for all the misunderstanding that simmers between us. Especially with those eyes and his smile, both of which are concentrated on me.

Patrick backs me up against the column. I'm pinned between his two arms that are bracing against it, and I can see the Olympic rings tattoo. A broken dream, just like my own.

The cold marble sends another shiver down my spine, even though I feel warm and tingly inside. We listen to the others squeal and laugh in the distance as we catch our breath.

"You are an athlete," I comment.

He raises his brows in affirmation, still panting.

"So, you never told me, why don't you swim anymore?"

"I didn't on purpose. I told you it was a long story."

"All we have is time," I say in a cheeky tone, throwing his earlier words back at him.

He snickers and looks off in the distance as though contemplating.

"Because of my father. We had a bit of what you might call a falling out," he says, looking back at me.

"What happened?"

His jaw tenses, but eventually he decides to answer.

"We had our differences, and then I went my separate way. I've basically been on my own since I was fifteen."

"What do you mean by on your own?"

"I left home. Finished secondary school and worked. I crashed at different friends' houses till I could manage paying for a place. I've done my own thing since then."

I can't even begin to imagine doing something like that. What would he think of me, knowing that I've been silver-spoon-fed my entire life? I almost feel envious of Patrick and his self-determination, but the thought of breaking completely free of my family is terrifying, even in light of the Hoff's lyrics.

"That's—"

"Crazy?" he finishes, in a knowing tone.

"Yeah, but I wasn't going to say that. I was going to say I thought it was cool."

He smirks again.

"I don't know if I would call it cool, but it was the best decision I could make for myself at the time."

"What did your parents have to say about you leaving home? What happened that was so bad with your dad?"

Patrick leans in a little closer and his look changes slightly. He has a suggestive and devious spark that flits across his face.

"You're athletic too," he says, avoiding my question.

"I see. Deflecting much?"

"Another time. I don't want to ruin the moment. I'd rather learn more about you."

Patrick keeps moving in closer and drops his arms to let his hands find mine, and we curl our fingers together. He's so close to me, I can feel the heat and sense the pheromones coming off him.

"You played tennis once, but you don't play anymore . . ."

"No," I say more seriously, and just like that the air between us gels and grows thick with intensity. He stops moving in closer.

"Why?"

I knew the question was coming. We've both equally avoided the parts of our life that feel too raw to share yet seem to be at the forefront of everything. But Patrick's given a little, and now it's my turn.

Patrick moves his fingers around my hand with the scars, his fingertips brushing against the tiny lines and ridges. Immediately I tense up.

"That's why I don't play tennis anymore . . . something happened."

He pulls the hand with the scars up, dropping hold of my other hand, to examine the scars under the scant lighting.

"What happened?" he asks after spending a few minutes studying me. "You get into a fight with a hedge trimmer?"

I can't help the short broken laugh that escapes me.

This past year I've avoided talking about it, except when I can't. I've ignored it because it's painful, and I don't want it to be real. But looking up into Patrick's eyes, I know he sees me and that he's not judging me. The words dance at the tip of my tongue, ready to pour out and unchain themselves from the deep reaches of my heart.

For a second, I think it's the alcohol. But no. There's something about us that just clicks. He's a complete stranger. But I want to let go and let him into my world.

Patrick takes my damaged hand and moves it closer to his lips. He kisses the scars.

"It's okay. Another time," he says softly, with gentle eyes reassuring me.

As Lauren's laughter grows closer, I don't know what I feel. Relief, maybe? Even though I know the things I want to say are starting to unearth. They're ready to be heard, instead of staying compartmentalized.

My eyes grow moist at his tenderness, and it's the first time in I don't know how long, I feel safe from all the hurt, all the pressure, and all the guilt.

Patrick drops my hand and leans in. My heart is pounding. I'm staring at his lips. I want him to kiss me so badly, it's a physical ache.

"Hey, Cinderella, I got your shoes . . ." Lauren says, swooping in, out of breath. She has my platforms and extends her arm to hand them over, shooting a quick, appraising look at our semi-embrace. Patrick backs away and straightens. "You too, Prince Charming. Let's go. We got places to be."

I slide out from standing against the column, letting go of his hand.

"Thanks," I say, taking my shoes and slipping them back on.

We join back with the others, who are out of breath, a bit drunk, and laughing and joking like hooligans. It doesn't take long before our traveling caravan is on the move again, making our way toward Brücke.

The city feels like a beating heart, pumping with energy. Every time I look at Patrick the pulse of everything that surrounds us quickens. The adrenaline is palpable.

Patrick holds my hand as we duck and scoot around cars and motorists. We talk and flirt. Everything just feels easy with him. And I know, unequivocally, I'm in way deeper than I want to admit.

CHAPTER 18

The Troll

We walk a couple of blocks from the underground tram station to the club. I rarely get to ride public transportation when I'm at home—my mother finds it disgusting, offensive, and unequivocally beneath her; ergo I am not allowed to use it—and since I've been on my travels, it's been something I've sincerely relished. Yeah, sometimes the trains or buses smell. I even saw a guy throw up early in the morning at the back of a bus in Paris. But there is something normalizing about being packed in with all the other passengers, just another face in the crowd.

The neighborhood we're in feels industrial, and as the streets empty out, I start to wonder if we're even in the right place. But then we're there. Brücke. It's much bigger than I had envisioned. It's on a large plot of land, with overgrowth, and seemingly hidden in plain view. It reminds me of a haunted house, especially with the high wrought iron gate that wraps around the outer perimeter.

As we walk along the sidewalk, passing by the metal fencing, I can see that it's old and rusted, with slivers of metal chipped away. The tops of each rod are spiky and stand at attention, like they're ready to take down any intruders.

"You okay? I think you're cutting off the circulation in my hand," Patrick says.

"I'm sorry," I say, loosening my grip. "This place is a little creepy, don't you think?"

"A little."

"You know it used to be an old communist prison?"

"*Really?*"

"Yeah. The woman who helped me with my outfit, Violet, was telling me about it. She even said she had family that had been imprisoned here."

"That's crazy."

"I know, right? Apparently, it had been a castle, but when Russia occupied East Berlin, they used it as a garrison. Then eventually it was converted into a prison. People were tortured in there. Died in there, too."

"Now you've made it creepy," Patrick says, giving me a chilled look as we pass under a streetlight.

Around us it's eerily quiet, though the faint tremble of music increases as we get closer.

"Hey, Pat . . ."

"Hey, Lauren," Patrick says.

Lauren is walking just ahead of us, with her arm looped through Erik's, and she's talking over her shoulder.

"Where are all your Aussie friends tonight? Isn't that Lizzie girl usually glued to your side?"

Lauren completely turns around, walking backward, and looks from Patrick to me. I give her my fiercest glare, even though she is right to ask. Still, when we are alone, I will dismember her. One long, tanned limb at a time.

She widens her eyes at me. The read on her face is obvious. *Well, you still haven't asked, have you?* Urgh.

"Max and I are traveling together. The girls like a bit of company at times, but that's all it is," he says smoothly.

"*Company*, huh? Interesting," Lauren replies, spinning back around, but not before looking at me with a suspect look.

Just like that, Lauren leaves the exchange for me to uncomfortably navigate like a minefield as we all walk through the opening in the gate onto a gravel path toward the club.

Thanks, buddy.

I have mixed emotions. Part of me feels like I should press Patrick a little more because it's clear he's not being entirely truthful. I know it; I can feel it. But the other part of me is leaning more toward Alda's philosophy of feeling more and thinking less.

There's a long line to get into the club, but Alda tells us to keep walking.

"I know the bouncer," she informs us as we walk straight past all the would-be patrons that snake back pretty far from the entrance.

Our casual stroll past the crowd garners some ugly looks.

"Awkward," I say, unsure if I'm referring to the crowd or the uncomfortable silence that's been growing since Lauren lobbed her grenade between us.

"Brutal," Patrick replies, a little too quickly, seemingly relieved that I've said something—*anything*—unrelated to his travel companions.

I keep the conversation moving forward, trying to get us back to where we were just moments before Lauren's sneak attack.

"Violet also told me a little about the bouncer," I continue breezily. "But she said she didn't want to ruin it for me—whatever that was supposed to mean. That it was part of the experience or something. She also said I needed to ask about why it's called Brücke. Do you know? I didn't look it up and Violet wouldn't tell me because—well, again, she said it was about the 'whole experience' and all."

"I think—if I remember right—the bouncer has a nickname

that's related to the theme of the club. Something like that."

"What's the inspiration?"

"A Norwegian fairytale," Lars interjects.

He and Alda are behind Patrick and me, looking rather chummy with one another.

"Yah! *De tre bukkene Bruse,*" Alda says with a grin, staring up at her hulking date.

"Should I know that story?" I wonder aloud.

"You probably heard it. *Three Billy Goats Gruff,*" says Lars, his Scandinavian accent undulating like a sweet lullaby.

Mom was never big on reading bedtime stories (that was for the nanny to do, anyway), but I have a dim memory of a hungry troll that lived under a bridge and the goats that outsmarted him and crossed to the other side.

"I don't think I know it," Patrick says.

"This was one of my favorites when I was a kid. We like trolls in Norway," Lars says cheerfully and then proceeds to give a full recap of the story as Patrick and I slow and walk along with him and Alda.

Lars's recanting aligns with my recollection of the story. By the end he's being cute with Alda and feigns a nibble at her neck, making flirtatious chomping and gnashing sounds that make her giggle wildly. "And each time, the goat says, 'Ah! Wait for the next one, he is bigger and fatter than me!' The troll then lets each one pass, waiting and waiting for the biggest and fattest one to arrive so he can eat him. *But,* when the biggest and fattest one gets to the bridge, he knocks the troll over the side and down the river. So, the goats pass anyway." Lars pretends to take another bite of Alda's neck, like a vampire, and Alda obliges him with more giggles.

"Is there a moral to the story? Like an Aesop's fable or something?" Patrick asks.

Lars lets out an ironic snort. "Yes, of course. Don't be greedy."

"So, I still don't understand. What is the inspiration? How is the club themed around the fairy tale?" I ask.

"Well, there is a bridge to get in and you have to outsmart The Troll by following the rules," Alda explains.

"There's a *bridge*? And a *troll*? I'm still confused . . ."

"Well, The Troll you meet in a minute. He is the bouncer. *Brücke* means bridge in German. I let you experience that part on your own."

"Why does everyone I talk to keep saying that? 'Experience it on your own' or 'experience it for yourself'?" The irony of posing this question out loud is not lost on me; I know I need more life experience, though this isn't exactly what I had in mind. I don't know what I had in mind, actually.

Alda gives another of her girlish giggles. "You will understand shortly," she says with a reassuring grin. "But for now, try not to be scared of The Troll. He's not as scary as he looks."

Even though Alda's still giving me a reassuring smile, it doesn't reassure me at all.

We keep winding our way past the crowded line, and I feel as though we are slowly trekking upward, on a slight incline. I'm reminded of the recurring dream again for the second time tonight. The house I grew up in is on a hill, placed ominously and looking out on the rest of the world below it. Not a beacon but its own type of prison.

As we get closer to the front of the building, Alda untangles herself from Lars's side and breaks out into a sprint, bounding up a short set of stairs into the arms of a giant. Not just a giant, but a man armored in tattoos and piercings all over his face and presumably in places I can't see.

"That's The Troll?" If I ran into this guy in a dark alley, I'd probably wet myself.

The Troll is posted at the top of the short set of stairs with a giant medieval-looking door behind him that I assume is the entrance. The vantage point allows him to look out over the mass of humans hoping to get into the club, but he doesn't see Alda right away. He's caught off-guard as she lunges herself at him, but then his stoic face melts away as he sets her down and the two talk familiarly with one another in German.

"O-M-G. This is happening! I am so fucking excited!" Lauren says in a low voice as she scooches up next to me.

Lauren simmers then nods toward Patrick, who's distracted talking with Varun and Grady.

I shrug, and she gives me a concerned look.

"It's okay. I'm okay. It's cool."

"Sure?"

I nod and smile, though I'm feeling a mix of emotions I'd rather not go into.

We start to file in to go through an ID check and pat-down with The Troll. Patrick and I are at the back of the group, and somehow Olivier has ended up with us.

I start thumbing through my waist purse to pull out my passport for the ID check.

"Ms. Smith, you look like you have quite a number of stamps in your book, no?" Olivier comments, looking down at my worn-out passport.

"*Ms. Smith?* Is that like a code name or something?" Patrick jokes.

My insides squirm, as I remember that I gave Olivier a false name that day in the museum.

"No. Brooke Smith. This is her last name, yes?" Olivier queries in his superior tone.

Patrick and I exchange a look.

Fuck. He saw my passport when we first met. He knows my last name.

"Maybe. I don't know her last name," he says. "Just made me think of that Angelina Jolie spy movie for some reason—Mr. and Mrs. Smith. I think there's a remake coming out soon."

Patrick winks at me. He is, in fact, holding up his end of the bargain and keeping my secret safe. I breathe a sigh of relief, but when I turn to fake a smile at Olivier, he looks like he's seen a ghost.

My passport is splayed wide open to the front page. *Crap.* I flip it closed.

Olivier doesn't say anything. My heart is pounding. We stare at each other for a moment. There is no mistaking that he knows exactly who I am, and as we stare silently at one another, he knows I know he knows. Meanwhile, Patrick seems none the wiser because he's busy getting his own passport out.

Olivier quickly turns back around and gets ready to hand over his ID to The Troll and do a pat-down.

"That was close," Patrick comments in a low voice.

"Yeah. Totally," I reply, every fiber of my muscles aching from the tension I'm feeling, even as Patrick places his hand on the small of my back, and all I want to do is enjoy the moment.

Finally, it's my turn. I walk up the steps and stand in front of The Troll. He's no smiles, all business, even though we're with Alda.

I hand him my ID. I can't help my eyes locking on to the matching tattoos of dragons snaking down each arm. The one on his right is red, and the one on his left is green. Each has its mouth open with the flames extending over the tops of his hands and curling out to his fingertips.

I don't really know anyone with tattoos, except one of the girls on the Yale tennis team who has a few, but they are small and look more like they belonged on a charm bracelet.

As The Troll flips open my passport and looks at the information, I can see a series of dates on the inside of his wrists, along with names.

The Troll clears his throat, growls at me slightly with a gold grill on his teeth, and hands my passport back to me.

"Sorry. Um, they're really pretty," I say, realizing how hard I've been staring.

His no-nonsense face disintegrates into a giant grin and he laughs heartily.

"Ha! Never heard them described as pretty before," he says with a mild German accent, obviously amused with my choice of words.

"Sorry," I reply, and then I remember something. "Violet said to say hi."

I'm hoping maybe this continues to soften him, and he forgives me for my gawking at his body art.

"Ah! I can see she helped you with your look, yah?" he says, eyeing my ensemble.

"Yeah," I reply sheepishly.

"I like Violet. She is good people."

I bite my lower lip because curiosity has got me. "Can I see them?" His smile disappears. The jovial laugh dissipates. "Your tattoos. I'm thinking of maybe getting something."

I make this up on the spot without thinking. Whether it's true or not, my admission has the giant laughing supremely at me again. *Thanks, doofus* (me, not him).

He collects himself. "I'm not a zoo animal, you know?" He shakes his head, as if pitying me, and extends his two thick arms, giving me the opportunity to inspect the two dragons. When he turns his arms over, I see that the name 'Inge' is on his right wrist and the name 'Fred' is on his left, each with the dates appearing to expand a lifetime.

"My mother, Inge. This is Alda's grandmother. Alda is my niece," he says, pointing at Alda, who's waiting a few paces away at the door, apparently standing by to ensure all of us make it through the gauntlet. "My father, Fred. This is to remember them. They are my protectors," he continues with a proud grin and proceeds to roll his arms back over and ball his hands into a fist so the flames are pointed straight at me.

"Pretty," I repeat, smiling back, even though I feel my heart ache thinking of Liam. "Thanks."

I wonder to myself if I would, in fact, ever be brave enough to get a tattoo. I think I could. One day, when I was ready.

The Troll does his pat-down of me, and Patrick steps up and does an ID check and pat-down as well.

Having made it past the The Troll, we enter Brücke through the medieval double doors that lead to a small corridor. It's dark, a little crowded, but I can see there is a booth with a glass window, and inside is a woman sitting perched on a stool. She's fluorescent from the blacklight that illuminates her small space. Already I can feel the music vibrate through my chest from somewhere deep inside the building.

The woman waves for Patrick and me to approach and points to a piece of paper on the glass with the cover price.

Before I can do anything, Patrick slips a hundred-euro note under the opening and motions that it's for both of us.

"You don't have to do that," I say, leaning up to his ear, taking the opportunity to inhale a little bit of him.

"I know. But I am anyway."

The woman gives him a few notes in change back and motions to the right. As Patrick stuffs them away, I can't help but feel bad that he's spending money on me when he's probably on a budget and I have plenty to burn.

There are doors flanking the booth on either side, the right side apparently being the entrance and the left, I'm assuming, the exit. Before we take another step, Patrick holds my elbow.

"Why don't you go ahead. I'm going to use the toilet real quick," he says, close enough I can feel his breath on the nape of my neck. "I'll meet you in there."

"I can—" I start.

"No, no. You go ahead. There might be a line. I don't know how long it'll take. I'll meet you in there."

I blink at him in confusion, but he leans in and kisses me on the cheek. In the rush of his heady warmth and scent, I find myself turning and walking off, as ordered.

I push against the door, but as I walk through, I look over my shoulder and see Patrick inconspicuously kneeling as if tying his boot, but instead he slips a cell phone out. He shields the screen, but I can see it. He's texting. He doesn't look at me or notice I'm staring back at him.

There is no line to the bathroom because there are no bathrooms in the lobby.

Patrick is private, verging on secretive. But everyone has secrets. Me, most of all.

I wonder if I really care about Patrick's secrets, or if some part of me just wants to use him to discover parts of myself I've never known.

Perhaps in the end, it doesn't really matter.

This is life experience.

CHAPTER 19

Soak Up the Glory

Don't think, just do.

Don't think, just do.

Don't think, just do.

Don't think, just do.

I stared across the net at my opponent, ready to return the serve. My mantra repeated on a broken loop in my head as I rhythmically breathed in and out.

I inhaled through my nose, exhaled through my mouth. Everything was instinctual. Every shot in my arsenal ingrained in my muscle memory. I could anticipate the shot coming to me and where to hit it back on my opponent's side of the court before having to think about it. Where I'm over-analytical in my day-to-day life, on the court, there is no time for that.

My eyes narrowed as my opponent tossed the ball in the air and hit a powerful, flat first serve wide on the deuce side, grunting as she made contact with the ball. I split stepped, stepped in, took a short back swing, and smacked the ball down the line out of her reach.

I was the last one on the court. My teammates screamed and cheered from the sidelines like a pack of wild animals. The stands were full too, and the crowd erupted. If I won my match, we won overall, and our team would advance to the national championships with a high-seeded position in the tournament.

I grabbed my towel from the sidelines and wiped my face and tossed it back to the ground. I walked to the AD side of the court, concentrating on my strings and fixing their placement.

"AD, Ms. Neville," said the chair umpire.

Don't think, just do.

My opponent changed it up. Heavy spin into my body. I split stepped, jumped back out of the way of the ball, and slammed an inside-out forehand to her backhand side. She got to it, sliced it back. We rallied cross-court, forehand-to-forehand. The tension on the court and in the crowd was intense. I progressively made my balls heavier and deeper until my opponent was far back on the court. Then I took her by surprise with a disguised drop shot. She raced to catch it before a double-bounce but she was too far back. My point. Game.

I allowed myself a small, discreet pump of the fist, though inside, I was roaring.

I was up 5-4 in the second set. I won the first set easily, but my opponent had been putting up her best fight to save the match. There was a lot riding on the win.

I grabbed my towel from the ground and made my way to my seat for the changeover.

As I sat down, my coach and her assistant were already chirping at my side, encouraging me to close things out and making minor suggestions on my shot selection. I listened, but as they stepped back my eyes went to the crowd.

I saw her. Sitting amongst the crowd dressed to the nines in her usual garb of glamour and sophistication, the LV of the Louis Vuitton monogram imprinted all over the blouse she had on. I was a younger version of my mother. We both had the same soft, long, wavy blonde hair, though mine was pulled back into a bun, soaking wet with my sweat, and her hair was perfectly shaped and ironed out.

She looked impeccable. But I could see through it all. She was a fake, a snob—a control freak who would rather be cruel than vulnerable. Even as I gave everything I had on the court, she was looking down at her phone, scrolling, totally unaware of the people cheering and talking around her. As if she could feel the penetration of my stare, she paused and looked up from her phone.

She stared at me, cocking her head, as if to try to make sense of her strange daughter. When I didn't respond, she let out a small— probably fabricated—yawn, politely hidden behind her bejeweled hand. Then she picked up her bag and left.

Bitch.

It's a violent word, but those types of feelings, the numbness and internal conflict I felt toward her, had all intensified to a whole new level by then.

"Time, ladies," said the chair umpire.

Yes, time.

I got up from my seat and grabbed my racket and towel. It was time to set aside my feelings like I always did. It was almost second nature.

I dropped my towel off to the side, grabbed two balls, and stepped up to the service line. I was back to focusing. I had to win—despite her, and for her. It was what everyone expected.

Don't think, just do.

Four points later I had the match on my racket.

"Forty-fifteen," declared the chair umpire.

I looked across the net, my expression stone cold and resolute. I picked my spot and served up the T. My opponent barely got a racket on it. The ball she returned was short, a sitting duck, and I easily put her out of her misery.

I walked up and shook my opponent's hand as my teammates stormed in from the sidelines to congratulate me.

Of course I was happy I won, but mostly I felt like I was going through the motions. At the end of the day, none of it really mattered. Eventually Mom would put her foot down and send me into whatever job, marriage, or arrangement she decided was best for me. Those little moments of apparent freedom and rebellion were chump change for what I was really giving up.

I glanced up in the stands as my teammates celebrated, wondering if perhaps she'd just left to use the bathroom. But she was gone.

What did it matter? Even if she was there, it wouldn't have changed how I felt.

I walked to my seat, packed my tennis bag, and headed to the locker room. I left my coach and teammates behind, along with the parents and people from the crowd who had swarmed down onto the court, giving congratulations. I doubted anyone noticed that I was gone.

I lean against the dark hallway wall, growing increasingly impatient. Patrick's still on the other side of the door behind me.

Is he texting Max? Lizzie? The Ghost of Olympics Past? Okay, that's a little harsh, but seriously.

I let out a deep, confused breath of air. Not only is my head confused but I feel physically disoriented. I'm in a dark hall. My eyes look straight ahead at the green dot at the other end. It's small.

Under my feet the floor is shiny like a black mirror. I take a step and the floor lights up, and at the other end of the hall a corresponding light illuminates. Beneath my feet the image looks like boards, bound loosely together with water visibly rushing between the slates. It's a screen, made to look like real-life. At the other end, the light is green, and I can see vegetation protruding and snaking out from the walls on either side. I don't know if the growth is real, but it certainly looks it.

The vibration of bass from the hidden bowels of the building is calling me in. I take another step and again the path lights up as does the far end of the hall, exposing more flora and fauna. As I take the next step it dawns on me: a bridge to greener pasture.

The green is brightest at the far end as I continue to walk down the hall—or rather the "bridge"—and the lights simultaneously brighten the space. I reach the far end of the hall, where the greenery is thickest and double doors stand in front of me. My hand is pressed against the leathery skin of the right door. The vibration of the music on the other side courses through me.

For some reason, the whole moment and what comes after feels pivotal. As if I'm not just stepping into a different room but a different future.

Everything confusing in my life right now feels like it could be distilled from this moment.

I can worry about whether Lizzie is Patrick's boyfriend . . .

I can fear my mother's threats to cut me off . . .

I can keep blaming myself for letting Liam down . . . for hurting so many people.

The *something* feels as fresh in my memories as if it just happened. Like an out-of-body experience, I can see myself walking into the locker room after the match and . . .

Music pounds. A vapor of sweat, perfume, and booze seeps through the door.

Let it go.

Just beyond the threshold humanity breathes, shouts, and dances as a single heaving organism. Life, in spite of death. Freedom, in the face of surrender.

My hand is steady, pressed against the door, ready to push it open. I'm ready to take control of my own life, to make decisions for myself, embrace the consequences, and find my greener grass, so-to-speak.

My mind clears. My heart is pumping with adrenaline, along with the music that is beckoning me to walk through to the other side, to whatever awaits.

I push the door open and breathe it in.

Fuck it, let's dance.

CHAPTER 20

Like Globules of Mercury

My hands are raised in the air, my head tipped back as I surrender to the rhythm. This might be one of the most exclusive clubs in the world, but the dance floor is packed. One guy's back is pressed to mine, another girl's hair brushes my shoulder as she whips her head in time to the music.

I don't care. My body has never moved this way before, and I love it.

I don't know how much time has passed when I feel someone grab my elbow. It's Lauren.

"Dancing queen! Where's Patrick?" She leans in, close to my ear.

I do the same, leaning in close to her ear, explaining the whole bathroom excuse to text on his hidden cell phone thing.

She gives me an unimpressed look. "Whatever. That's your mistake to make, girl. Come on. We're all at the bar."

We head down the flight of stairs and squeeze through the mob of humans till we're at one of the bars along with everyone else in the group, except for Patrick.

Immediately, when I join the others, Olivier approaches me and pulls me to the side.

"It is true? You are Brooke *Neville*? As in the family that—"

"Why does it matter?" I say sharply, cutting him off.

His face is soft and sympathetic, contrary to the intrusive and gossipy person I've taken him for. I can tell he's trying to figure out how to say whatever is on his mind.

"Um—I'm sorry. About what happened—everything. Especially your—your brother."

He's looking at me, and I can tell from his look that not only does he know the tabloid bits, but he knows the finer details. The stuff people ignore in favor of the juicier headlines.

I can feel the tears.

No! I swallow and turn away. Not now. Not tonight.

"Hey!" Patrick says, walking up and settling his hand against my hip, as he pulls me close to his side.

Olivier floats away as I focus on Patrick. His face is cast in shadows, but I can see the outline of his mouth, and he's grinning. I struggle to smile back.

"SHOTS! SHOTS! SHOTS!"

Alda and Lauren surround us, chanting as loud as they can. Shot glasses with clear liquid are passed around and I break from Patrick to take a whiff.

Never in my life have I smelled alcohol so foul.

"AQUAVIT!" Lars announces. "Scandinavian special!"

Patrick leans in. "Throw it in the back of your mouth and don't let it touch your taste buds. Best advice I can give you."

"SKOL!" shouts Erik and we all raise our glasses and repeat the same in unison.

I down it. I try my best to follow Patrick's advice but fail miserably. If I knew what formaldehyde tasted like, I imagine this would be it.

I open my mouth, not sure how to make the awful taste go away. There are two extra shots sitting on the bar.

My mouth is burning. My brain is on fire.

And. I. Don't. Give. A. Damn.

"Who are those for?"

"Me and Erik," Lars replies with a charming smile.

"Here," I say, handing him a fifty-euro note I pull out from my waist purse.

He starts to protest, but I take the two shots and tell him to keep the money.

I hand one of the drinks to Patrick, who responds with a raised brow. Oh yes, it's going to be one of *those* nights.

I can feel the warmth of the liquor sink into my body and flow out to my extremities. This is followed by a tingling sensation, as if I've shed my old skin in favor of a new exterior. The feeling is transformative.

I place the empty shot glass back on the bar and wipe my hand across my mouth like a savage. Patrick neatly swallows his shot and places it on the bar, staring at me warily.

I want to beat a drum, hunt a beast, and sink my teeth into a raw hunk of meat.

Who the hell am I? Kesha?

"You're looking at me differently," he says.

"I'm looking at you how I want to look at you." I shrug.

But then Olivier reappears. He steps right up to me and leans in close to my ear, for only me to hear.

"I'm sorry. I did not mean to upset you. I'll keep things to myself," he promises, his French accent turned ingratiating.

"It's fine," I grit. A girl is passing by with a tray of drinks, and I grab one, downing it.

"Hey!" Before she can complain, Patrick steps in and hands her a bank note. She stalks off with a final dirty look over her shoulder.

I roll my eyes with a dismissive, flirty smile at Patrick and turn to Olivier.

Our eyes are locked and I'm giving him a bland, stoic look. He gets the message and leaves.

The DJ is talking to the crowd for a second and whatever he says in German ignites everyone into a frenzy as he starts the next track.

Before I know it, our group is in the thick of the pit and I'm watching Alda and Lauren move carefree with Lars and Erik. Even Varun and Grady are dancing. Olivier is swaying but mostly he's standing nearby nursing a mixed drink. We exchange another look.

"You and the French bloke have something going on?" Patrick says into my ear from behind me.

His breath sends a chill down my spine. His body is mere atoms away from mine.

I drop my head and turn my eyes over my shoulder up to his.

"Not really. More of a misunderstanding."

I enviously watch Lauren as she moves like water and wonder if she's ever experienced a moment of insecurity in her life. It's almost like the world was designed for her pleasure.

The beats and bass start to take me as the music rises and folds, peaks and drops. Thunderous bass pulses through the sea of humans like globules of mercury—thick, dazzling, and hypnotic. It's chemical.

An ethereal voice calls out through the notes, growing in volume. I answer with my body, barely aware of Patrick and the others moving around me.

When his hands brush up my sides, every nerve in my body comes alive. I was dancing for the siren, but now I dance for those two hands. Strong, curious, and mind-numbing.

My eyes are closed and my blood is on fire as Patrick's hands smooth and press, slipping under the edge of my lace top, warm against my skin.

The beat is sex, and I am the song.

As I slow my movements and shift closer, Patrick's lips brush against my neck. The heat from his body mixes with mine, thick and electric.

I am smiling. I am numb.

Nothing else matters, except this song.

CHAPTER 21

The VIP Lounge

Lauren, Alda, and I are queued up in the bathroom. Lauren may look like a goddess with superhuman powers, but she must have one of the smallest bladders in the world.

"God, this place is huge. Don't they have more bathrooms?" she says, hopping up and down, wincing.

"Yes! Follow me! I have an idea. Why I did not think of this sooner!" Alda replies and motions for us to follow.

"Thank goodness because my bladder is literally about to explode," Lauren comments, still bouncing.

We follow Alda farther down the corridor until we reach a roped-off area with two guards blocking the way. One of the guards is Black with dreadlocks and the other is a white guy with fiery red hair in dreadlocks. Their clothes and facial expressions are the exact same; each is dressed head to toe in black and both have a snarl on their faces. Must be a prerequisite to employment.

Alda lets go of Lauren's hand, who has hold of my hand, and runs up to them just like she did with The Troll. She flings herself up into the arms of the Black guy first, who only at the last second seems to recognize her. His face immediately softens from being a toothy Doberman to a friendly Lab, as does the other guy, who also gives her a big welcoming hug.

"Seriously, Alda knows everyone in this place. How fucking

lucky is it that we met her at the concert," Lauren remarks, as Alda chats with the guards.

"Well, *you* met her. I took off from the concert. Remember?"

Lauren drops her wonderous and admiring gaze from Alda to turn and look at me.

"Have you asked him about Lizzie, yet?"

"No," I say, somberly. Suddenly I feel completely sober, even though I'm still swaying.

"Well, if you're not going to ask him, why not ask *her*." She says it all nonchalant.

"Ask Lizzie?" I gawk at her. "No way."

"Why not? What's the worst that can happen? You'll get the truth? Though she may fabricate things a little like she did with the whole beer ordeal. Still."

My mouth is still hanging wide open, stumped by her words. I slowly close my gaping piehole. "Even shitty experience is experience in life, chica. Don't be afraid. We all need a little bit of it." Lauren gives me look like "buck-up buttercup."

Like a flip of a switch, I suddenly feel every bit of my drunkenness return with a vengeance. There's a throbbing in my head, and I'm wobbling in my platforms. Only now there's no Patrick to keep me standing. I have to do it on my own.

"Hey! Let's go!" Alda hollers.

"Where are we going?" Lauren asks, walking toward Alda, leaving me behind feeling whip-lashed by the advice.

"VIP lounge!"

Lauren's eyes immediately light up, and her grin stretches from ear to ear. "No fucking way!" she screeches, bouncing up and down in place like she's won the lottery, to which Alda immediately pacifies her.

"Calm down! We must be *cool*, remember? The rules!"

We take an elevator that opens up to a dark room that is different than any other part of the club we've been in so far. It feels like a cocoon, cozy and secluded. The music is low and way more chill.

I can see that the theme of greener pastures continues. There's a circular bar in the middle of the room with a tree in the very center. It looks as if it has grown up into the ceiling and covers nearly the entirety of the overhead, with small lanterns strung in the branches.

The mood lighting is a soft emerald, and there are designated areas for individual parties, with plush couches and lounge chairs. But the thing that has caught my attention is the bartenders. Each is dressed like a woodland creature. I see a fox, an owl, another is a deer—and, of course, there's a goat. The goat is arguably not a woodland creature, but still, totally appropriate to go along with the theme of the place. The costumes are not gimmicky at all, more like real masterpieces that took time to perfect and could easily be on the set of a Hollywood film. Germans sure take their club scene seriously.

We wind our way through and make it to the bathroom, where there are plenty of empty stalls.

"Oh! Sweet relief!" Lauren calls out from her stall.

I feel the same—even though I don't announce it to the world. In fact, there's a little bit of a sobering effect that I feel paying homage to the porcelain gods, which I probably need after all the Aquavit shots.

We finish up in our individual stalls and emerge to wash our hands. There are some girls who look like models in a little alcove of the bathroom that has a chaise lounge and floor-length mirror. One girl is fixing herself up in the mirror while two of the other girls look to be strung out on the chaise.

I look at myself in the mirror. The light is not super bright, so it's forgiving of my makeup that is slightly damp, a little runny, and not quite as crisp as when the night started. I can tell my eyes are a bit bloodshot from all the alcohol, and immediately I feel how thirsty I am for water.

I'm not the only one feeling dehydrated, so we decide to grab some aqua before leaving the VIP lounge, and Alda says she has something she wants to show us afterward.

"Is it a surprise?" Lauren asks.

"Yah." Alda gives Lauren and me an impish look as she finishes retouching her makeup.

As we make our way to the bar, I see the rail-thin models fling themselves into a packed seating area and at the center is . . .

"Landon! Baby, you were supposed to wait for us!" squeals one of the models as she fawns all over him.

"You know that guy or something?" Lauren asks me because I've totally stalled-out staring at him and his entourage, starstruck.

"Yeah, I do. That's Landon Simon. Top men's tennis player. He just lost at Wimbledon."

"Looks like a real winner," Lauren replies into my ear, her tone snarky, and tugs at me to move.

My eyes don't leave him as we scoot past. But then he and I make direct eye contact. His gaze is locked on me, and he nods—a "hi," "hey," "what's up." I freak out a little inside, but then his head stealthily dips, and he runs a finger under his nose and snorts.

"Come on, Brooke." Lauren tugs more forcefully.

We grab a couple of waters from a bartender dressed as a badger or a skunk, who Alda also knows, then follow her outside.

"VIP rooftop lounge!" Alda announces.

"Way cool," Lauren says.

It's intimate, not a big space at all. There's a bar to the right with a green wall of ivy covering it. The deck is a sleek teak wood, and the furnishing is modern. The space is enclosed by a glass wall perimeter. There's an inviting fire pit with a few people seated around it. Yet again, the space is completely different than any of the other spaces inside Brücke.

We walk out to the edge, and the view is spectacular. The whole cityscape is visible, along with the iconic Berlin Fernsehturm (TV Tower) that is lit up in all kinds of crazy alternating colors.

"Wow, bet the guys would be jealous," Lauren observes.

She then starts sniffing the air like a hound and steps over to someone smoking a cigarette to bum one.

"Hope you ladies don't mind. I like one every once and a while. Only when I'm drinking, though."

She takes a long drag and exhales, closing her eyes.

"Can I have drag?" I ask, after having gulped down most of my water.

"What! Really? Would never imagine Brooke the tennis player and athlete as a smoker."

"What about you? You do PT every day," I fire back. Lauren gave me a short tutorial on basic military acronyms, so I know a little of the "alphabet soup," as she calls it. PT means physical training.

"Well, I'm a mess and you seem more like a . . ."

"What? A saint?"

She doesn't answer but hands me the cigarette. I take a long drag and similarly exhale, closing my eyes.

"Can I have a drag, too?" Alda asks.

"Of course," replies Lauren as I hand Alda the cigarette. "It's the least I can do for everything tonight."

We pass the cigarette back and forth, each taking a drag and staring out at the incredible view of Berlin and above at the twinkle of stars visible through the city light pollution.

"I remember the last time I had a cigarette," I say out of nowhere.

I can feel the alcohol snip at my inhibitions and unchain my internalized thoughts.

"So, you're a regular smoker?" Lauren jests.

"No, definitely not," I say with a smirk, glancing in her direction. "Just, something happened between me and my mom that's hard to forget."

"Why? What happened?" Alda asks.

"We had a fight. Well, I guess I was arguing *at* her. My mom is not really expressive."

"Preaching to the choir, girl," Lauren says, trying to make O rings with the drag she's just taken, but failing.

"Maybe, but I heard my mom say something to someone after our fight that's sort of hard to forget."

"Oh yeah? What's that?"

I can see myself—like an out-of-body experience. I'm looking back at my parent's estate. The holiday extravaganza is over. There are staff swarming all over cleaning up, and the guests are gone. I know where everyone is—at least I think I do. My mother is in my parents' room going through her pre-bed beauty regimen, my grandmother has just left in a private car, and my father is in his library with my grandfather, and the two are smoking cigars and drinking brandy, congratulating one another for their various capitalistic conquests.

Meanwhile, I'm outside in the gazebo. It's cold. Freezing, really. There's a light layer of snow across the sprawling lawn. The festive holiday lights and decorations are still lit up all over the house. I'm staring at the expansive estate and mansion feeling defeated, small, and insignificant, still in my glamorous dress, wrapped in a big warm coat.

Liam kept cigarettes and a lighter in a plastic bag under a loose board when we were in high school. I find it. The cigarettes are stale, and the Bic lighter is nearly empty. I smoke one of the terrible tasting cigarettes. Liam had them for his friends, not for himself. He was too good for that.

The musty taste of the cigarette deadens my feelings that are cracked and frayed after having finally attempted to tell my mother about what she ended up calling my "silly dream." I go to stub the cigarette out and hear my mother's voice and quickly duck behind some hedges. She's on the phone with her friend Claire Beth Jeffries. Claire is younger than my mother. She idolizes my mother because of the power she wields—a ruler in our world who needs no brandy, cigars, or congratulations.

Claire was missing from the party. I figure out from the bits of conversation I eavesdrop on as to why she didn't make it. She found out she can't have children of her own. My mother is trying to be supportive but then says the most hurtful thing I can imagine. "Most of the time I *hate* being a mother. Think of the news as a blessing, not a curse."

I can hear her cavalier tone speaking into her cell all over again as I stare up at the sky over Berlin. I've let the story tell itself, minus giving anything away about my family's wealth—I keep that to myself.

"Wow, I have no words. That is fucked-up, Brooke. I'm sorry."

"At least I know why she treats me like she does," I reply, remembering the feeling of the hot end of the Bic lighter pressing into my palm as I listened to my mother's words.

Both Lauren and Alda shake their heads in disbelief.

Saying it out loud makes me feel less trapped. *I'm alive. I am here. I am now. I am present.* Lauren takes the last puff of the cigarette.

"So, what was the silly dream you and your mom were arguing

about to begin with?" Lauren asks, putting the cigarette out in a nearby ashtray.

"Honestly, it doesn't matter. It's not important." I'm not sad, but my tone is rather gloomy and reflective. I don't know if what I thought I wanted to do with my life matters anymore. Or at least, if it matters right *now*.

"Well, if it makes you feel any better, my dad and I butt heads all the time. He hates that I'm majoring in sustainable philosophy. He told me it was a waste of time and not a real thing."

"What is 'sustainable philosophy'?" Alda asks, sounding a little tipsy.

Lauren's already explained it to me three times, and I still don't understand. Before I know it, she's repeating the same spiel for Alda. "Anyway, when I told my dad that's what I was going to do, he started calling me Greta Thunberg."

Alda laughs. "I like her!"

"I don't know who she is."

"What the fuck, Brooke?"

Lauren is staring at me with her mouth twisted, completely aghast. "Girl, what planet do you live on?"

"Greta is the Swedish climate activist. She is very cool. I follow her on Instagram," Alda tells me.

I shrug my shoulders dismissively. "Doesn't ring a bell."

"Seriously, when we get back to London, I'm giving you a tutorial on being Gen Z."

"Thanks," I say cynically.

"Speaking of Instagram . . ." Lauren launches into telling Alda all about her trying to earn sponsorship, etcetera for her social media account and recruiting Alda as a new follower.

I'm looking at my two new friends, realizing I'm not alone and that I don't have to be anymore. *Look at where you are and how things changed in just a matter of days.*

When I started this whole journey, I didn't know what I was looking for. I just knew I needed to go, if not for me then for Liam. Whether I've been consciously looking for something—friendship, love, forgiveness—or not, it's apparent in this moment that what I needed most found me.

My inebriated eyes drift out toward the city lights. It's beautiful. Defiant. Torn. Ugly. Splendid. It's not one thing. It's more. It's definitely not perfect. But it's a place that was built up from being broken.

"I'm ready," I say, my thoughts coalescing and suddenly consumed, thinking of him—Patrick. I'm not asking him, and I'm not asking Lizzie anything. Let's just be reckless. There is something defining about Berlin and the people I've met here. No need to complicate the magic, though deep down I know I want more. The drunk me definitely wants more, anyway.

We start to retrace our steps back through the VIP lounge, but then someone shouts in our direction.

"HEY!" It's Landon Simon. He's waving at us to come over, but he's looking directly at me.

"HEY! I know you! You're that girl! The *super*-rich college tennis girl who—"

I immediately grab Lauren and Alda by the wrist and start dragging them away, while Landon continues shouting and starts with an exaggerated laugh, saying things like "TOTALLY MENTAL." *Okay, pot calling the kettle black.*

Tennis is a popular world-wide sport, but nonetheless can feel like a small community.

The three of us girls are out of the VIP lounge. I can't even look at Lauren and Alda. I go to press the elevator button, but I miss, my hand shaking slightly.

"Stop," Lauren says. I pause. I feel myself well up with tears, completely and utterly mortified. This can't be happening.

I turn slowly and look at them. The one thing I don't see is judgment.

"Fuck that guy, and fuck whatever happened. And you know what else? Fuck your mom, too." She and Alda step closer and embrace me. A few tears escape, but I'm suddenly ensnared by a weightlessness that takes hold of me. *I am not trapped.*

A solid minute passes. Lauren releases me and holds me in front of her, my arms cupped in her hands. "You good?"

I give a weak smile and nod, feeling like I've somehow absorbed a smidge of her confidence through osmosis or something. There's nothing fake about it, or me, right now.

Alda is affectionately twirling the end of one of my braids. Lauren is still looking straight at me, face hardened. "You *are* good, and you are going to be okay," she says in an affirmative tone.

I nod again. A few more tears slide down my face. Then a smile breaks free, but mostly I just feel relief.

Lauren lets go of me and presses the elevator button. "By the way, I called that shit," she remarks with a smirk.

"What's that?" I say, wiping my face as Alda hugs my waist.

"That you were rich, bitch! 'I saved for this trip'—blah, blah, blah! You didn't have anyone fooled. Certainly not me."

I snort. "Really?"

"Really. I mean c'mon. Mayfair?"

Figures. I'm a terrible liar.

"And, I mean, no one's asking you for anything, but ya know, if you want to pay for a round on Mommy dearest's dime again or whatever . . ." she teases as we step into the elevator.

"Why not?" I shrug, turning to my new BFFs. "Fuck her, right?"

CHAPTER 22

Truly Distilled

We wiggle our way across the dance floor through the crowd toward the bar, where the two hulking Scandinavians tower over everyone else like lighthouses in a rough sea squall.

I can feel my anticipation.

Fuck it. I'm kissing him. It's happening.

I feel pumped. Like I'm on top of the world. No more lies. The burden has been eliminated, and I have real friends on lock.

I spot the broad angle of his shoulders and skip toward him. But I've only taken a few bouncy steps, when I stop dead in my tracks.

Patrick is not alone. Lizzie is with him. All the empowerment and confidence I just felt a second ago washes away like a sandcastle into the sea.

I see the other Australians, Max and Abby.

Lizzie reaches up and puts her hand on Patrick's cheek. I can't tell if he's smiling back at her, but his hands are on her waist just like he had his hands on my waist earlier. She wraps her hands around his neck and then they kiss.

I'm such an idiot.

Max spots me standing there. He starts to smile and gives me a nod like "what up, bro," and has that stupid backward ball cap he always wears.

I immediately turn around and shove my way through the crowd. I bolt up the stairs to the wraparound balcony, through the doors that cross the bridge, and out the exit.

There's still a long line outside and I can feel people watch me as I start out in a power walk then break out into a jog-slash-run. By the time I turn the corner out of the gate leading into Brücke, I'm running. The platforms are no longer an obstacle because I need to get as far away as I can. As fast as I can.

My lungs feel tight from the cigarette I just smoked. Or perhaps I'm just choking on my emotions.

My rational brain reminds me that Patrick and I haven't even kissed. I have—*had*—a stupid crush on a douchey Australian guy, who's in some kind of open relationship. It's not a big deal. This stuff happens every day of the week. So why am I crying?

Patrick never promised me anything. I was the one always pressing with the questions. I'm the one who wanted it to be something more, as if we were two kindred spirits connecting over our broken childhoods and our love of sports.

I'm being melodramatic, but I also feel as if my chest is about to burst open. To top everything off, I'm also drunk and running through an unfamiliar city in glorified lingerie.

I'm only half paying attention to my surroundings. I see the Berlin TV Tower and run toward it because I know the hostel is nearby.

A car honks at me as I dart across the street. The streetlights flash—green, yellow, red. The walk sign changes. Some young people are laughing, having fun. I smell fast food from a food truck I pass. A homeless person jingles a cup at me.

I feel like I'm in a movie. Like everything that is happening around me is on a screen that is separate from my own reality.

I collapse against a wall and rub my eyes. I'm standing alone on a dark street, but my mind is back in the locker room. The numbness is too much. I'm numb and crying uncontrollably. I need to feel more than just my tears.

Distilled. Everything is distilled in this moment.

I see myself drop my tennis bag. I'm breathing hard, staring at my locker in front of me. My name is on polished gold plating across the top: BROOKE NEVILLE.

Who are you?

I loathed who I was in that moment. My life was a farce. All pretense with no substance, even though I felt all of who I was and wanted to be aching to pour out into the world.

I snapped in the locker room. I cried. I never cried. Till then.

Those tears . . . That day . . . The satisfaction of release.

I hit my locker over and over again, my right hand landing hard, harder. The pain was shocking and satisfying. My hand bloody, my knuckles exposed as I picked up my rackets one at a time and smashed them against my locker and the floor, splintering each one into tiny pieces.

Everything was a blur, and all I could hear was screaming.

But then I knew. The release came at a cost. Everything has its equal and opposite effect.

CHAPTER 23

The Villain

Walking up the steps to my room feels like summitting Mount Everest. My eyes are clouded by an inky film of mascara, and one of the fake lashes flaps sadly each time I blink. I need to get this ridiculous outfit off my body and clean the mess from my face. I'm going to dissolve under a hot shower for a good hour, until I've disappeared down the drain.

As I get closer to my door, however, something is off.

I don't remember leaving the light on.

A warm glow seeps out from under the door. Then a shadow passes. Someone is moving around inside.

I take a deep breath and remind myself I'm in a densely populated building. This would not be an ideal place to try and murder someone. It could be one of the hostel staff, perhaps doing a welfare check after experiencing more harassment from my mother. Or it could be something more sinister. There is a reason that girls like me are usually followed by an extensive security detail, especially when traveling abroad. I have about 1.2 billion targets painted on my back. Okay, truthfully, a bit more.

Enough. I am not going to spend my life swinging between fear and despair. I place the keycard against the sensor and kick the door open.

Two terrified screams rip through the night. It's only once my lungs are empty that I realize one of them is mine.

"Oh my God. . ." I gasp, hand clutching my chest.

Sitting on the bed is my mother. She's wearing a designer linen suit. Her hair is back in a bun and her makeup is muted.

It's a serious ensemble for a middle-aged woman in a Berlin hostel, who appears to be in the throes of a panic attack.

"'I AM FINE?'" she gasps, and for a moment, I'm confused. My mother isn't one to share her feelings, even if she is hyperventilating.

"'I AM FINE!'" she shrieks again, her anger starting to ground her. She takes a deep breath, and I realize she's not fine at all. She's quoting my single-line email.

Her eyes sweep up my mostly naked body, and she looks away, as if the vision is too painful to bear.

"Running up your credit card? On dozens of drinks in a single night at this *place*. Pictures on social media with you looking like you are totally out of control, which—thank you very much—are now circulating like wildfire across the internet and amongst everyone back at home." She scoffs. "Oh, yes, you're *just fine*."

She pulls out her phone from her Gucci bag, holds it up and scrolls through the pictures. I see a glimpse of the Insta account she's looking at: @milgirlbratluv.

I gave into the one picture after our run together but didn't realize Lauren had been posting others of us and the group without me knowing. The latest is a photo of me dancing at Brücke, with Patrick's hand slipping under my top, his face hidden behind me. Just some random hand moving up my skimpy top.

"Uh . . ." I let out a groan and close my eyes but don't say anything else.

Damn you, Lauren. Hypocrite. Rule breaker.

"Who is this Lauren?" My mother pushes aside her disgust to soften her voice. "Is this some kind of rebellion?" She waves a glittering hand at my ensemble. "Some kind of self-inflicted humiliation? You promised you weren't going to lose control again. We made a deal."

I can feel the fumes furl from my nostrils at her mentioning me losing control. We both know what she's talking about.

"Pack your things right now, young lady. We're leaving."

"Mom, give me two weeks. That's all I ask. I know this looks bad, but I can't go back home yet." I'll give up on London, wear her stupid Chanel dresses, and play the Good Daughter. But I am not leaving tonight without a word, like a ghost. I am finishing my time here in Germany.

"Not an option."

Looking around now, I see that my mother has already packed my things. No doubt there is a limousine parked downstairs waiting for us. Rage radiates from my chest to the tips of my fingers. I curl my hands into fists.

"No."

She doesn't react; she just stares back, but I see her nostrils flare in return at me.

"Get out," I say resolutely.

Tears are streaming down my face, all over again. The pain is real. But this time, I am taking the axe to my life and breaking it apart with my own hands. That, at least, feels good.

"I'm not perfect. We both know that," I say and shake my head. "I'm not Liam, your golden child." I almost choke on my brother's name, but I push through. "But he's dead, Mom. He's gone."

My mother recoils, as if I've physically hit her. "Brooke!"

"He's gone, and you killed him."

A tiny part of me softens at the pain in her eyes, but this needs to be said. She was the one that made him believe he could never quit. That he had to be number one, so as not to embarrass the family. Through pain and injury, through multiple concussions. "If you're going to be a savage on the field, Liam, you can at least be the best one out there," she had told him.

"You killed him, but I won't let you kill me."

The tears are stinging my eyes, but I feel myself smile—ironically—ready to push the limit and lay my last blow, releasing everything that I've been holding onto since the funeral.

"Kill you?" My mother clutches her throat, eyes darting around the room.

"You came all this way for an email. But where were you when Liam collapsed at training? You knew . . . you *knew* something was wrong."

Her eyes flash up at me, filled with hate. "And where were *you?*" she hisses. "The beloved sister he shared everything with? If anyone could have known the truth and done something in time, it was you. But you were too selfish, Brooke! Always have been." My mother stands up, towering over me even though she's a good foot shorter. "He shared everything with you. But you never deserved Liam's love. You sad, lonely, selfish, ungrateful little wretch!"

She throws back her hand and for a moment, I think she's going to claw at my face. But she catches herself and picks up her handbag instead.

The two of us stare at one another, breathing hard. I don't fight the tears; I just let them fall down my face. The only sound is the late-night rumblings of the bar downstairs and an ambulance siren somewhere in the city.

"You won't 'let me kill you.'" She laughs softly, as if she's never heard anything so ridiculous. "The girl who's been handed every pleasure and opportunity in life, on a platter." She stalks past me and walks to the door but pauses. She doesn't look me in the eye but keeps her back to me. "I don't need to kill you, Brooke, because you are dead to me. If this is the life you want so badly—dirty hostel rooms and cheap clothes—then take it. But I won't play the villain in your story, or be your enabler. You can self-destruct all on your own, young lady."

"I'm not scared of you," I say.

She laughs. "Let's see how brave you are when you're broke, alone, and have no one else to blame."

"GET OUT!" I scream as the door closes behind her with a soft click.

I've finally found my voice, but the room is empty.

CHAPTER 24

Cut Off

The following morning I am hungover and hollowed out. The events of the past twelve hours feel surreal, and as I look around my empty room, it's hard to believe my mother was ever there. Did I dream the whole thing?

My stomach is rumbling, and eating feels like the only obvious choice, so I leave the hostel and walk until I find a pastry shop.

"*Entschuldigung?*"

I'm not really paying attention as I stand at the register to pay.

"*Hallo? Entschuldigung?*"

"I'm sorry. Yes?"

"Your card," the girl says, handing it back to me, shaking her head. "Not working."

My stomach drops as a wave of nausea rolls through me. My mother wasn't bluffing. An idol threat no more.

"Sorry," I say, embarrassed as I see my face turn red in the mirror that covers the wall behind the counter. I pull out some emergency cash from my little day bag and hand it to the girl, who returns the black card. I look at it in my hand, now nothing more than a worthless piece of plastic.

I try to act cool as the girl hands me my change. I find a seat and wait for my food, which I devour, along with a big mug of coffee and two glasses of water, on top of trying not to think about how much of my remaining funds I just wasted on a fancy patisserie meal.

It doesn't matter. I'm not giving into her. I'm not playing her game.

I spend most of the morning walking and wandering aimlessly. I walk past portions of the Berlin Wall that stand as relics of the city's brutally divided past. Eventually I find myself back at the Gemäldegalerie Museum, standing before a familiar painting.

Portrait of a Young Girl by Petrus Christus.

I pull out my camera from my bag and flip through the pictures of me and my new friends, of Patrick, some saved pictures I have of my tennis team, and then I go to the oldest ones I keep on the digital load of me and Liam.

I'm fucked up.

It hits me like a ton of bricks that in all my attempts to be perfect and control my life and my future, I'm tortured by things that have happened in my life for which there is no easy solution or fix. Maybe my mom was right. I thought that this trip was about healing myself, but instead I'm just self-destructing.

I glance back up at the portrait. The girl's empty eyes stare right through me.

I can't bear to spend another moment with her, so I turn to leave but find that my escape is blocked by a pair of intense eyes and a pissed-off expression.

"Hello, Patrick."

The Freshman Phenom

My first instinct is to run, even though my body aches from the last twenty-four hours. Then I remember that Patrick can't hurt me, not after everything I've lost. Besides, if anything, he's the one who should be embarrassed and explaining himself.

I fold my arms and wait for him to speak.

"Shall we sit?" he says, his hands stuffed in his jeans pockets. "Sure," I say curtly, joining him on the bench facing the paintings. "How'd you find me?"

"Olivier," he answers. "He didn't really think you'd be here, but it was the only place we could come up with."

I nod, embarrassed by the idea of the group coming together to try and puzzle out yet another erratic disappearance. I must look like a total diva. Par for the course, I suppose.

A few minutes pass and we stay silent. A mother and little girl walk by holding hands, stopping to look at the Petrus Christus painting. The little girl points at the painting—I think she's pointing to the funny hat that the subject is wearing—and they discuss it in what sounds like Italian, then continue to the next exhibit.

"Can I explain some things to you?" Patrick says.

I don't want to hear excuses, but I do want him to explain. I don't care if it'll hurt more at this point. I need the truth. Besides, I have nowhere else to be. I turn my gaze toward Patrick, and we look at each other eye-to-eye. I hate that I feel all the aching feelings and compulsions from the night before—even after everything I've seen.

"The truth," he promises, like it's a covenant he's now sworn to and can't break. His gaze slips away from me and he takes a deep breath, then rubs his hands together nervously. "So, Max—he's the best mate I'm traveling with. He's also engaged to my cousin—Lara. Anyway"—He gulps down air and is still rubbing his hands nervously—"Max, he's always been a bit wild, and he was getting cold feet about the wedding and all, so he decided he wanted to take a bachelor trip through Europe before getting married—one last romp as a 'free man' sort of thing."

Patrick swallows the dry air again. Meanwhile, I can feel myself instinctively roll my eyes at the misogyny, completely unamused.

"I know how it sounds," he says, clearly sensing my disgust. "They have a complex relationship—Max and Lara. They've been together forever. They've broken up and gotten back together, I don't know how many times. Anyway, I came because Max is my best mate, but also, I'm like the middleman—I'm his *babysitter*, I guess you could say—for Lara. I'm supposed to make sure he doesn't do anything too stupid, even though she wants him to get his impulses 'out of his system.'"

"How's that going?" I say sarcastically.

"Not very well," Patrick admits.

"Sounds messed up and pretty patriarchal, if you ask me," I add.

Patrick shrugs, his gaze concentrated forward. "I agree."

I shake my head in silence.

"Anyway, as you probably might have guessed, we met Abby and Lizzie early in the trip, and Max hooked up with Abby."

"And now you're trying to say you've been stuck with Lizzie?" I scoff. "You guys are true gentlemen."

"We *all* have our own shit, right?" he says, looking pointedly at me. "I try my hardest not to hurt anyone, but sometimes life gets messy."

I don't respond. Let him dig his own grave. I'm done.

"I don't want to lie to you, Brooke. Lizzie has feelings for me, and we've kissed. But that's it—I swear. I'm not interested in her. It just happened because of the circumstances."

"So, you've been leading her on because being honest might make things awkward for your best friend, who is cheating on his fiancée? Is this supposed to make me feel better?"

"Well, when you put it like that . . ." Patrick drops his head and rubs his eyes.

"Whatever your explanation, you shouldn't have been flirting with me last night and kissing her a moment later. That was cruel."

"I wasn't kissing her last night. I was trying to explain to her that I wasn't interested, and then she kissed me."

I mull this over for a minute.

"I don't know how long we'll be in Europe, Brooke, or if you're even interested in me after all of this. But I think we have a connection, and I don't want to blow it up over a stupid misunderstanding." He turns so we are looking at each other again. "Tell me you don't feel it, and I'll walk away."

I swallow, trying to work out what I feel and if any of it has even been real. Even on a bench in the middle of a museum, I can't deny that his physical presence has an effect on me. It takes considerable self-control not to scoot over and climb into his lap.

"I feel something."

Patrick gingerly takes my right hand into his and smiles. He turns it over and traces the lines of the scars. "Just something?" We both watch as the hairs along my arms rise up like a tiny army of traitors. "I went back to the hostel after it was clear you left the club last night. I heard shouting and an argument coming from your room."

Something inside me slumps, even as I'm heartened by knowing he followed me back. There is so much bottled up inside me, and I have been carrying it all alone. I have no friends or real trusted confidants. No one to go to for advice, or to lean on when things feel too hard. Up to now, I've used money as a way to keep myself distracted with new experiences. But I no longer have that either. In a couple of days, I won't even have a roof over my head.

"What's going on, Brooke?" Patrick lifts a finger to wipe at a tear that's rolled down the side of my cheek, and in that tiny moment, I decide to tell him everything.

About my family and our wealth. My "silly dream" to be a professional tennis player and embarrassing breakdown.

About Liam—the boy who broke my heart into a million tiny pieces.

As I talk and cry, vent and complain, Patrick's expression turns from shock to something far more complex. I confess every terrible thing I've done. The final call from Liam that I missed. The agony of smashing my fist into a bloody mess, only to look down and see Alex at my feet, covered in blood and crying. The panic of being pulled away by forceful hands and cuffed by the college security guards. Then being pinned down as the campus doctor arrived with a syringe, my mother screaming at them to release me. The cries of my teammates as Alex was taken from the room on a stretcher.

He doesn't ask any questions, he only listens, and eventually—miraculously—I run out of words. The revelations settle between us.

"I'm sorry for your loss," he says finally. "You and your brother had a special connection."

"There's *more* though," I say, choking out words that are barely audible. "My mom had left the stands during my game because—because she'd gotten a call from the police. It was the same day Liam killed himself." My sobs are broken by a laugh. "What are the chances? That I would have an epic meltdown, at the same time my brother . . ."

I feel Patrick's eyes on me, his hand squeezes tighter, and with it I feel my own breath taken away.

"Mom thought I was falling apart because I'd somehow heard the news. But I was mostly just angry at her for ignoring my game. Ignoring me. Like always." I look up at him, tears rolling freely now. "How stupid is that?"

It was only after Liam's autopsy that we learned he had a brain tumor that had likely caused his deep, chronic depression. The change had been so sudden, all of us had missed it.

Manipulate your mind to do more than what your body can handle.

That was Liam's favorite athletic quote. He literally did just that.

Like me, Liam had his own sports diary, the entries of which changed dramatically in the last six months of his life. Reading his journals, it was clear he minimized what was happening by thinking he could mentally forge through whatever was wreaking havoc inside himself. He ignored the intense headaches and the pain. He thought he could deal with the dark thoughts on his own. Like everyone in our family was forced to. Pressure and arrogance—it has a tipping point.

I blame my mother for that, especially the arrogance. She was the one priming us our whole lives to not only act perfect but telling us we must *be* perfect—no matter what. Flawlessness, excellence, and being beautiful—that is the Neville way. It's a disease. It's *her* disease, and Liam succumbed to it in the worst way by ignoring how he was feeling for the sake of being what the world wanted. Mr. Golden Boy, King of Perfection. Until he couldn't.

I refuse to end up the same way. I won't give into her. Ever again.

"How would you have known, if he never told you?" Patrick says gently.

"I should have known. I should have just asked him how he was feeling. But I was in a place where I was too selfish and focused on myself. Just like Mom—in her own little world."

"Your mum sounds like a piece of work, but even so, do you really think that's fair? Maybe your brother craved a bit of independence, and that's why he went across the country to find it."

"Maybe," I say, pausing to contemplate this perspective. "I haven't thought of it like that before."

"Seems like there's a lot of blame that could get passed around. But it doesn't change anything at the end of the day, eh?"

Patrick gently strokes my hair, and I feel warm curled up next to his ribs.

"I'm just so sorry for it all," I say, looking directly at the girl in the painting.

"Sometimes remorse is healthy, but you have to learn to forgive yourself, too."

"I know," I say softly, and I do know. It's just so much easier said than done.

Patrick tips my chin up to look at him. I must look miserable and washed out, and the revelations about my life are pretty ugly. But there's warmth in his eyes.

"Do you want to get out of here?"

I sniffle, wipe my face with the back of my hand again, and clear my throat.

"Where do you want to go? I'm not sure I'm really in the mood for any sightseeing right now," I say.

He waves me off.

"No, not *here*. I mean do you want to get out of Berlin?"

CHAPTER 26

Farewell to the Berliners

From that moment, my life becomes a whirlwind. It takes a couple of days to rework all of my preplanned logistics, which I'm glad for because I didn't want to ditch my new friends without a proper goodbye. Plus, my room in Berlin is already paid for, and I certainly am not going to turn my nose up to free things given my circumstances.

The last stop on my grand adventure was Prague and so that is where Patrick and I are headed—just the two of us. It's both thrilling and terrifying. But for different reasons than when I first arrived. I'm traveling with a guy who I barely know but one that I've already hurtled through an entire emotional rollercoaster with, which has in a real way, strengthened the initial spark and bond between us.

Everyone in the Berlin crew now knows who I am—who I *really* am. Brooke Antoinette Neville. It didn't seem to come as much of a shock. Apparently, I'm a little too weird to pass for normal, and my real identity explained a lot.

Lauren gave me shit for being a "one-percenter" but admitted that her following on Instagram had increased like crazy because of it. I forgave her for effectively ruining the Neville name forever and promised to email her from the road. I also tried to get her to tell me how she managed to sneak her cellphone into Brücke. All I got was "it was uncomfortable but worth it to prove I was actually there." Alda was pissed for a hot minute but got over it.

I don't know if I'll make it to London now, or what the future holds in store for me. But as I squeeze Lauren goodbye, I know I've made a friend I'll do my best to try and keep.

Lauren pulls me back, after holding me in her arms. "Have fun but be careful. Make good decisions." She points with her eyes at Patrick.

She knows all about what Patrick had told me in the museum, which she acknowledged with a curt "I see." If the feminist in me was offended by Max's behavior, then I can only imagine how Lauren must see it. But one thing I've learned about my new friend is she is protective of me, just like Liam used to be.

It's strange, but across most of my new Berliner friends, I've felt some small part of Liam reflected back at me. Lauren the sage, confidante, and protector. Varun the charmer. Grady the comedian and jokester. Alda, Ms. Congeniality, who can speak four languages, meld into any group, and be adored everywhere she goes. Even the Scandinavians, the brutes, the monstrous gladiators who are totally fit. And Patrick. Patrick, the kindred spirit, and the person who seems to really *see* me.

Of course, even though Patrick reminds me of my brother in some ways, I don't *think* of him like that, and I'm still waiting for him to kiss me, which for some reason still hasn't happened. My body tingles at the thought.

"I will . . . *Mom*," I say to Lauren.

She and I exchange a look.

"You can just call me 'ma'am' and salute next time," she jokes, giving me a wink.

"We'll see you in London, darling," Varun adds.

I hope that's the case, but I doubt I'll be living in Mayfair.

Thankfully many of the forward reservations I made in Prague were pre-paid (thanks to my overzealousness to plan accordingly), and Patrick has promised to contribute to our budget. Part of me feels horribly reckless going and living it up with a sexy stranger, when I should probably be looking for a job and saving like crazy. But this is the first time I've felt half alive, and I'm going for it.

I give both Varun and Grady a hug, as well as Alda.

"*Auf Wiedersehen!*" Alda says. "You and Lauren should come to Germany for one of the *big* music festivals. I get us the hook up!" she adds, with her usual impish smile.

Lauren almost melts with excitement, and I laugh as we pick up our bags and leave them waving madly. Patrick and I are taking the early train, and the Scandinavians are absent. We stayed out late last night, plus—I'm assuming—when we all got back from the bar, the couples (Lauren and Erik, Alda and Lars) probably stayed up late doing who knows what for who knows how long.

Also missing are Max and the other Australians. Patrick apparently confronted Max about his behavior and told him that he was done babysitting. The conversation with Lizzie was also apparently difficult, but after the way she tipped her beers on me, I can't say I feel that bad. What goes around comes around.

Our group says final goodbyes as we wave from our Uber—Patrick insisted on an Uber versus public transportation—back to the group, who are all standing on the sidewalk.

Thank you, friends. Thank you, Liam.

CHAPTER 27

Ditto

It's a little over a four-hour train ride from Berlin to Prague, or as the conductor keeps saying on the train intercom, "*PRRRA-HAAA!*" with a sharp roll of the "r."

At some point, I reach into my bag and grab the romance novel I've been sluggishly reading. I get ready to settle back into my seat, nestling up next to Patrick, but upon seeing my book, he immediately snatches the beat-up and dog-eared paperback from my grasp.

"What is this?"

I grab at my book.

"Maybe you'd call it inspiration," I say cheekily.

"Oh, lucky me," he replies, keeping it just out of my reach and fanning the pages with his thumb.

"Yeah, lucky you," I tell him, as he easily lets me take the book back. Meanwhile, I'm stretched across him and can feel his face close to my neck.

"It's actually not bad," I comment, falling back against my seat.

"Oh yeah?"

He glances down at the contemporary cover art, with the muscular heartthrob of the story clutching the face of the female protagonist, the two engaged in a steamy kiss.

I feel a wave of heat hit me. Like so many times since we've met, I can't help but think of Patrick doing the same thing to me.

I flip to where I'm at in the book, but before I get too far along Patrick is reading some racy bits in a low voice from over my shoulder. It's a pool scene. There's mention of gentle caresses that elevate to passionate grabbing of various body parts. Mouths exploring. A deeply sensual kiss.

I'm panting, but I'm not the only one. He keeps going, even though there's an audible tremble at the back of Patrick's throat as he reads. Suddenly, the air feels so thick and steamy between us that a butter knife could break in two.

For God's sake, kiss me! I'm staring at his lips, licking my own, desperate for him to pull me into him and move his hand higher from where it is resting on my knee.

"PASSPORT!"

A border officer suddenly appears. We scoot away from one another like two teenagers caught by their parents.

The officer looks unfazed. *"Cestovní pas!* PASSPORT!"

Patrick and I each fumble through our belongings. I hand my passport over, and the officer searches for the elusive free spot. At least this time I don't feel so much like a fake. I feel like a real wanderer, an adventurer on a path of self-discovery. I've been places, and I've done things.

After the officer moves on, I nestle up under Patrick's arm and start to read but am hypnotized by the gentle rocking of the train car. I wake up to Patrick stirring me as we start to pull into the main Prague train station.

We gather our things and make our way off the train. It's a little past midday. The sun is out and shining through the glass panes overhead under the dome-shaped cover of the platform. The fresh summer air wafts in from where the trains arrive and depart. Meanwhile, all around the sounds of people coming and going, plus the intercom announcements, echo up and down the long belly of the train station.

I drop my big Osprey backpack on the ground and start to pull out my travel diary. But Patrick looks at me, shaking his head.

"No." He's staring down at my carefully crafted and upcycled guidebook. "Look, Ms. Lonely Planet, I get not having a phone or tablet or whatever, 'cause you need space from your mum, but we can just go ahead and use *my* cell to figure this all out."

"I bet I can figure out where we need to go faster with my notes than you can with your phone," I challenge. "Also, I take that as a compliment. Though I think my diary is better than a Lonely Planet guidebook."

Patrick snorts.

"Those sound like fighting words."

"A little," I say and flip my book open to the tab for Prague.

A second or two later, just as I'm about to start directing us on our route, a guy forcefully pushes into Patrick.

"Oh, no you don't."

I'm still nose down in my diary but look up to see Patrick has caught up to the guy and twists him into a pretzel with a fancy karate-type maneuver. A small crowd circles the scene as Patrick lifts the guy off the ground and takes back his wallet and phone. There's an applause from the crowd.

The thief looks like a teenager, and Patrick shoves him off with a few harsh words that seem impactful despite the language barrier.

"What was that all about?" I ask, one brow raised.

"Ah, nothing. Just an aspiring pickpocket."

"Yeah, I wasn't talking about that. I mean the—" I try to imitate the slick movement but end up looking more like a demented Marvel character.

Patrick laughs. "Oh. That."

"Where'd you learn *that*?"

"Enlisted in the military. Royal Australian Air Force."

I give Patrick a peculiar look. *"Really?* Are you still in?"

He sighs. "No."

"Well, how long were you in?"

He presses his lips together and squints his eyes at me. "Listen, Ms. Twenty Questions, you can interview me when we get settled at the place. Let's get out of here first."

I frown. "Okay," I say with an admonishing look. "I'm just curious is all. You should have told Lauren. She might have liked you more if she knew that, with her dad being military and all."

We shuffle off. This time I insist on public transit even though Patrick says he's happy to pay for an Uber or taxi again. We head into the heart of Prague where I have a penthouse suite reserved.

Since Prague was my last stop on my travels, I splurged and picked a luxury place to stay, which would have been my mother's preference for each of my destinations. Somewhere clean, pristine, and on par with her daughter's status in our privileged world. Not a place crawling with a bunch of young, out-of-control twenty-somethings ready to party day and night—which, ironically, my mother thinks I am now, anyway.

Emotionally I still feel like I'm processing what happened back in Berlin. The utter disgust on my mother's face. The words and vitriol we exchanged. It all comes back in mini flashes. The occasional wave of guilt passes over me, but it's fleeting. I made the best decision for myself that I could have, and each time I look at Patrick I'm buoyed by my resolve.

The only real issue is what happens next . . . I have no money and I've never worked at anything in my life, except school and tennis.

Patrick and I emerge into the light from the Metro tunnel and just like every other city I've been to, it's bustling. There are new smells, shops, people, and even tastes that cling in the air and ignite the feeling of adventure and excitement. Only this time it's amplified because I'm here with Patrick.

I flip my travel diary open and check it against the street signs and building markers around us.

"You got it?" Patrick asks, lurking over my shoulder, spying at my cut-outs and notes.

"I got us this far, haven't I, Cobra Kai?" I say, giving him a side-eye.

"That's silly," he says, picking up on the Netflix reference (one of the many shows I binge-watched after the locker room incident but would have otherwise been oblivious to), with a smirk and gives me a kiss on the cheek. "I trust you."

Ahhh, Patrick you are killing me. Wish you would just give me a real kiss already!

We continue down a block or two, then past a big open park. The area is in the hub of things but just south of the main city center. I picked it because of the view it had of the Vltava River that runs through the center of Prague—not to be confused with the Danube, which apparently a lot of people do.

My heart is beating a little faster as we walk into the building. It's ultra-modern, with white, clean aesthetic lines, large windows, textured by wood and stone architectural design. It reminds me of a spa, the way it feels very calming and serene.

I can see Patrick checking the place out as we walk through the big automatic glass doors and head in the direction of the front desk.

"You okay?" I ask, feeling every bit in my element.

"Yeah, I guess. I've never stayed in a place this fancy. Nice, just a little out of my element—and *price range*."

I'm not sure how to respond so I squeeze his hand to comfort him and give him a meek smile. A part of me feels a little embarrassed to think that this is normal for me.

"It's cool," he says cheerfully. "Just different. That's all."

We walk up to the front desk, and the guy starts to talk to us both in Czech but soon realizes we have no idea what he's saying.

"English?" The guy's facial features remind me of a baby bird, and he gives us both a circumspect look.

"Yes, thanks. My name is *Ann* Neville. I have a reservation for the penthouse suite."

Patrick and I exchange a look.

"Ah yes, identification and payment, please."

I feel my heart stop.

"I thought the card had already been charged and everything was paid for? I called to double check the other day."

The attendant shakes his head.

"No, ma'am. The deposit was made but we need a credit card on file for final payment. We will run it and charge a nominal fee for incidental room service fees now. Then charge final payment when you check out. Do you want to use the same card you used for the deposit?"

I feel my face burning. His English is perfect. There is no mistaking the policy. I have no way of paying for this. I thought everything had already been paid for and I was just going to use what cash I had on me for now, then try to see if I could pull cash out from a currency exchange place using my debit card. I start to recant my conversation when I called to verify the other day, but quickly learn that the person I spoke to was fired for apparent incompetence. Just my luck.

"Here," Patrick says, handing over a credit card.

"What are you doing? You just said—can you *afford* this place?" I say in a low, hushed voice to Patrick, not wanting to sound rude.

Patrick doesn't look fazed. "It's fine. I got this."

"Patrick, we can go someplace else—"

"Brooke—*Ann*—I got this. Now it's your turn to trust me," he says pointedly, curling a loose strand of my hair back behind my ear.

The guy runs Patrick's credit card and hands it back to him. Meanwhile, I'm still staring at Patrick confused and filled with dread. This place is a couple of thousand dollars a night. Does he know what he's done? I take a breath. It might take a while, but I'll make it up to him.

We finish in the lobby and make our way to the elevator. We get in and head up to the top floor.

I'm still perplexed. I feel guilty but also a touch curious.

"Do you have some secret trust account you didn't tell me about?" I say half-jokingly.

Patrick laughs. He shakes his head at my jest.

"I thought you said you did some type of—what was it again?"

I don't want to be demeaning, but I really am curious how the guy who told me in casual conversation a few days ago that he does construction work somehow can be nonchalant about paying thousands of dollars a night for a penthouse suite.

"I told you, construction work. I build homes," he replies, but he doesn't offer any further explanation. "Hey, let's just enjoy ourselves, eh? Don't think about it, alright? It's fine."

I nod. I'm too self-conscious to say anything else. Not being able to pay for something and having to rely on someone else is a new thing for me. Plus, Patrick asked me to trust him, and I do, but it doesn't stop my mind from dissecting. *Military. Construction worker.* What am I missing?

The elevator opens up directly into the penthouse suite. Straight ahead is a breathtaking view of Prague. The entire penthouse is encased in floor-to-ceiling glass. There is nowhere to look that doesn't have a view. It's spectacular.

We walk into the huge open living room that's connected to a chef's kitchen. Everything has the same luxe feeling as the downstairs lobby. It's minimalistic but expensive.

"Well," Patrick starts. "So far it feels like it's worth selling a kidney for."

He gives me a cheeky smile as I jab him in the ribs.

We drop our bags—the front desk attendant tried to insist on bringing them up for us, but Patrick declined. That apparently was a step too far into my privileged world for him. "Yeah, mate, I got it. I got two arms and a good back. No worries," was his response to the attendant. I followed Patrick's lead.

We wander from the exquisite living room and chef's kitchen, through several of the oversized bedrooms with spa-like ensuite bathrooms with big closets, a library, dining area, a sauna and indoor hot tub, a greenspace at the very center, and then find our way to a set of stairs leading to the rooftop.

"What's up there?" Patrick asks.

I shrug with a mischievous look because of course I know. I picked the place.

"Guess we gotta go up to find out."

"Guess so," he says and lifts me over one shoulder and proceeds to carry me up.

I feign resistance but instantly give in. Not that I was really resisting to begin with.

We get to the top where the stairs open to the rooftop that leads to a grassy area, a pool, and a sleek wood deck. The area is encased with a protective glass surround. It is pure extravagance, with the same spectacular three-hundred-and-sixty-degree views as inside.

Patrick slowly lets me slide down his chest to stand on the deck.

"Wow, this is incredible."

"Yeah, it is," I agree.

We're holding hands and he turns to face me. I think for a minute he's going to kiss me, finally.

"I'm really glad I met you," he says.

"Ditto."

He smirks and brushes a loose strand of my hair behind my ear again.

I can see his chest move up and down taking in deep, rhythmic breaths. I feel myself knotting up inside with anticipation.

But he drops his gaze, and so do I.

"Should we go explore a little?"

"Sure," I say, with just a sliver of disappointment evident in my voice.

"Did you have something *else* in mind?" he asks probingly, sliding his hand around my waist.

"No," I reply with a grin. "Let's go have a grand adventure."

CHAPTER 28

Hand-in-Hand

"Are you a virgin?"

Lauren had straight-up asked me when it was just us three girls—Alda, Lauren, and me—hanging out in Berlin, a day or so after the whole Brücke incident.

I'm not, but I am inexperienced—I totally admit that. Though, yes, I am on birth control. Not because I'm out having a whole bunch of wild sex. Like a lot of female athletes, I have irregular periods. The pill helps regulate my cycle. Supposedly.

I assume I'm like most girls my age, or at least I think I am. I want things—sexually, that is. But I'm not entirely comfortable or confident in my own skin, and my inexperience is clouded by my own judgment of myself.

I definitely feel my face flush and everything below my waist tighten at the thought of Patrick kissing me, and more. I have ideas of what an experience with him would be like, but how does it start? Is it my move or is it his? Is he hesitant because he senses naivety in me? Do I need to tell him outright that I want him?

My insides groan, and I realize I'm experiencing something I've never felt before.

Sexual frustration sucks.

I'm analyzing my hormones as Patrick and I walk through Old Town Square to go see the Old Town Hall Tower and the

Prague Astronomical Clock. He's pointing out different shops, and we're making small talk while holding hands. I can't help that in the back of my mind I'm nervous and anxiously wondering what happens when the day is over and we go back to the penthouse suite—just the two of us, together, sleeping in the same place. No one else around.

"So, Ms. Lonely Planet, what's the story about this clock we're going to see? What was it you said you had? FOMOOI—fear of missing out on information?"

"That's right," I reply, refocusing. "From what I can remember it was built sometime in the fifteenth century, and one of the clockmakers that had a hand in building it was *blinded*—like, the townies gouged his eyes out, or something—so he wouldn't go off and build anything like it anywhere else."

"That's fucking weird," Patrick comments, shaking his head with a disgusted look as he stares up in the direction of the clock.

"Well, we are talking about medieval times. People were f—I mean, *really* weird, back then."

Patrick laughs. "You're so cute. Not going to drop the 'f' word?"

"No, I'm going through a detox. I think Lauren's abuse of the word was rubbing off on me a bit too much in Berlin."

He laughs again, and I bite my lip because the sound makes me feel giddy and girly, and altogether warm inside.

"Anyway, there are three different kinds of time displayed." We've made our way across the big open square to where the tower and clock stand tall above us. I point up at the face of the ginormous clock. "You see there? That outer ring?"

"Yup," he answers, shading his eyes from the sun to look where I'm pointing. "The Arabic numerals, you mean?"

"Yeah, that's right. How'd you know? Do you know Arabic or something?"

He's still looking up. "I deployed to the Middle East. Lived there for a bit, too."

Just like earlier at the train station, I want to ask more, but I can sense Patrick wants to keep it light or that perhaps he's hesitant to open up with abandon, even if I'm not.

I turn back to the clock without further pressing. "You can see that a day for them was twenty-four hours—if you count all the numerals—but a day would start with the setting of the sun."

"Cool. What about those? Are those Roman numerals just on the inside of the outer circle?" he asks, pointing and squinting.

"Right again. The Roman numerals represent time as *we* know it."

"Do we actually *know* time?" he says, all philosophical.

"Well, I don't know about you, but I've met her personally multiple times," I say slyly without skipping a beat.

"Time is a *she?*"

"Of course," I say, as if it's the most obvious thing in the world. "'The two most powerful warriors are patience and time'. Clearly, Tolstoy could have only been referring to a woman."

"Romance novels and *Tolstoy?* You have a very broad range in your reading tastes."

I nudge at Patrick. "My college coach used to send out morning emails with our training schedule for the day. She always started her email with a motivational quote. That one stuck with me. It's from *War and Peace*, I think."

"I take it you never read the book, then?"

I shake my head. "No, but my grandfather has a rare first edition in his library," I casually admit but immediately feel myself flush. Not because of the implication of my family wealth—Patrick knows. I'm wondering who in the family my mother's told about our fight and me being officially cut off.

Patrick, who seems mostly immune and indifferent to the frill of my background, snickers. "I'll have to remember that time is a *she* and you love motivational quotes."

My thoughts cut back to the present moment. I playfully nudge Patrick again. "What can I say? I'm an athlete. Don't all athletes like motivational quotes?"

Patrick gives me an indifferent look.

"Anyway…" I finish telling Patrick about the astronomical clock—it's all very mystical sounding—including an explanation about the animated figurines that come to life on the hour, every hour.

"Looks like we have about five minutes or so," I say and can see Patrick studying the figures.

To the left of the clock face are two figurines: a man looking at himself in a mirror, meant to represent vanity, and another with a bag of gold to represent greed. To the right of the clock face are two other figurines: a man with a stringed instrument to represent lust and a skeleton to represent death. But unlike the others, death has his bony hand on a thin wire rope.

"Hmmm. So, you said the figures were meant to represent things that were frowned upon at the time the clock was built? I'm assuming then it had some religious basis?" Patrick says.

"Yeah."

"You religious?"

I'm a little caught off-guard by the question, mostly because I thought he was avoiding anything heavy.

I shake my head. "Not really. I grew up Presbyterian. But I stopped going to church regularly when I started playing tennis tournaments on weekends and when Liam had football games."

I think of how Liam and I would get bored out of our minds sitting in church when we were really young and end up playing sword fights with our fingers or tick-tac-toe on the back of the church program to pass the time. Then how, in a blink of an eye, I was sitting in the front pew with my family staring at his casket, center stage. Time. *She* moves like that—fast and unyielding.

"You?" I ask.

Patrick shrugs. "Catholic. But I wouldn't consider myself religious. Spiritual, but definitely not religious. The institution of the Catholic church never really sat well with me growing up, especially hearing all the coverup stories about priests abusing kids and stuff. Just seemed like a bunch of bullshit hypocrisy to me. Plus, my dad is pretty devout." Patrick pauses. "I think because of that I have a bit of a negative association. My dad is not exactly the type to practice what's being preached, or what *he* preaches, anyway."

I'm looking at Patrick. His gaze has drifted off.

It's obvious Patrick is supremely guarded, especially about the nature of his relationship with his dad, but I feel each time when we talk more intimately that he wants to give more. We both do. I can appreciate though that the newness of our relationship—whatever it may be—only allows us to expose so much. The nugget is another small glimpse into his life and into his world. I'll take it.

The skeleton figurine starts to pull on the thin wire rope, and two small doors open. More figurines twirl around inside, each appearing at the opening of the doors.

"And those are the twelve apostles," I say.

"Cool. Should we take a picture?" Patrick asks. Wherever he disappeared to in his thoughts, he's returned.

"Sounds like a good idea," I reply, pulling out my camera.

"Well, I was thinking more like we would just use my cell phone and I could text them to you, ya know?"

"Are you trying to ask for my cell phone number, Patrick?" I fold my lips and narrow my eyes at him, trying to be quirky and cute.

"Maybe. If you're lucky."

We go Dutch and take a selfie with both my hot pink digital and Patrick's cell. But before Patrick can drop his phone in his back pocket, I swipe it and input my number. He looks a little tense with me holding his cell.

"There," I say, handing it back. "Don't worry, I'm not planning on going through your phone."

He doesn't say anything but gives me a smirk and shakes his head.

"Where to next?" I wonder aloud, keeping my travel diary safely packed in my bag.

"Charles Bridge and the Prague Castle?" he suggests.

We head off, hand-in-hand, making our way in the direction of the infamous Charles Bridge and the Prague Castle. The Charles Bridge is packed with tourists, artisans, and musicians, and we funnel across from one side to the next like cattle. Then we climb a horribly jagged cobblestone road and transport back in time a couple thousand years, spending the rest of the afternoon meandering Bohemian cottages, gazing up at church spires, and perusing dreary medieval art and royal jewels.

We're both starving by the time we decide to leave Prague Castle. However, before food I want to find a currency exchange to try and take out money on my debit card and exchange some of my emergency cash that I still have in U.S. dollars.

I didn't do this when we were in Berlin. Between rearranging travel and Lauren's demands that we hang out every second of every day, I didn't have time. Plus, the crew rallied behind me, so I didn't have to worry about paying for things. I know, the poor little rich girl accepting charity. So shameful.

This time we use Patrick's cell phone to google and search for a place and quickly navigate to a spot.

I step up to the debit card machine, insert my card, and punch in my PIN. It doesn't take long before I get an error message and the machine spits my card back out.

A sinking feeling settles in my stomach. Now I know for sure she's told my grandfather. He helped me open the account on my tenth birthday and is the only other person with access to it. I turn back around to Patrick, feeling my face grow hot, perturbed and angry.

"So, it seems like my mom put a block on my debit card, too."

"Don't worry about it. I got it," he says calmly.

"I just don't understand her," I say, frustrated. "I don't get how she thinks cutting me off like this will help anything. All it's doing is putting a bigger wall up between us."

"She sounds like a bit of a control freak, but she's also grieving," he adds carefully.

"You're taking her side?"

Patrick smirks and shakes his head. "I'm on your side. I just know sometimes the people we hurt most are the ones we love most."

"You don't know her like I do," I say, sounding a bit snarky. "I don't think she's capable of love."

"Maybe."

"*Maybe?*" I scoff. "The woman is a monster. And you can hardly talk—you're not even on speaking terms with your dad."

I see Patrick shift away and know that I'm acting defensive, even though I don't mean to. It's been an amazing day so far, and I don't want to ruin it. Maybe I crossed a line.

"I'm sorry," I say.

"You don't have to be. It's fair—what you said, I mean. But what I would tell you is, it's just different. Me and my dad. Isn't there another *Tolstoy* quote about that?"

"All happy families are alike; but each unhappy family is

unhappy in its own way. Or something like that." *Anna Karenina.* That one I did read.

We stare at each other for a minute without saying anything else. I know he's not going to say whatever the issue is between him and his father, especially not in the middle of some random currency exchange store in Prague.

I exchange the remaining cash I have and suppress my groan at my dwindling savings. If I don't find a way to make money soon, things are going to get tough. Even so, being free of my family feels like a ten-ton elephant got lifted off my chest.

"Where do you want to eat?" I ask, feeling a little bashful from our first "spat" as a couple. Or whatever we are.

"Why don't we go to someplace on the other side and walk across the Charles Bridge before we eat?" he suggests.

I agree, and we head in that direction.

My stomach is growling, and my legs feel wobbly from the trek up and down the old historic cobblestone streets. It's late; the sun is not yet setting but dusk has blanketed the city, and the Charles Bridge for the most part has cleared up from all of the human traffic and mayhem we encountered earlier.

There's still a group of street performers out, some instrumentalists who are playing music and collecting tips in an open guitar case. The group is made up of a classical guitarist, a percussionist, a bassist, a violinist, a flautist, and a very enthusiastic guy with a tambourine. The sound is classical, but the group is playing modern pop tunes.

Patrick and I are hand-in-hand, but I stop in front of the group to drop some money into the open instrument case, ignoring the fact that this is probably a reckless expenditure for me right now, and listen to the music. Patrick stands behind me with his hands on my shoulders. But slowly we close the gap between us, and I let my back press against his chest as he wraps his arms around me from behind.

The music is soft, romantic, and soulful. For so many days on this trip, I've walked, eaten, slept, shopped, and explored alone. To have a strong, warm presence holding me is enough to make my eyes moisten. In some ways, I've lost more in the last year than most people lose in a lifetime. So why is it that my life feels fuller, and richer, than ever before?

We let the song finish and applaud with the small audience that has gathered then continue on our way. We walk, our hands still entwined, both of us looking at the different statues that line the bridge. About halfway across the bridge, Patrick stops. He sweeps me around so I'm standing in front of him, close, like we're doing a flamenco dance.

He's looking down at me, and I can feel my heart pounding as I stare up into his eyes. The sky has a touch of the same periwinkle that tints his irises. There isn't a cloud in the sky, only a few stars twinkling far off in the distance.

"Can I kiss you?"

I feel my breath catch.

"Yes."

Patrick leans down and presses his lips to mine. My eyes fall shut as the soft warmth of his mouth fills all my senses. He kisses me like I've never been kissed before, with a gentle but growing hunger that promises so much more between us. His hands run gently through my hair, and he holds my face. I maneuver my hands gently around his neck. We fall into our own little world and somewhere far off, I can hear the musicians start up again.

CHAPTER 29

Sleepwalker

My heart is racing. I'm breathing heavy. There's a thin layer of sweat over my body, and my chest is going to explode.

I jolt up in bed. *This is a panic attack. 100%.*

My mind is going a mile a minute. *What am I doing? What do I do when this ends?*

My flight is set up to go back to London, but then what? I have no money.

Would my mom cancel my flight? She wouldn't care about the cancellation fee. I can't put anything past my mother at this point. I am fucked. Also, I am apparently failing miserably at my detox from being around Lauren's potty mouth.

I lie back in bed, wide awake, tossing from one end of the king-sized bed to the next.

I grab the romance novel, turn on the bedside lamp and read a couple of pages. Bad idea. That has me panicking about a whole other issue.

Think, Brooke.

An hour later, at 3:37 a.m., I'm struck by a stroke of genius. I jolt back up, climb out of bed, and slip on the complimentary silk robe hanging in the closet.

I quietly edge out of my room, careful not to make any noise, and sneak past Patrick's room, that's down the hall from my own.

It's completely quiet when I pause in front of his door. *Good.* I keep moving and head to the opposite side of the penthouse to the office like I'm on a spy mission, and there are unforeseen booby traps waiting for me with each step I take.

Once there, I plop down into the executive chair positioned in front of the antique desk with an oversized Apple monitor on top and check my flight. She hasn't cancelled it. *Okay, good.* Then I sign on to my email, type up my message, and—fingers crossed—press send.

This has to work.

Since I'm here and not sleepy at all, I drop a line to Lauren, too.

I leave the office, but I'm still wired so I head to the kitchen. These types of places will usually stock the fridge with anything you want, and I had provided a short shopping list ahead of us arriving. It looks like they packed it with more than what I asked for.

I grab the milk and find a mug, pour, then set it in the microwave. Warm milk has always worked like a charm to help me sleep. Big matches, school tests—it knocks me out.

Before the beeper on the microwave goes off, I press stop and pull it out.

"Brooke?"

A little scream escapes me as all of the lights come on, and I drop my milk, the mug shattering everywhere. *Holy. Shit.* Not the milk. Him. Patrick is standing in the kitchen in nothing but gym shorts.

"Stay there," he instructs and makes his way over to me, bare-footed and bare-chested.

The milk is everywhere and so are shards of the mug. He swoops me up. I see him wince.

"You okay?" I ask, wrapping my arms around his neck.

"Fine," he says in a strained voice, walking to the living room.

He gently places me down on the plush couch and goes back

to the kitchen. My eyes follow him. The Olympic rings are not his only tattoo. His whole back is ornately covered.

I hear him in the kitchen cleaning up. "What were you making?"

"Um, warm milk."

"*Warm milk?* That must be an American thing."

A few minutes later he's back. He hands me a new mug, and I can see he's made himself some tea.

"What are you doing up?"

I take a sip of my drink and try not to stare at his exposed body. He has one tattoo on his chest. Covering his heart are the Australian and British flags, crisscrossed.

"I couldn't sleep."

"Yeah? Something on your mind?" he says sleepily.

A moment ago, my brain was going in circles like a dog chasing its own tail and now all I can concentrate on is remembering to breathe and not gawk. "Just trying to figure some stuff out. For when I leave."

"Not planning on sneaking off in the middle of the night, are you?" he teases.

"No," I say, giving him an ironic look. "I mean, ya know—" I start but realize I don't like the way it sounds that my time with Patrick could ever end. "When I go back to London. I need to figure out what to do for money and where I'm going to stay and stuff."

"Hmmm," he mulls, taking a slow sip of his tea. "Have you come up with a plan then?"

I'm holding my warm mug between my hands with my mouth twisted. "I think so."

"Well, let's hear it. Unless it's top secret."

I give him a wry look. I want to say, "Who's the one being top secret?" but it doesn't seem like the right time. "Well, when I was eleven, I was a ball girl at Wimbledon."

"*What?*" he says. "Like one of those kids in the baggy clothes running around gathering the balls for the players?"

"Stop. Yes." *God, he's making this difficult. Flirting. Barely dressed.* "Anyway, I stayed with a host family. The husband was one of my dad's friends from college. They really liked me, and I've stayed in contact with them."

"I see," he remarks, taking another casual sip of his drink.

"Anyway, I sent an email to see if maybe I could stay with them. At least until I figure out a few things. Maybe they can help me with finding a place to work while I go to school. Or I can work for them—cleaning, doing whatever—ya know? Earn my keep, so-to-speak."

He laughs. "Billionaire heiress turns into maid?"

"Not funny," I reply, grimacing at him.

"Come on, Brooke. I'm only kidding," he says lightly. "You have to admit though, it sounds a little desperate, eh?"

"Well, I am desperate, aren't I?" I set down the mug and turn to look at him, ignoring his smoldering body. "I'm not calling my mom, and I'm not going back. I'm starting over. Isn't that basically what you did?"

I see him tense up, as I've quickly turned the tables back to him. Something we seem to do to one another with regularity.

"Yeah, but I told you. It's different." He sets his tea down, and I can tell he's getting serious.

"How different? Competitive swimming with prospects of going to the Olympics to then joining the military? And now a construction worker? If that's not starting over, I don't know what is. Besides, you seem happy. You made your own choices."

He rubs his face and clasps his hands together. "I joined the military to get away from my dad. It was an easy way out but not an easy choice. The minute I was of age, I joined. But I did that because there was no one in my family to fall back on. I could only rely on myself. I don't think that's the same for you."

"How would you know?"

"A feeling, maybe."

We don't say anything else for a few minutes. We just sip our drinks in silence. I'm not sure if maybe that was our second spat, all in a single day.

The warm milk starts to work its magic. I'm crashing from the buzz I've been hopped up on for the last couple of hours trying to sort my life out.

"You're tired. I can see it."

He's right. I can't fight it.

He sets his mug down after a final sip, swoops me back up, and takes me to my room. I settle in bed, and he kisses me on the forehead. "Try to get some rest, Princess. We have a bunch more exploring to do tomorrow."

Part of me wants to ask him to stay, so I can feel his body snuggle up against mine, but I am truly exhausted. The adrenaline has run its course.

"Are you going to tell me about the tattoos?" I ask, yawning, as he pauses at the light switch.

He smiles back. "Sure. Goodnight, Brooke."

"Goodnight, Prince Charming."

CHAPTER 30

Live the Big Dream

I wake up and unfurl my legs from being clutched tightly to my chest. I'm in my balled-up fetal position, per usual. I'm groggy from the fragmented sleep I got. Even before the late-night rendezvous, Patrick and I had stayed up till just past midnight talking on the huge wraparound living room couch, with a fire going in the modern fireplace and a panorama view of the city skyline twinkling under the night sky. We also spent a good amount of time making out, which was A-MA-ZING.

My eyes flutter closed as I imagine Patrick kissing me all over again, and also about his sculpted body and those tattoos.

O-M-G! Had no idea I'd ever be this into tattoos.

I'm completely smitten as I roll my hand out across the giant bed, finding nothing but an expanse of cool, empty sheets. I shouldn't be disappointed; just like in Berlin, even after confessing our feelings for one another, Patrick chose to give me space and sleep in his own room. Each night it took forever to say goodnight and go our separate ways—for the record, I would have been perfectly fine with his arms wrapped around me all night. *I should have asked him to stay last night when he tucked me in.* Though knowing my habit of bad dreams and strange sleeping positions, perhaps it was for the best. *Damn heavy emotions.*

I just can't work out if he's being chivalrous, protective, cautious, or something else. We're meant to be enjoying a holiday fling together, but I feel more like an Elizabethan maid being courted by a gentleman. Neither of us knows how much time we have together. He lives in Australia and will eventually have to return to work. My life is a mess, and my future is in London—I hope. *Shoot, I need to check my email later.* It's the hard reality that neither of us really wants to face.

I open my eyes and rustle my legs under the thousand thread count sheets. My whole body feels like it's sinking into the down of the pillow and the perfect balance of the coils beneath my body, and I instinctively bite my lower lip, continuing to think of Patrick and him kissing me in this cool, sensual place. It sends a different kind of flutter through my body now that we've actually kissed, and I can feel between my legs a pulse spring to life, wanting more of him.

Oh my God, I want him so badly.

I rustle around a little more under the covers.

What if I went into his room and jumped on him? Surprised him and woke him up? It could be playful and lead to other things . . .

I'm still pinching at my lower lip with my teeth, thinking, and my heart is pitter-pattering with adrenaline, even though I've just woken up.

Then I hear something and push the covers off.

Ring-ring-ring.

It doesn't sound like a cell phone—well, it doesn't sound like Patrick's cellphone, anyway, which I've heard a number of times since we've been together.

Patrick usually takes whatever calls he gets alone, stepping away. He's always made light of it and explained that it's Max calling to check in, or his mother (whom he seems to be somewhat close with, despite the strained relationship with his father), or work, which is some sort of management job in construction. He doesn't talk much about work, other than complaining that his boss is a bit of a jerk. I've given him a hard time here and there and made it a point to say he should just ignore their calls if he's on vacation—I mean "holiday" (per Patrick's correction). He's explained that that's not an option, for whatever reason.

Ring-ring-ring.

I slide out of bed and throw on the silk robe and walk out to the kitchen where the ringing is coming from. It's just me who's up. Patrick is nowhere to be seen. I'm staring at the phone affixed to the wall, nervous as to who is on the other line.

What if it's my mother? Why does she have to ruin everything?

I take a deep breath and remind myself it's probably just the front desk.

My mother said I was dead to her, and while I don't believe her to be that ice cold, I also know she has way too much pride to contact me so soon.

I let out a heavy sigh of resignation and pick up the receiver.

"Hello?"

"Hello, dear."

An old and rusty but thoughtful voice scratches down the line. My grandfather.

"Pop?"

"Yes, dear."

"How did you— I mean, why are you— I'm sorry, that was rude. How are you, Pop?"

I'm not sure what to say or what he's been told, though I know he's obviously been told something. I'm wondering if my mother put him up to this and what their agenda might be.

"I'm fine, dear. How is radical independence going?"

I throw my head back, knowing full well that this is my

mother's doing. She's called in reinforcement from the patriarch of the family to mediate.

"Wonderful," I say, looking around the beautiful suite that Patrick paid for.

"I'm sure you know why I'm calling. By the way, that was nice of you to call from Berlin."

I breathe heavily into the phone and shut my eyes. My grandfather is one of the few family members I share some kind of closeness with, and it's disappointing my mother would shamelessly weaponize that.

Of course, I feel my own sliver of guilt since he's the one I called from the hostel manager's office in Berlin, feigning a call to my mother and asking if he would pass to her that I was fine. I definitely didn't intend to put him in the middle of things, but it seems like he already is.

Before I can say anything in response, I feel myself jolt to life as Patrick's arms wrap around my waist from behind, and he kisses my neck.

"Good morning," he says, soft and sweetly, close to my ear.

I frantically pull away and motion for him to stay quiet, pointing at the phone. I mouth a "sorry" as he backs away from me with his hands raised, as if he's surrendering to a siege. I mouth a "thank you."

"Sorry, Pop, give me a second," I say, walking to the penthouse office.

"Are you with someone?"

"No, no. I accidentally hit the TV volume on the remote. Sorry."

I've never lied to my grandfather. Lying to my mother's father—the central bloodline of my privilege, the person who gave me my first tennis racket and set the course for my love and obsession of the game—feels like the ultimate betrayal. Plus, I love and admire him.

Even though we're on the phone and he has no way of seeing

me, I feel his presence. My grandfather has that kind of effect. He is, after all, one of those billionaire-class, master-of-the-universe types. He doesn't have to say or do much; it's like an ethereal omni-presence that clings to him and projects out into the world. He's seen and done a lot in his life.

"Brooke, I know—" He pauses, his voice sounds slight as he clears his throat. "Excuse me."

"You okay, Pop?"

"I'm fine, just a little tickle in my throat. Anyway, what I was going to say is that I understand. I know you are dealing with a lot. The episode at school . . ."

I wince.

I hate hearing him even mention the *something* because I know how embarrassing it must be for him—as it is to the rest of my family and my own self—to have his grandchild (his favorite, no less) attend the school he's donated millions of dollars to, only to have her throw a tantrum in the women's locker room and attack another player. *Monster.*

". . . and your brother. I know what it's like to lose a brother."

He pauses again but this time there's only silence. My grandfather lost his older brother in World War II, and he rarely speaks of it. From what I understand, they were close, like Liam and I were close.

"Brooke, have I ever denied you anything? Besides, you've always been able to talk to me. Is there really something you feel you can't talk to me about?"

I let out another big sigh. "It's a little tough when you put it like that, Pop."

My eyes are combing the books on the shelves but stop on a collection of fantasy books.

My grandfather introduced me to the genre. I remember him

showing off his first edition collection of J.R.R. Tolkien's The Fellowship of the Ring. I can see him walking the twelve-year-old me around his library and stopping at the collection, housed on the second story wraparound of his library, selling me on the grand adventure of Frodo and his company of hobbits. It was one of those rare occasions that my grandfather talked about his brother—another Liam, and my brother's namesake, who was also a huge fan of Tolkien.

"What is the dreamer dreaming, dear?"

I take yet another deep inhale, and with it I catch the scent of something delicious.

Is Patrick cooking?

"Dear?"

"Sorry, it's just—it's not easy to talk about. Mom and I . . . things haven't been good for a while."

"Okay. What were the issues?"

"Mom—and Dad, for that matter—they have this whole plan for me. Like they've already decided my future for me, and well . . . there's something I really want to do. I want to try at least," I qualify, building up my nerve.

"What is it?"

"I want—I want to play tennis for real, like go on the pro circuit. I mean, I want to be a professional tennis player."

He's quiet on the other end, and I feel like an eight-year-old who's asked for a zebra for her birthday. Wait, I had one of those at a birthday. A joy ride to the moon, maybe?

"Mom is against it. She's completely forbidden it. She and Dad won't support me and basically have said that if, or rather *when* I fail at it, it'll just be an embarrassment to the family. That I don't have what it takes to endure the pressure of the pro circuit, especially after the whole school thing. They want me to go to work for Dad or you and then settle down and marry, have kids, and be a country club wife. Like that's all I'm good for or destined for because that's my pedigree. That's my lot in life."

He's quiet for a moment but then finally says, "I see."

This time it's him letting out a deep sigh on the other end of the phone. Knowing him, he's probably trying to resolve the problem or come up with a way of fixing the issue. But instead of offering a solution, he simply says, "You know, you're a lot more like your mother than you think."

I smirk and roll my eyes to myself. "I doubt that."

He lets out another cough, this time there is the faint sound of phlegm that catches at the back of his throat.

"You sure you're okay, Pop? You should call the doctor to have him come out and check that cough."

"That's what your grandmother keeps telling me."

There's silence and it seems we are at an impasse. I can't help feeling a little disappointed. I always wondered if my grandfather was a potential ally or just another puppeteer with a gentler touch. But it seems he's keeping his cards close.

I remind him to go to the doctor and promise to think about forgiving Mom, though I sincerely believe that ship has sailed. He tells me he loves me, and I say it back, though a little bit of my heart has cracked over the course of the call.

Before we hang up, I muster my courage one more time. "Pop? My debit card—"

"You know what you need to do, dear."

Urgh.

We hang up and I sit there, thinking. Eventually the smell of bacon and toast calls me to the kitchen. But there are other notes that are unfamiliar and enticing.

"There she is," Patrick says as I saunter over. He cheerfully mans the stovetop, spatula in one hand and pan in the other. Also, completely clothed. A little disappointing.

"I meant to ask you last night, but did you know the fridge was stocked with food?" he says, astounded. "And the wine fridge down there, too?"

"Oh yeah, that's to be expected in a place like this." I wink at him. "Don't worry, you're paying dearly for the privilege." I take a seat at the oversized island on one of the bar stools. "What's cooking? Eggs Benedict with smoked salmon and caviar?"

"One of my specialties. Egg and stuff."

"Ooo," I coo. "You have specialties. So, you're a chef?"

He laughs, turning in my direction. "At your service."

I return the laugh. "Well, just make sure it's not dry. I like mine a little runny and wet."

"Who said this was for you?"

"Funny. You better be making some for me. I could smell how delicious this was all the way from the library."

"Speaking of which, who was that on the phone?"

The receiver is sitting on the island in front of me.

"Family stuff. But can we talk about it later?"

He turns back to me after having turned his attention back on the omelet-thing.

"Of course. It's slightly creepy that they know you're here, but whatever."

Patrick finishes cooking and makes plates for the two of us, along with some toast and fresh-squeezed orange juice.

I gobble up the food, feeling replenished after feeling both physically and emotionally drained by the conversation with my grandfather.

"A girl could get used to this," I tease, even though I'm not sure if the sentiment is a bit more commitment than what our relationship entails.

"Oh yeah?" he replies with a curious grin and raised brows. "Good to know."

What does that even mean?

I can't tell if all new loves, or new relationships—whatever this is—are weird, or if it's just me and my awkward lack of experience. The coded talk. The insinuations. The teasing. All the little nuances that add to the mystery, the thrill of what is possible or what could be. It's both exciting, confusing, and exhausting.

We finish our food and go over our plans for the day, get ready, and head out. We wind our way through religious relics, edifices, cemeteries, and synagogues in the Jewish Quarter. In Old Town, we find a trendy place to eat lunch in the square and watch the routine of the astronomical clock play out again. We settle in with a beer and spend some time people-watching, making up background stories of people we see walking by. It's playful and fun.

"What about that guy over there?" I say from behind my shades, stealthily signaling to a tall thinnish middle-aged man with stylish glasses, mostly bald, looking contemplatively across the square with his arms latched behind his back and a paper map in one hand.

"Hmmm . . . Let's see. Bestselling non-fiction author who writes about microscopic bacteria in the Arctic that are going extinct but are critical to the ecosystem. He's been having a long-distance relationship with a woman—a *scientist*—he met at a conference in Russia. But the thing is, she's not really a scientist . . ."

"What is she?" I say, playing along.

"A hooker with a heart of gold."

I laugh. "You idiot. But, admittedly, you're pretty good at this."

"What?"

"Making it up as you go."

We watch as a young girl runs up to the man, followed by a woman with a baby in her arms. The girl and the baby are wearing matching dresses, and the man and woman kiss.

"There goes your plot line."

"Nah, it's just a few chapters further along," Patrick says. "She gives up turning tricks and picks true love over money." His face clouds over momentarily, but he shakes it off. "You want to get out of here and check out some more stuff?"

I watch him closely, wondering what that was all about. "Sure."

We call the waitress over, and she brings the bill. I suddenly feel awkward. I only have so much cash, but I don't want Patrick to feel like he needs to keep paying for everything. He hands her his card automatically.

"Can I at least pay for the tip? I can afford that on what I have," I say, fumbling with my wallet and feeling like a fool.

I've literally never contemplated the word "afford" in such a context, as in questioning my ability to pay for something.

"I'll pay you back," I say, meaning it.

Patrick gives me an empathetic look. "Look, you don't have to . . . *but* I'll let you pay the tip if you tell me who it was you were talking to this morning."

"*Really?*"

"Come on," he says in a coaxing tone.

"You're that curious?"

"Suppose so," he says, leaning back in his seat trying to play cool even though it's clear he wants to know.

"Fine. It was the KGB. I was reporting back to Russia. I've been collecting intelligence on you—the ultimate honeypot trap." He laughs and shakes his head, though he looks strangely uneasy. "I'm joking!"

He rolls his eyes. "Obviously."

I hand over some Czech crowns to pay for a tip, and Patrick accepts them.

"Later. I'll tell you later. *Promise.*"

Patrick relents, and we pay our bill and head out. We spend the rest of the afternoon wandering through Old Town, visiting a gallery with a mix of collections ranging from heavy religious depictions to contemporary streaks of paint on canvas, then head to a peaceful church with an adjacent public garden filled with lush flower beds and a small playground. We loop back toward the square as the day wears on, making sure to pass the rotating head sculpture of Franz Kafka.

"Wait!" I say as we pass a sign that I happen to catch in-between our casual conversation.

"What is it?"

"I know who that artist is," I say, pointing. "Banksy." I can't believe it, but there is apparently an entire museum dedicated to the graffiti artist.

"Brooke, who *hasn't* heard of Banksy?"

"Me, apparently," I say, feeling slightly deflated because I thought I was onto something cool and obscure. "You do realize you're talking to a girl who wasn't even allowed to create a social media account till she was sixteen and had all of her electronics and tennis rackets taken away for three months for making *one* B in high school—straight As the rest of the time, mind you."

His eyes sort of pop.

"I told you—control is her M-O."

With a bit of sympathy, he asks if I want to check it out.

We wander through the museum that's full of graffiti images depicting satirical commentary on politics and humanity in general. We—rather, I—learn that no one knows who Banksy is, though there are plenty of theories.

That must be nice. Notorious but anonymous all at the same time. Seems like the way to be.

We pass a copy of the same piece that caught my attention at the hostel in Berlin; the one with the CANCELLED sign over a FOLLOW YOUR DREAMS slogan. It makes me think of the fact that I've revealed my deepest desire to my grandfather, and he seemed completely indifferent, verging on siding with my parents. I don't know why I would have expected a different reaction. Besides, even though it is truly what I want, there's a darkness that looms over it. How could I follow my dream when it's clouded by so much sorrow, pain, and shame?

"So, I wonder, is there anything you do actually like about your mum?" he says, sort of out of nowhere. I give him a scandalized look. "Well, I mean, I understand everything that's happened and that there's tension, but you are on this all-expenses-paid holiday, right? That's gotta count for something."

I know I'm pink. "Sure, although obviously the circumstances of that have changed. But there were compromises."

He gives me an unimpressed look. "Compromises aside, there has to be something you like about your mum."

A heavy breath unfurls from my nostrils like a bull ready to charge. My eyes lower. "Her confidence. She's unapologetic for who she is. If she wants something, she won't let anyone stand in her way—no matter what."

"Like mother, like daughter?"

"Hardly," I reply, though I can hear my grandfather's comment from earlier echo in the back of my mind; that she and I are more alike than I think.

We round our way through the remainder of the museum and get to the end, where there are signs leading outside and information about participating in an immersive experience.

"Hi!" says a girl in coveralls that are splattered with paints of all shades and colors.

"Hi," I say.

"Would you like to try out spray painting? Do your own graffiti?" she asks. "We just started the program last week. There's plenty of space to pick from on the wall," she adds.

We're at the side of the building on the opposite side we walked up from coming into the museum, so we wouldn't have seen the whole set-up.

The girl in coveralls has different cans of spray paint, stencils, masks, and some make-shift coveralls-slash-smocks, and the wall has all kinds of weird designs, words, and symbols, clearly left by other patrons who've participated in the literal immersive experience.

I look at Patrick with a big grin.

"Go for it. I'm not sure I'm that sort of artistic."

"Come on," I plead. "It'll be fun."

"How about I just provide constructive feedback?"

"Boo!"

I roll my eyes then proceed to get dressed in the coveralls and put a mask over my nose and mouth. I feel like a deviant. I like it.

"So, what are you thinking?"

"I don't know," I say, scanning the cans of paint before deciding on a purple. "I'm not exactly artistic either, but I have a few ideas."

"Oh yeah?"

"I think I'm going to do a mix—tag and stencil," I reply like a pro.

I search the stencils and find a peace sign, and a heart stencil, which the girl helps me tape to the wall in an open spot. Next, I pick out some additional spray paints: a yellow (my favorite color), lime green, and white.

I step back when I'm done.

"Peace. Love. Tennis?"

"That's my tag," I say, shrugging but beaming, proud of my mark: a purple peace sign, a yellow heart, and a tennis ball that I freestyled.

"I dig it. But how long has it been since you played?"

I groan and ignore him. "Your turn."

"Fine," Patrick relents and proceeds to get dressed in the graffiti gear.

He grabs a bright red color and finds an open spot and starts. No hesitation. He just starts writing, and when he's done, he steps back. We all admire it.

"I like it," says the girl from the museum.

The red writing reads "Live the Big Dream." Sort of like an equal and opposite answer to Banksy's FOLLOW YOUR DREAM—CANCELLED piece. But also, I think he's sending me a not-so-subtle subliminal message in response to my own tag.

"Me too," I add, letting my hand slip into Patrick's.

CHAPTER 31

Other Specialties

We finish up at the Banksy Museum and stroll aimlessly back in the direction of the place we're staying. It's getting late and we're both hungry again.

"Do you want to get food?" I ask, though the cost of spending money on food is weighing on me—or rather, the cost of *Patrick* spending money on food is weighing on me.

"I have a better idea."

"What's that?"

"Why don't we eat back at the hotel? That fridge is full of food. I can cook us something."

I give him a questionable look. "You mean you can cook more than just an omelet?"

"I have other specialties, thank you very much," he says, puffing out his chest with a bit of bravado.

"I'm intrigued."

"Then it's a yes?"

I nod.

We get back and Patrick inventories the fridge and pantry, then sets in motion cooking dinner for the two of us. Meanwhile, I pop open a bottle of expensive wine that's been chilled in the wine fridge and pour us each a glass. Even though we're in Eastern Europe, Patrick manages to concoct a Middle Eastern dish, with rich, aromatic notes that are making my tastebuds water.

"This looks amazing. I'm assuming you learned this when you deployed?"

"Yes and no."

"Cryptic much?"

Patrick pauses from stirring. He looks positively domestic with a dish towel thrown over his shoulder. "Yes, I was in the Middle East. No, I wasn't on deployment. I was traveling."

Then I remember. "I believe I was going to be allowed to interview you once we got settled in this place. And from where I'm standing, you look pretty settled," I say with a cheeky intonation, taking a sip of my wine.

Patrick laughs but ignores me as he plates our food. We carry our meal up the stairs to the rooftop to sit at the patio table next to the pool so we can look out at the cityscape and setting sun as we eat.

"So?" I prompt. He knows where I'm picking up from and indicates as such with an ironic smirk as he finishes a mouthful of food.

"I was doing some contract work sort of related to my military service. It required a lot of travel throughout the region. During my downtime, I liked to go to the bazaars and try different foods, pick up different spices and stuff," he tells me, taking another bite of his food. "I learned how to cook some of my favorite meals while I was there." His eyebrows arch suggestively, as his eyes point to the food.

"Whoa! How about that? A few more dribbles of detail about Patrick. Does that mean I have nineteen more questions I get to ask now that you finally answered my one question?" I tease.

In fairness I have learned more about him, but it feels like the scales are tipped more in my direction and I've shared far more about myself. That being said, I have learned his mother is an English teacher, hence the annoying corrections on definite articles when I referred to New York City as The City. I also learned that they are relatively close, even with him going off on his own at a young age. He has a younger sister, but they're not close. His father is some sort of mechanic and has his own shop, I think. Again, Patrick has been stingy with the details.

"Yeah, well you still owe me an answer on who it was who called you this morning."

"Still on that, huh?" I say, taking a bite of my food.

"An ex?" He says it casually.

"Yeah, he's eighty-two and a billionaire. Jealous?"

I raise a brow between sips of wine.

"Intriguing," Patrick replies, taking a sip of his wine and letting his eyes slide to look out at the city.

It's beautiful. The evening is peaceful, and the sky has a warm glow. The view is starting to twinkle from the city lights, and the noise from the traffic is a hushed muffle below.

"It was my grandfather," I finally fess up.

"Really?"

He looks across at me surprised but gives me a look like he's waiting for me to divulge more, which he prompts for because I don't say anything else.

"*And?*"

"And what? We talked," I respond, setting down my drink. He shakes his head at me and has a sarcastic grin on his face. "Okay, okay," I relent, and proceed to tell him about our conversation, my mom using him to get to me, but also a little about my relationship with my grandfather.

"Your mother isn't a good person, is she?"

I'm about to take a bite but put my folk down. "No, Patrick. That's what I've been trying to tell you. She's incredible manipulative."

I lower my gaze, unsure if I should say what I'm about to say.

"When my brother—"

I break off because I can never say the words. *Died. Dead. Gone.*

"—everything happened, I had to go see a therapist. It wasn't necessarily a choice, but I was open to it because it seemed like the right thing to do. One day I showed up, and the therapist was in hysterics. My mother was paying her to tell her *everything* I was saying. She felt terrible and wanted me to turn her into the state ethics board or whatever."

"*Jesus.* Did you?"

"No. I told her to keep telling my mother everything I said. If that's the only way I could communicate with her, then so be it. Let her hear the truth. I mean, I didn't tell her *every* single thing I was feeling, but at least it was better than most of it staying on the pages in my tennis journal."

Patrick shakes his head, confused, like he doesn't know what to do with everything I've told him. "What about the money?"

"I told my therapist to keep it. She probably deserved the extra benefit with having to deal with our family. But . . ." I break off because I know this part makes me no better than my mother. "I did use the fact that she kept the money to my advantage."

Patrick gives me an uncomfortable look. "How so?"

I suck in a deep breath. "Look," I begin, feeling the only way to make this sound remotely okay is to preface it. "I've always thought about it like this: My mother has three sets of rules." I pause, holding my hand up and ticking them off. "Rules for our society, family rules, and rules for *me*. I've been suffocated my whole life by her dominance—*everywhere* I go. No escape, always under her watchful eye and unending criticism. I needed to get away after everything happened. I needed to get away from *her*. I asked the therapist—"

"If she would get your mum to support you going off abroad for a bit?" he finishes for me.

I nod, slowly. "There were strings attached to the agreement, but honestly—" I start to choke up and laugh a little, throwing my hands in the air. "What does it matter? I have nothing to my name at this point, and it's the best I've ever felt in my whole life."

He watches me for a solid minute, studying me. Then he reaches over and grabs my hand. "I'm glad, Brooke. You deserve it. To stand on your own two feet and have some space," he replies, smiling gently.

"You know what it's like, don't you?" I surmise as a stillness passes between us.

His gaze drops from mine but returns almost instantly. "I know what it's like to have a strained relationship with a parent . . ." His words trail off and he shakes his head to himself and blows out a deep breath. His eyes are moist. "My relationship with my dad is something that can't be fixed. It's unforgivable what happened."

For a second, I think he's going to tell me what horrible thing transpired between him and his father. But then he says, "I hope it's not the same for you and your mum, in the end. Maybe she's just worried about losing the only child she has left."

I immediately feel deflated by his response. "Maybe. But like I said, it's been this way my whole life, Patrick. Something major would have to change. And even then, I don't know if forgiveness is possible."

He nods solemnly, then lets go of my hand.

We finish our meal in silence. The romantic rooftop dinner feels slightly spoiled by the seriousness of the conversation. When we're done, we take everything back inside.

"I'll clean up," Patrick offers.

"You sure?"

"Yeah, no worries," he replies with a cheeky smile, lightening the mood.

Swoon. I've already admitted to him that I love the quintessential Australian phrase, "no worries."

"Okay, I'm going to take a shower."

I stand in the shower for a long time, thinking of Patrick's sliver of hope for me and my mom's relationship. Even if it was salvageable, right now is not the time to do anything about it. Everything is just too perfect being here with him. I don't want to spoil it with another emotional dust-up with her.

When I'm done in the shower, I throw on a bedtime tank top and matching pajama shorts. It's cute and flirty. I walk to the kitchen, but Patrick's not there. I wander a bit more, searching for him around the penthouse and even poke my head into his room that is immaculate, with his belongings neatly laid out and organized. Meanwhile, over in my room, everything is strewn all over the place, like a bomb went off. Even though I'm a Type A personality, I can sometimes be a bit careless when it comes to clothes, especially since I've been vetting what to wear around Patrick.

"Patrick?" I call out, as I make my way down the hall.

"Up here!"

It sounds like his voice is coming from the rooftop.

I head up and look around but don't notice him till he pops up from the pool and splashes me with water.

"Hey! Watch out now! I just took a shower!"

"More the reason to get in the pool," he says, pulling himself out from the water, his shoulders and biceps flexing. I'm still ogling his muscles as he walks toward me.

"Oh no. No, no, no," I say.

"'Oh no,' *what?*"

He has a huge grin on his face, and water is dripping off his body. Meanwhile, the material of his gym shorts is suctioned against his body. I feel my cheeks turn hot as my eyes spy the contours that his body makes under his shorts.

He keeps walking toward me, and I back away, playfully shooing him off before it turns into a bit of a chase on the artificial turf that covers the ground.

"No!" I shriek.

"Yes!"

"You're not supposed to run around pools! It's dangerous! You might slip and fall!" I say before he nabs me and throws me over his shoulder and starts toward the pool.

"Rubbish."

"Patrick, no!"

It's the last thing I say before we both plunge into the pool together. When I come up from under the water, Patrick still has a huge smile.

"You got me all wet."

"Did I?" he says, swimming closer.

My legs find him and wrap around his waist, and he pulls me in. We start kissing, and the sound of the astronomical clock is tolling somewhere far off in the background.

"Yes, you did," I say pulling back from his lips for a moment. "See, told you my romance novel could inspire . . ."

CHAPTER 32

You Sound Like . . .

"So, what does the one on your chest mean? I mean, I get the Australian flag. But why also the British flag? Is it some sort of homage to the motherland or something?"

Patrick laughs heartily, setting the dinner he's made for us on the coffee table, then heads back to the kitchen to grab his drink and the bottle of wine we're drinking from.

The last couple of days have been amazing. Each day with him is better than the day before it. Not only do we find comfort in one another because we have so much to talk about—we share many of the same thoughts and views, likes and dislikes, and similar experiences as athletes—but we find comfort in one another physically, too. However, the same routine continues: late nights staying up talking, kissing, and caressing with true tenderness exchanged between one another, but then Patrick ultimately escorts me to my room, bows, and retreats to his own room. *Urgh.*

The idea of sexual frustration is the sort of thing that makes a girl like me blush and shy away because I am a bit prudish, but I feel like a grenade has gone off in my body, and my hormones have been sent into a chaotic flurry.

Of course, as magical and wonderful as all of the time with Patrick has been, the flipside is that time is counting down. *Damn her.* We only have a couple of days left until I fly back to London, and Patrick is going to meet up with Max, minus Abby and Lizzie. We've discussed this, and I believe him. Mostly.

"My mother is from England, actually. I have dual citizenship," he replies, reappearing and taking a seat next to me on the couch.

I also want to ask him about one of the other tattoos I'm most curious about. A black beetle that he mentioned in passing had something to do with his spirituality. But my stomach lets out a terrible rumble, feeling tortured by the delectable untouched meal set in front of me, with all the delicious smells emanating from it.

"Dig in."

I do, forgetting the question and conversation, and pick up my plate like I'm under a spell. Cooking truly is a specialty for Patrick, and after our exhausting day I feel like I might not be shy about asking for seconds or even thirds.

Today we took a short train ride out of the city and explored a thirteenth century Bohemian castle. The day was glorious, so we also went for a hike, enjoying some alone time secluded in nature. It was wonderful but made for a long day, so once again Patrick volunteered to make dinner so we could just chill out and relax at the penthouse.

Tonight, we're doing a dinner-and-movie night. Patrick said he was picking the movie.

I barely finish gulping down my food when a thought occurs to me about his answer. "So that means you can just go to London whenever you want, right? Stay as long as you want?" This immediately has my wheels spinning.

"Well, I mean, yeah. Still have to pay to get there, though."

I've mentioned a potential visit to Australia at least twice, but just like now, he seems evasive, neutral, or plain uninterested. It's weird considering our chemistry, but I guess he's not into the long-distance thing, though I haven't quite given up on the idea.

Patrick grabs his phone, connects to the streaming platform with the TV, and lowers the lights in the room with a remote that controls just about everything in the high-tech, swanky penthouse. I take a healthy swig of my red wine as he grabs his plate.

"Ready?"

"What are we watching?"

"It's a surprise. I think you'll like it." This coming from the guy who told me he likes classic horror movies. Definitely not my thing.

I twist my mouth and give him a skeptical look as I set my glass back down and get comfortable.

He presses play. As the intro plays out, I turn in his direction. *"Really?"*

I can't contain my amusement or judgment. "This is the worst tennis movie ever."

Patrick has chosen the movie *Wimbledon*. A rom-com that centers around two tennis players meeting at Wimbledon and falling for one another.

"You've seen it before?" he says, sounding a little disappointed.

"Of course. Probably a million times," I exaggerate.

"Well, it can't be that bad if you've seen it a million times."

"No, it's fine," I admit, touched by Patrick's choice. "It's super campy. Also, you're going to see some serious diving on the court, which no one does in real life. Like they do it *every* single point."

We settle in, and within five minutes we exchange a look. The lead love interest's name in the movie is none other than Lizzie.

"Sorry, didn't realize," Patrick says.

I roll my eyes. "I forgot too. Well, we're in it now."

By the end of the movie, I'm snuggled up, lying with my head pressed to Patrick's chest, listening not only to the movie but also to the steady pace of Patrick's breathing and his heart. The rhythm is lulling and settles a peace over me.

"Do you feel inspired?"

"What do you mean by inspired?" I say, sitting up and stretching. I glance back at him with a leering look, hopefully wondering if maybe he's referring to the sex scenes.

"I mean, I know it's been a while since you played, but you're not in the same boat as me. Seems like you want to get back out there."

My expression immediately prunes. It's been 162 days since I've had a racket in my hand.

"It's complicated."

"Why?" he responds almost immediately, his tone a little pushy.

"Patrick, the last time I played was literally the worst day of my life. I lost my brother, I lost control over myself, and I seriously hurt someone. And—"

"What?"

"I don't want to talk about it." I don't say it angrily, but my words are firm.

He doesn't give up. "Talk about what?" he asks in a more coaxing voice.

"Why do you have this effect on me where I feel the compulsion to tell you everything? All of my dark secrets. Yet, I feel it's hardly reciprocated."

"What do you mean?"

"Your father," I say but almost immediately regret it because I don't want him to feel like I'm prying too deep. "Sorry, I shouldn't make you feel like you're under some sort of obligation to tell me."

Patrick sighs, looks away for a moment, and turns back to me. He's fidgeting with his fingers and hands. "I promise, I'll tell you. But not right now." He reaches out and twirls a lock of my hair in his fingers and settles a strand behind my ear. *Sure.*

I snicker, ironically. "You know what I wouldn't give to have a father like in the movie? The tennis parent that wants it as much as, or maybe more than, the player."

"Why would you want that?" he asks, almost like he's put off by the idea.

"Because, Patrick, I already told you, my mom doesn't support my dream at all," I start, reminding him of the recap I gave him of my conversation with my grandfather. "She has no doubt that I *will* fail. She doesn't want me to embarrass her or our family. Even though I've done a supreme job of that already, according to her." I shake my head to myself.

"What about your dad? What does he think?"

"He defaults to whatever my mother believes or says. He's too busy to get involved." I love my dad, but it's the truth. He may hold weight out in the world, but not in our household. Everything is under the weight of her thumb. "Bottom line is what she wants is for me to be like her—marry rich and look good for society pictures. End of story."

This explanation is far more blunt than my recap. I can see a hint of hurt in his eyes, and I feel a stab in my own heart.

Reality check. Even if Patrick wasn't opposed to a long-distance relationship, the truth is my mother would never accept someone like Patrick for me. No one in my family would. This—me and Patrick—could literally never be more than what it is in this moment.

"You should go after what you want." For a minute, I'm not sure if he's talking about tennis or himself.

"You sound like him." I drop my gaze, sniffling.

"Who?"

"Liam," I reply, smiling to myself as I think of him.

We sit quietly for a moment. Patrick reaches out to hold my hand and glides his fingertip over the scars. I don't recoil. They are what they are.

Patrick lets go of my hand then leans forward. My little day bag is on the coffee table. It's unzipped and inside is my tennis diary turned travel diary. He pulls it out.

Silver Gilt. What a silly name. How many times I've fallen asleep imagining myself hoisting a Grand Slam tournament trophy over my head and bringing it to my lips with an enthralled crowd all around me.

Patrick opens it and runs his fingers along the ripped ends like he did the first time in Berlin.

"You said something the other day about it being better than keeping it in your tennis journal."

"Yeah."

"What were you keeping in there?"

I sit back against the couch and hug my knees to my chest like a little kid, alone and scared of the world.

"All the bottled-up emotions I couldn't hide from anymore. I thought it might help. Clearly not," I say, my eyes narrowing onto the scars.

"You shouldn't be so hard on yourself."

I smile sardonically.

"What?"

"Now you sound like her."

"Who?"

"My therapist."

Patrick smirks and eyes me sympathetically. "How was it— therapy? Did it help?"

I shrug. "I think it helped, some. But I don't know if there's any real recovery for everything that happened. It's more a matter of finding the best way to cope."

"How so?" he asks gently.

I shrug again, arms still folded around my legs. "Learning to sort through and recognize the different phases of grief and find peace in the present moment, I guess. Sometimes I'm incredibly sad because Liam's gone, and other times I'm furious with him. Sometimes I feel shame and guilt because of what I did to Alex and my family. Other times I feel relief, which is a horrible thing to say. But it's true. That moment in the locker room changed the trajectory I was on. I wouldn't be right here right now, which I'm glad for."

We both fall silent for a moment.

"What about how you feel about your mum?"

"My feelings about my mom tend to be one note, but coping is more complex."

Patrick nods and turns back to the missing pages. "What'd you do with them?"

I slowly uncurl, walk to my room, and return a moment later with a small stack of folded pages. I set them on the coffee table and sit back down, staring at them.

Another long silence. "Still trying to figure out how to let it all go."

CHAPTER 33

Love All

I wake up to the sound of movement, presumably Patrick in the kitchen. I pick up my watch from the bedside table.

5:36 a.m.

I flop my head down onto the pillow. My routine of early morning workouts has been completely thrown off ever since Patrick and I arrived in Prague. Especially with us staying up as late as we have . . . talking and what have you . . .

What the hell is he doing?

I lay there for a few minutes with my eyes closed. It's obvious he's whipping up something. I can smell the beginning aromas of breakfast being cooked.

"What are you doing out there?" I shout.

There's some more shuffling around and then footsteps coming down the hall, followed by a gentle rap on the door.

"Come in."

Patrick opens the door just enough to poke his head in. He has a big goofy grin.

"What are you smiling about? It's stupid early in the morning."

He laughs. "I know. But I have a surprise for you today."

I scrunch my brows at him and pull myself up on my elbows.

"A *surprise?*"

He nods.

"At 5:45 in the morning?" I agonize.

"Well, I wanted to make sure you—I mean, *we*—had a good breakfast beforehand and had enough time to get there."

"You are being so weird. What is this *surprise?*"

"I can't tell you what the surprise is, otherwise, it's no longer a surprise, silly," he replies, still with the ridiculously big grin. "Come on. I'm finishing making breakfast."

With that, he leaves the door ajar, so the aroma of food is more apparent and rousing, as it fills my room. I slowly pull myself out of bed, slip on my robe, and head down the hall to the kitchen.

"Have I mentioned that I hate surprises?"

Patrick laughs as he turns to look at me over his shoulder from the stove, where he's fussing over the eggs he's cooking. "I feel confident you will appreciate it—love it, in fact."

"Mmhmm. I'm not so sure."

Patrick multi-tasks and makes me a cup of coffee from the automated espresso machine while finishing cooking. We eat, but I don't stuff myself. I'm skeptical about whatever it is he has in the works.

"A hike? Some special castle? Bungee jumping?"

He continues to laugh at my guessing but doesn't give anything away.

"I'm not telling. You'll just have to find out when we get there."

"I told you, I hate surprises." I groan and decide to try a different tactic. "Well, what should I wear for this surprise?"

"Wear whatever makes you feel comfortable."

"You really aren't going to give me any hints, are you?"

"Nope," he replies, chomping down on a big bite of toast, completely self-satisfied.

I groan again and when we're done eating, he sends me off to get dressed while he cleans up the kitchen. I throw on my usual daytime garb for when I know we'll be out walking most of the day.

Something cute but functional, with a pair of comfortable shoes. By the time we head downstairs it's getting close to seven.

As we walk through the lobby hand-in-hand, Patrick lifts my hand to give it a kiss. I can see he is as giddy as a teenage boy with a new video game, totally geeking out and pleased with himself and the surprise he has planned for me.

As I gaze side-eyed at him I immediately think of the couple I saw in Berlin when I was checking in at the hostel and first met Patrick. It feels like ages ago now. In context, I got exactly what I was wishing for, but I feel how fragile it is in this moment. Even though Patrick has a firm grip on my hand, I know time is unthreading the hold we have on one another with each passing second. This will all be gone in a matter of days. It is quintessentially bittersweet.

The glass doors automatically open for us. We walk outside, and it's as if we are on the other side of a wormhole in our own mysterious and cosmic world of new, enigmatic love. It is absolutely perfect and, just like the girl from Berlin, I look at Patrick adoringly, desperate to ignore reality.

This has to be real love. But why does it feel so unfair and heartless at the same time? Answer: Because it is real, <u>real</u> love.

We make our way to an Uber that Patrick already has waiting for us. We pack in, but my adoring look fades, and I give him a wary expression.

"Did I mention I hate surprises?"

"A few times. But you'll survive."

I groan one more time for good measure, and the car departs. Thirty minutes later, Patrick tells me to close my eyes.

"Oh, so we're getting close?"

I give him a raised brow as he checks his cell phone, which he keeps out of my sight so I can't see the pin on his iMap, showing our final destination.

"Yup."

I begrudgingly give in and shut my eyes. Admittedly, even though it's true that I really do not like surprises because it goes against my Type A personality, it's all a bit romantic and sweet. I imagine maybe it's some romantic or scenic place to walk or hike and he wants to get to the place early, before it's loaded up with tourists.

I'm listening to any sounds that might give me a clue since our back windows are cracked open. I try to decipher any movement of the car that might also be a clue. About ten minutes later the vehicle slows and makes a turn, and I hear something. It's a familiar sound. A sound more intimate to me than most, and I immediately feel my whole body stiffen. The car stops.

"Hold on," says Patrick, and I can hear him get out and scoot around the car, while I hear the sound repeat rhythmically like one of those Newton's cradle desk pieces.

He opens the door and helps me out.

"Okay, you can open them."

I open my eyes and feel myself tighten and recoil. We're in front of a building, and all around us are tennis courts. I can feel Patrick's eyes on me, but I'm in too much shock to look in his direction.

It's now been one-hundred-and-sixty-six days since I've held a tennis racket in my hands, and I can feel a phantom pain run across the scars as if the skin has just been torn wide open.

"Patrick . . . what . . ."

I'm at a loss for words. I really don't know what to say. I know I talk about wanting to take things to the next level—go pro—but this is happening too fast. I'm not ready. It's too soon.

He steps closer, cupping his hands gently around my arms.

"Brooke, I know what you are probably—"

"I can't. I told you last night. It's complicated. No."

I know he has to see the absolute panic in my eyes and on my face. I feel as though the blood has drained from my body, and my anxiety is shooting through the roof every time I hear the sound of a ball being hit in the background. It's one thing to watch and listen to it on the TV, another to be here.

I shake my head feverishly. The car has already rolled off, and it's just us standing in the parking lot of this tennis facility.

"Yes, you can," he says, staring into my eyes, genuine belief in his voice.

I feel myself getting emotional and slip out of his grasp, with a slight tremble in my hands.

"Why? Why would you do this? Why would you take me here?" I'm breathing heavily, but my speech is calm. I'm stunned more than anything.

He reaches for me, but I shift away. He runs his hands through his hair, vexed, and drops them to his side.

"Brooke, you can do this—"

"Patrick, no I *can't*."

"Brooke—

"Patrick, you don't get it. I—I was obsessed. It was like an addiction—a *drug*," I say, stammering in my explanation, which probably doesn't make sense. "The high of hitting the perfect shot and winning a match. I—I ignored *everything* else, everyone, including the people around me I cared about and loved. Nothing else mattered. Plus, my mom . . ."

"What about her, Brooke?" he says, sounding a touch irritated. "You were right last night. You have to figure out how to let go of the grasp she has on you. You are not a failure, and you won't be if you just give yourself the chance out there."

My eyes are wet. I shut them. I haven't even hit one ball and I feel physically drained.

I open my eyes. "I feel like if I do this, I'm betraying them—*him.*"

"What do you mean?" he scoffs. "*Betray?* From everything you told me, Liam wanted this for you because he believed in your dream as much as you did." Patrick hesitates, sweeps me up and down with sympathetic eyes. "His death has nothing to do with your dream—*nothing* at all to do with tennis. Same with your teammate, Alex. This is about *you,* Brooke—plain and simple— and whether *you* want this or not. Stop punishing yourself for things that have already happened."

Some people pass us in the parking lot and glance our way. I'm a hot mess and quickly wipe my cheeks with the back of my hand. In the last two weeks, I've cried more than I have in perhaps my whole life.

"Why are you pushing me into this?" I say defensively, once the people are out of earshot.

He looks defeated. "I'm sorry. I'm not trying to push you. If you don't want to do this, we can leave. I just—" He breaks off.

"Just what?"

His shoulders slump, and he sighs. "If this is all we have, I just want you to remember me for being some small part of the best part of what makes you, *you.* I'm not trying to save you from all the hurt you feel inside yourself, Brooke; only you can do that. But I wish you could love yourself and see how wonderful you are, 'silly dreams' and all. Just as much as—"

He breaks off again. Looks directly in my eyes. His gaze pierces straight through me, shatters everything that's been binding and choking me all this time. He walks toward me, and I let myself fall into his arms, crying. He holds me tight. *Please don't let go.*

"You have to learn to trust yourself, Brooke. You *can* do this and not lose yourself in it at the same time."

My mouth is saturated with the salty taste of tears. I'm limp in his arms, and even though his body is muscular and defined, his embrace feels like a soft landing.

"You sound like her again," I say after a minute or so passes with us standing there. Me, an emotional wreck, and Patrick, the anchor keeping me from drifting further into the abyss of my dark thoughts and feelings.

"Don't worry, all my advice is free. Though I don't know if it's worth much."

"It means something to me," I say in a muffled voice and feel him squeeze tighter.

Patrick holds me back, wipes my face, and gives me a light smile. "Ready to let go? Live the big dream?"

I inhale deeply through my nose and exhale through my mouth, letting myself absorb the familiar sound of a tennis ball being hit. "Yes."

Between us there's a silent exchange, seemingly reflecting on so much of ourselves that we've just poured into one another. The moment is intense until I finally break the reprieve.

"I don't have anything to wear or a racket to play with—"

Patrick raises a familiar brow at me and gives me a mischievous wink.

"That's all been taken care of. There's a tennis outfit and sneakers in the locker room, and you can pick a racket to borrow."

I shake my head and fold my hand over my mouth, hiding the smile that is eager to find my face even as the tears continue. I feel so much emotion at the thought of stepping back out onto the tennis court after all this time—joy, nerves, but most of all, relief.

"I guess you thought of everything," I say, dropping my hand, sniffling with a few tears sliding down my face.

Patrick nods proudly, smoothing away my tears.

"You deserve it, Brooke."

He kisses my forehead and pulls me into another embrace.

My heart and mind are racing as I listen to his heartbeat. Even with this huge emotional breakthrough, I can't help but think of what he's made clear—there is no future for us. But my mind is unwilling to accept it because he's also made something else clear to me—this is real, real love. So, what is the hesitation?

What if he came to London? If I'm on my own, we could figure things out.

The idea nestles into the back of my thoughts while we pull back from one another, and he gives me a soft peck on the lips.

"So," I start, exhaling deeply. "What's the deal?" I ask, gesturing toward the building.

He takes my hand in his and leads me toward the doors to the facility. As we make our way inside, he explains that he's set up a private lesson for me to hit with one of the pros. A way for me to ease back into things and clear off the dust.

"Wait," I say, stopping in front of a bulletin board in the lobby. There's a poster, and I can't make out most of it because it's in Czech, but I see the date and a picture that implies a competition of some sort.

I feel my heart flutter. I'm nervous but instantly feel hungry for the fight looking at the poster image. It's a sentiment I haven't felt in such a long time. That sweet yearning and rush of stepping on the court, warming up and trying to assess what I can from my opponent before the match even begins. I miss it terribly, but more than anything I need to prove to myself I won't get carried away. I can play. I could win or lose. But I can turn it off at the end of the day and remember the bigger world around me. The people in it, too.

"What about that? Looks like it's today."

"You want to jump right into competing?" he replies, circumspect.

"If I'm going to do this, I need to own it. Besides, you said it—I have to learn to trust myself, right?"

Patrick and I check in, and the pro is more than happy to have me join the open round-robin competition they have set up. I go to the locker room and sure enough, there is a change of clothes for me—stylish too, I might add. There's also a brand new pair of tennis shoes—also, stylish. I bend them in my hands, trying to break them in a little.

I step in front of the mirror.

I missed you.

I've missed this girl something fierce. Missed this part of me that got buried the day the *something* happened. My eyes peer down at the scars over my hand. I think of Liam, and I think of my mom. I think of Alex and of my team.

I need this.

This is for Liam because he believed in me, and this is for my mom because she won't. This is for Alex and my team because I let them down, and I need to set things right. This is for me because, like Patrick said, it's who I feel I'm really meant to be and it's time to start over.

Yes, I can.

I head out of the locker room and find Patrick waiting for me.

"Wow, you really do look like the real thing."

"Thanks."

The sexual tension between us is so obvious, and my skimpy tennis outfit is not helping.

We walk to the pro shop, where I pick a racket from the available demos.

"That one looks cool," Patrick comments.

I screw my face up at the electric blue racket. "It might look cool, but it's not about the look. I need the right grip size and weight."

"Okay, Goldilocks."

"Ha-ha."

I pick up a few until I finally settle on one that feels almost like my custom rackets that are sitting in my closet back home. Holding the racket and going through a few practice swings makes me feel like I'm no longer missing a limb. I'm whole. "This one."

At the check-in desk we make introductions. The competition is a little bit of a mixed bag. A Czech lady—maybe late thirties—two teenagers who are apparently pretty good and looking to play college tennis in the states, and one of the pros who coaches at the club, who played briefly on the women's pro circuit.

The top seed gets the first-round bye, which is one of the teenagers, a sixteen-year-old boy, coincidentally named Novak.

I play the Czech lady first. Her name is Tereza. She's super nice, athletic, and played tennis at a top-ranked American university once upon a time. Based on a ten-minute warm-up, I can tell she's good and has been keeping up with her game since her college days.

She spins her racket so we can decide who will serve first.

"Up," I say.

"Up, it is," she replies, picking up her racket from off the ground. "What would you like?"

"I'll serve first."

I head to my seat, wiping my face with a towel because I'm already starting to sweat, and take a quick sip of water before heading to the base line. As I walk to the baseline, I look in Patrick's direction. He gives me a dorky smile and thumbs up.

"You got this!" he shouts.

When I'm playing, I'm usually oblivious to what's going on around me, but seeing him there gives me the confidence and balance I need in the moment to really do this—to start over and be who I believe I am really meant to be without hurtling down a dark, isolated, and lonely path.

I step up to the baseline.

"Love-all."

"You are fucking awesome!" I hear Patrick say loud enough just for me to hear as he walks up behind me from the stands.

I laugh, completely giddy. "Thanks."

He kisses my cheek even though I'm sweaty.

"I mean, no joke—you are *really* talented, Brooke. I'm—" There's a glistening in his eyes. "I'm so glad I got to see you play."

I look up at him admiringly from my seat and then stand up. We're staring intently at each other, and I give him a tender smile. I feel overwhelmed by so many emotions after the day that I throw my arms around him.

"Thank you," I say, softly into his ear, tearing up like the mush puddle I've become since Berlin.

He wraps his arms around me, and I sink into his body, feeling both physically and emotionally exhausted all over again, just like this morning. The difference is I feel more myself than I have in a long time. Even before the *something*.

He kisses the top of my head. "Of course."

As we head out from the facility, the head pro flags us down.

"Brooke, thank you so much for coming out." He has an English accent, shaggy blond hair, and looks to be mid-forties.

"No, thank you for letting me join last-minute. This was a total surprise, and it was really wonderful. It's been a little while since I played."

"Well, it certainly didn't look like it from how you played."

I smile at the compliment, and there's a short awkward pause.

"Well, your boyfriend said you were good but not a ringer," he jests cheerfully. "The girl, Lucie—the pro that teaches here—she has several top fifty wins from the tour under her belt, and Novak made it to the finals in the junior French Open this year."

"Wow, I didn't know," I reply, genuinely impressed and humbled.

"Yeah, I'm probably going to have to cool some tempers," he kids with a sly grin. "Anyway, here, before I forget," he says, handing me 200 euros. "No trophy, and usually I do a gift certificate to the pro shop or a free lesson, but seeing as you're on holiday, I thought maybe you two could go out for a nice meal to celebrate the winning streak."

I'm taken aback. "What?"

"It's your prize money. Also, I threw in a little extra for beating up on Novak." He gives me a wry wink.

"Really? Thank you so much!"

He nods and walks off but turns back in our direction.

"Hey, and if you're ever back in Prague, stop by. Or if you're looking for a coach, let me know." He waves and walks off.

I turn to Patrick with the money clutched in my hand, still shocked.

"That's crazy. I've never won *legit* prize money before."

"Could be a start to something," he says suggestively with a coy shrug of his shoulders. "By the way, where are you taking me to dinner tonight?"

I play-slap at Patrick, and he grabs me, pulling me into him, and we kiss deeply. I pull back and look up into his eyes.

"Thank you, again. I needed this," I say. My sass has a grip on me, and I can't resist. "Boy. Friend." Then pull him to me and kiss him. The best prize of all.

My Shield

Patrick and I end up going out that night after my day of playing tennis, and we spend every cent of my winnings on a nice meal and drinks. I'm glowing with happiness, but I can't ignore a growing bud of anxiety. The countdown is bearing down on me. Patrick said absolutely zero in response to me half-seriously, half-jokingly calling him my boyfriend. The consolation was the kiss. It was a really good kiss. But still.

Soon I leave, and we have yet to talk seriously about, well, what happens next. My hints of something more continue to be avoided even though I am sure Patrick feels the same as me.

The question keeps circulating in my brain: What happens when the fairytale ends in Prague? I'm too nervous to broach the subject head-on and honestly, I just don't want to think about it.

The following day we pretend we have all the time in the world together and head out for more sightseeing. We briefly revisit a few of the stops we checked out the first time through but mostly wander to different buildings and exhibits attached to, and surrounding, the Prague Castle. When we've had enough, we pick up some food and wine for a picnic and go to Petrin Park.

We find a nice spot in the slightly overgrown grass. It's soft and a little dewy from staying hidden in the shade of the trees and is tucked away from the walking paths so that we are secluded and mostly alone.

We nibble, drink, kiss, and talk. There are ladybugs every-where that jump and tickle our skin as they land on us. It is sublime and terribly romantic.

"So, I want to know . . ."

"Uh-oh, what does Brooke want to know . . ." he toys, tossing a grape in his mouth.

I frown in response. "What do you think I want to know?" I ask, sounding brisk but flirty.

Patrick gives me a curious look. "What do you mean?"

I think for a minute about the best way to ask my question as I pick up a slice of artisan cheese and cracker to munch on.

"I mean—you really didn't want to keep going with swimming? You don't feel that spark at all, of wanting to get back into things? That rush from competing?" My voice is energized because I'm still a bit buzzed from playing tennis yesterday and now can't imagine having gone cold turkey for such an extended period of time. So much so that I can't understand why Patrick, with all his apparent talent, wouldn't feel the urge to get back into the pool.

Patrick does the thing where he fidgets with his fingers. "It's not that I don't miss it. It's just I didn't feel a sense of fulfillment. Or at least after a time I didn't. Watching you play yesterday, I could see it, ya know? You looked fulfilled out on the court. For me, it just turned into going through the motions. I stopped having fun. Stopped enjoying it. Stopped loving it."

"Because of your dad?"

Patrick's eyes flit up at me, still having not shared whatever dark secret that lingers there in the space between him and his dad.

"Yes and no," he says, sighing heavily. "I don't blame him for me not swimming competitively anymore. That was my choice at the end of the day."

A silence settles over us as we each take a long sip of our wine.

"The truth is, I don't miss it at all," Patrick finally says. "But you know what?"

"What?"

"I really liked watching you play. Even though I felt I was on pins and needles the entire time during the last match."

I give him a sarcastic look and roll my eyes. He's avoiding the subject, per usual. "Well, you don't have to tell me what happened. Even though you said you would," I say, razzing him. "But you know you can trust me, right? I care about you, Patrick. I won't ever judge you—promise." I don't know if it's the wine or my desperation for a sliver of hope that our journey doesn't end together in Prague, but the last bit ends up coming out sounding like a lifeline. Perhaps just for myself. Or us.

Patrick sucks in a deep breath and gingerly touches my hair, tucking a tendril behind my ear. It's something he does often, and I find it sweet and tender.

"It's hard for me to talk about, Brooke. I don't know if it's because I'm embarrassed by it or because I've never really let myself heal from it—*emotionally*, or whatever."

The way he emphasizes the word "emotionally" catches my attention.

Patrick bites his bottom lip. His trepidation is palpable, and I respond by reaching across to press my hand against his cheek.

I know I'm not seeing things. When I look at him, there's water glazing his eyes.

"Alright. Here goes," he says, blinking away the tears and turning his gaze off into the distance.

"I had just finished a competition. I won in each of my heats. The thing is, I had decided that I was done swimming and that that was going to be it—my last competition. The kicker is it was a qualifier for the Olympics. I was going to be going to the *Olympics*."

His eyes turn sharply to me as he emphasizes the stakes at hand. "Oh."

"Yeah. Anyway, I knew my decision. But, my father didn't know, and after I won, he was already planning the logistics—what my training would be like leading up to it, my sleeping and eating schedules, weight training, cardio—*all of it*. Complete and utter control."

Patrick's eyes have turned red, but his voice is steady as he continues to talk.

"The whole way back from the trials, he was going on and on about the schedule and what the plan was going to be for me, for the Olympics. Meanwhile, I just sat there absorbing what he was saying, feeling totally numb, knowing full well that it was never going to come to fruition. I was done, and I dreaded telling him."

"I can only imagine," I reply softly.

I don't know what else I can say even though a million things come to mind. But the thing is I don't want to say more in the moment because Patrick is finally talking about his dad. Although one thing is for sure, I can relate to the numb feeling and the pressure, even if mine is a slightly different iteration.

"We got home and before we went in the house, I said it out loud. I told him. Blurted it out. 'I'm done, I'm not swimming anymore'. And it—" He breaks, searching for the words to finish. "It just flipped a switch in him."

Patrick pauses and peers off into the distance again.

"My father—he started yelling. We both did. He told me that I was being selfish, that he and my mum had invested *time* and *money* in me. That they had *sacrificed* so much for me to get to that point and to have the opportunity to make something of myself. To be more . . . He was so angry that I was going to throw it all away. Just like that."

I'm holding Patrick's hand, and I can feel his grip tighten. I swallow. My throat closes, imagining the worst.

"The neighbors came out by that point—I mean, it all just really spiraled out of control. My dad got up in my face and said he was so angry that he could hit me. I egged him on and told him to do it, and . . . he did. Again and again. I didn't even fight back. I just let him hit me."

I can't keep a horrified look off my face at this revelation.

"He nearly broke my jaw. I don't remember how many times he actually hit me. But when it was over, I told him if he ever touched me again, I'd do what he did to me, only worse."

I can see the tears in his eyes have nearly breached. He lets go of my hand and wipes them away.

"But of course, there's more."

"What do you mean *more?*"

It's like we're back in Berlin at the Gemäldegalerie, me confessing everything about the *something*, only the roles are reversed.

"My dad was also my manager and had signed a fairly large sponsorship deal without me knowing. The deal put me on the hook for various appearances, interviews, endorsements—all based on my performance as this rising star swimmer for Australia. I had no idea he'd done that."

"How could he do that?" I ask angrily. "Couldn't you just give the money back? Break the contract?"

Patrick grimaces, shakes his head. "No, he told me the money was already invested. Couldn't tear up the contract or give the money back. I was stuck. Obligated." Patrick shakes his head again. "Looking back now, I don't know how much of that is true. I was young. I didn't know any better, and he had a strong hold on me."

"So, what? Did you have to keep swimming?"

"For a bit. But I had an injury that had me out for an extended period, which helped the hype die down. Then people forgot about me. Someone else took my slot on the Olympic team. I eventually broke ties with my dad and family and went off on my own."

"Injury?"

Patrick shrugs, dismissively.

"What about the money and the contract?"

"A loss. The price of doing business, I suppose. I never saw a cent of it."

I give him a confused look. "What do you mean, you never saw a cent? You said your dad invested the money."

Patrick scoffs as a ladybug lands on the tip of his finger, and his eyes focus on its little legs scurrying over his skin. "In himself. In his shop."

I don't know what to say. I've heard horror stories of *those types of parents*. The type that would run their kid ragged with the hopes of them achieving fame and fortune as a professional athlete and being able to live vicariously through their successes, to the point of destroying their own child. But this takes it to a new level.

Patrick watches intently as the ladybug crawls over his hand then spreads its wings and flies away.

I'm truly at a loss for words, and we sit cloaked in nothing more than the faint sounds of birds chirping in the background.

"You can see why I never talk about it. Sort of a mood killer."

Patrick tries to smile, but it's clear that rehashing the violent events and the manipulation that transpired between him and his father weigh heavy on him. His eyes are glazed again and red from the strain of holding back the emotions he must be feeling and holding on to. I feel an overwhelming need to be protective of him in that moment—no, not just in that moment. I want to protect him, always.

"I—"

I almost let the word "love" roll off my tongue, but I'm too scared, even though I feel it—*love*—for him and want the word to be my shield to defend him from such a dreadful thing to have happened.

"Thank you for trusting me," I say in a soft voice. I place my hand on him and draw closer until we are holding each other, and I know he's crying, quietly, and then we both are.

We leave the ugliness behind. I hope I never meet Patrick's father. I may kill him. Seriously.

Patrick and I arrange to have an intimate dinner at the penthouse, prepared by the hotel's private chef. We don't revisit the topic of parents or anything like that. We're back to our usual witty banter and joking around, sprinkled with affection. We finish our meal. The chef leaves, and we watch the city lights from the rooftop for a while.

Eventually, Patrick heads back downstairs to use the bathroom and I slip down behind him.

"Hey, you," he says, surprised to see me waiting for him.

I don't say anything. I take his hand and lead him to my room.

He stops at the threshold, still holding on to my hand. I turn to look at him.

"Brooke," he says, pausing. "Are you sure? Even if we feel—I don't know how this could—"

I step toward him and kiss him, with everything my heart has to offer. I pull away and stare up into his eyes.

"Yes. Even if this is all we have together."

CHAPTER 35

Good Morning

I wake up the next morning, and I'm not in a fetal position. I did not have my recurring dream of the house on the hill. Instead, I'm wrapped in Patrick's arms, admiring the Olympics tattoo, which he got after competing in the Junior Olympics and winning medals in several of his heats.

I trace the different colored circles with my fingertip, which causes Patrick to stir. I can feel his warm naked body press against me and pull me closer.

"Hmmm, are you awake?" he groans and kisses at my back and neck, nuzzling at me.

"Sort of. Not really." I'm thinking of how I had almost convinced myself that I could be satisfied with just a fling. After last night, nothing could be further from the truth. I'm all in.

I trace the tattooed circles again and kiss his arm where they are permanently etched into his skin. Then before I know it, he's rolling me over so I'm facing him. We kiss softly at first, and not long after Patrick is finding his way back between my legs and is inside of me.

As we move together with my legs wrapped around him, his lips circulate between my mouth, my neck, and my breasts. Our hands caress and grab at one another's bodies, and his fingers make me want to scream at him for mercy, just so long as he doesn't stop.

It feels erotic. I don't feel shy at all. I feel like a woman, not a girl. I am completely comfortable and at ease with our skin pressed together, naked, our limbs intwined. Meanwhile, the more we move together and the more he touches me, every part of my body wants to explode and splinter into a thousand, million pieces. I'm completely immersed in every moment of him.

When we're done, I roll on my back and glance over at him. We're both sort of panting, but he looks completely wasted, while I feel fully awake.

His eyes are closed, and he looks like he's concentrating on recovering, or possibly meditating.

I move my hand over to him and gently run my hands through his hair. His breathing eventually slows and returns to normal. He opens his eyes, turns his head to look at me, and strokes my hair in return.

"Good morning," he says.

"Hi."

We lie there staring at each other all googly-eyed for a few minutes.

"I'm going to take a shower," he says.

"You should. You're gross and sweaty."

"I blame you for that."

I bite my lower lip, and we kiss one more time before he gets up.

"Nice butt," I say as he stretches, his muscles flexing, and I feel myself getting all bothered again, wanting more of him.

"Glad you like it," he says, sneaking a look at me over his shoulder.

I get out of bed and throw on my sweats as Patrick goes into my ensuite.

"I'm going to make coffee!" I holler into the bathroom over the running water.

"Sure you don't want to join me?" Patrick hollers back from inside the shower.

"I think my body needs to recover for a little bit," I reply as I shut the door.

I make coffee for the two of us and sit down at one of the bar stools sipping my drink. My body feels like putty, and I'm blissfully happy.

Buzz . . . buzz . . . buzz . . .

I'm in my own little world and didn't even notice that Patrick's cell and wallet are on the island.

His cell buzzes again. I ignore it and focus on my nails. *I'm not that girl.*

I refrain for a good thirty seconds.

"Don't do it, Brooke," I say out loud to myself.

It's probably just Max, or maybe his mother.

I sneak a look down the hall to see if Patrick is there and listen quietly for the sound of the shower; the water is still running. I pick up his cell and look at the name and number displayed.

"What the—"

I set down my coffee abruptly and it splashes on the counter as I stare at the phone in my hand. I don't recognize the name, but I certainly recognize the number. I let it keep ringing as I stare perplexed at the screen. It stops but I can see he has eight missed calls from the same contact.

I put the phone down. I get up and look down at it like it's a hand grenade. My heart is racing as I think, trying to make sense of things.

I glance down the hall and listen again. The shower is still going, so I grab Patrick's wallet and start going through it. My hands are shaking. I pull out the credit card he's been using and can see it has a business name, and behind it there's a license. A credential.

Elite Security.

It's the international VIP company that's worked for my family for as long as I can remember. The phone number calling Patrick is that of my mother's head of security.

It can't be real. He can't be one of them.

In the distance, the shower switches off and a door opens.

"Brooke? How about you get your sexy arse back in here, eh?"

I stare down the hall, shocked.

No. Fucking. Way.

CHAPTER 36

Moving Backward

"Mom, why does Grayson *always* have to come with me everywhere? Why can't I go to the city on my own with my friends? Or just ride my bike down the street without feeling like someone is watching my every move?" I lamented.

I was sitting in the eat-in breakfast area, picking at my flaky quiche crust with my mom and brother sitting across from me. She was delicately nibbling at her egg whites and fruit.

"Brooke, we've gone over this a million times. You are *special*—"

"She's *special*, alright," Liam said under his breath.

"Shut up, Liam. You're—"

"Stop it, the two of you! You both need to understand this, and for that matter, come to terms with it now and for the rest of your lives," our mother said, looking sternly across the table at the two of us.

She was serious about whatever she was about to say, and I stopped picking at the fine pastry, while Liam looked to have been chastened by her words, too.

We were both tweens. Both that irritable age for any parent where we start to question our world and the decisions made for us and were altogether a little bratty.

Our mother had our attention and proceeded to lecture us on how we were "up against the world" because of the family we came from. Most of it sounded like a broken record; we had heard this all before.

"There will never be a time where you two are alone in the sense that some measure hasn't been taken to ensure your safety and security. Whether that means you are driven in a private car or followed by some sort of security detail or you're on a private plane or traveling first-class with a detail accompanying you, that is the life of a Neville. You can fight it, or you can thank the fates that you'll never be lonely."

I'm standing, arms crossed, looking out the big bay of windows at the Prague cityscape, still completely and utterly in disbelief. Patrick is a liar. Period.

It's an overcast day and the last full day Patrick and I have in Prague together, or perhaps anywhere together. Not something I was hoping for only thirty minutes ago.

I can hear Patrick open and close the door to my room and walk the length of the hall to the kitchen.

"Brooke?"

I don't answer. A moment later, I hear him again.

"Hey, there you are," he says as he comes up behind me and hugs my waist and kisses my neck.

I stiffen and close my eyes, feeling the tears burn as my shock starts to fade into a pain unlike any I've felt before.

Patrick loosens his grip and pulls back.

"What's wrong?"

I try to find my voice. It takes a minute, but I'm finally able to speak.

"Who are you?" I say, with as much courage as I can muster, as my mind is still pulling at strings to make sense of what is going on.

"I don't understand. Did I miss something?"

I close my eyes and let more tears roll down my cheeks, then turn to face him.

"I mean *who* are you, Patrick? *Why* are you here? Better yet *why* am I here with *you?*" My voice is steely and he's eyeing at me probingly, trying to make sense of my questions. I clear my throat and let the air that's been trapped in my lungs escape. "I'm so *fucking stupid.* You must take me for a complete idiot."

"What happened, Brooke?"

I can't tell if I'm angrier at him or at myself. But as he continues the ridiculous charade, my anger starts to find its target. I go straight for the jugular—I'm not in the mood for mincing words.

"I'm wondering if my mother paid you to fuck me, too? Is that part of the premium package? Security detail and escort services, all in one?"

I toss the business credit card and the security credential at his feet.

Patrick looks down and his eyes close momentarily, recognition hitting. He must have guessed I'd discovered something, but there is no escaping the truth glaring up at him.

"Brooke, it's not—"

"Not what, Patrick? It's not what I *think?* I'm pretty confident it's exactly what I think. Especially, since you have—what, I don't know, seven missed calls from 'Client 4227,' which is my mother's security detail."

He doesn't say anything, but his shoulders slump and he takes a step closer.

"Stay back. Don't you *dare* touch me."

We stare across at each other, and I feel like I'm going to detonate. Into what, I don't know—hurt, anger, resignation. I'm feeling all those things.

"Brooke, I understand what this may look like but please let me try to explain," he pleads.

"How long have you been following me?" I ask. "Was that whole story about Max and his engagement bullshit or what? And Lizzie and Abby, are they in on it too?"

The neurons are firing off in my head, picking apart every miniscule moment over the last couple of weeks since we first met in Berlin. Surely not Lauren and Varun, and—and—and Alda and Grady and the Norwegians . . . Were they all helping him follow me?

I think back to the music festival and how Patrick also randomly showed up. Did someone tip him off that I was there? Or for that matter, the night I went to Brücke, and he just happened to appear in the hostel lobby, dressed in black with combat boots. Even Alda, with her incredible connections and VIP all-access. A high security venue, the perfect place to give me the time of my life, without actually exposing me to risk. Then there were Lauren's guarded words, telling me to be careful with Patrick.

They were all in on it.

My voice is pitching from high to low, spewing out the possibilities of deceit. I laugh and shake my head to myself, pressing my palms to my head as I feel my thoughts spin out of control, questioning every part of my reality out loud, or rather what I've perceived to be my reality, over the last couple of weeks. He probably had some sort of dossier on me and knew everything about me without me having to tell him—it was never a secret of who I actually was because he *already* knew. But it wasn't just Berlin. I've been traveling solo for *months*. Plural.

I drop my hands and look up at Patrick. It was part of the bargain with my mother—a chance to be completely on my own, if I held up my end of things.

This is how I felt in the locker room—the walls closing in, the emotions trapped in my body too big, too painful to contain. A sob wrenches its way out of my chest.

My new friends . . . my first real boyfriend . . . my first real love . . . My mother's smug expression, as she sat in my room sizing up my choices . . .

My fists ball up. I need to break something. I need to destroy something before I'm destroyed.

No, I can't lose control again.

Somehow, through the chaos of my mind, I remember there is another person in the room. A stranger I barely recognize.

"Is Patrick even your real name?" I shake my head. Of course it is. I saw the ID card.

He runs his hands through his hair and folds them behind his head. He's taking deep, slow breaths. Controlling himself, like a pro. He's a man trapped in a cage with a lioness.

"Yes," he says, leaning back slightly. "I've never lied to you, Brooke." I choke out a laugh. Is he for real? I turn toward the windows, afraid of what I might do if I look at his face a moment longer. "The stuff about Max is not bullshit. He *is* really engaged to my cousin, and they have their issues. He and I work for the same company. We're both—" I whip my head around to glare at him because I want to see him say it. "We both work for Elite, protecting people . . . like you. We got assigned to take over from the detail previously following you. We were instructed to get close to you. Confirm a few things."

"Nice one. You must have been making bank with all that overtime getting so *incredibly* close," I sneer.

He lets out another deep sigh and chooses to ignore my comment. "We left for Europe a few weeks before the contract started in Italy, so Max could go get whatever 'out of his system' before his wedding. The stuff with Lizzie and Abby was an unforeseen complication. I warned him not to let it affect the job, but . . ." He catches his choice of words and winces.

"Yes, maintaining professional boundaries gets tricky, doesn't it?" He chooses not to answer, so I continue. "So, at what point did you decide to sleep with me? Was it after I poured my heart out to you about my pathetic life, or did my mom have to cut a fat check just like she did with my therapist?"

I had told him that I'd had a mental breakdown. I trusted him with things I've never shared with anyone, not even Liam. What kind of person pretends to care for someone who'd been through all that? I've been lied to and manipulated my whole life, but this level of cruelty is just . . . stunning. He should be sympathetic above anyone else, assuming the story about his father is actually real.

"Brooke, I understand you're angry, but I'm not sure this is helpful."

"You *used* me. You pretended to care for me, but I was just a big fat dollar sign to you."

He has the outright audacity to scoff and cross his arms. "Be honest, Brooke. We used each other."

"*What?*" I honestly can't believe what I'm hearing. He isn't just a liar, he's delusional.

"I tried to keep things light between us, but you weren't happy with a summer fling. You wanted the whole boyfriend package. I had to bare my soul to you, and I did. You wanted *love*." He spits out the word, like it's dirty. "But what exactly were you planning to do with *my* heart, Brooke? Pin it in your fucking scrapbook? You knew full well that there was no way I could ever exist in your world. Not really."

"I wanted to at least try!"

"Try what? Making me your little Australian pet?"

"Am I supposed to apologize for . . . for caring for you? For being born wealthy?" I sputter. "I'm confused."

He takes a deep breath. "I tricked you by hiding my identity. But you deluded yourself thinking we could ever be together," he starts, his words shaky. "And you didn't care if that destroyed me in the long run. Because you're *Brooke Antoinette Neville*, and you're used to getting whatever you want. It comes as naturally to you as breathing."

His entire body is trembling, and I can see that he's not just embarrassed by what's happened between us, he's hurt too. But as much as there is some truth to his words, he is not the victim here.

"I might be rich and entitled, but you're a liar. And you know what you just said couldn't be further from the fucking truth."

"She says, from high atop her lofty tower." He forces a laugh, shaking his head. "So easy to judge, when you've never had to struggle a day in your life."

I blink at the hard set of his jaw. At the realization that this is the first time I'm really truly *seeing* him. "You're an asshole."

"No, I'm a fucking idiot."

"Because you got caught?"

"No, because I love you." He says it with bitterness and regret. "I wish to God I didn't, but I do."

The tears I'm holding back sting terribly, and for a minute I feel myself soften—just slightly. But then I remember that this man held me as I wept about my family and gently tried to convince me to forgive them—or at least leave some inkling of hope open—and give them another chance. My abusers. His employers.

"You wouldn't recognize love if it bitch-slapped you in the face."

I swallow down the lump in my throat. I can barely hold back the tears any longer, and I keep trying to catch my breath, inhaling through my anger and hurt.

And then my mind goes to its default mode: self-preservation.

"I don't ever want to see you again," I say and turn my back to him.

"You won't," he says with a curt finality that makes me want to scream.

I hear him shuffle around in the distance, presumably gathering his things. Eventually his footsteps cross the living room to the front door, and I hear the *clunk* of the handle turning.

"Did you really think someone like you could just galivant around Europe, like a regular person?" His voice is full of scorn. "Do you know how many people in this world want to hurt you? How many potential threats I've reported in the past week alone? Or the fucking *mess* we had to clean up after Lauren posted those photos of you traipsing around Berlin?"

I stay silent, frozen. Tears are streaming uncontrollably from my eyes. But I won't give him another word. He's taken enough from me.

"Lauren, Alda, and that whole group had nothing to do with any of this, by the way. They're just your friends."

My eyes shut tightly, and I continue to resist the urge to turn around. I have no reason to trust anything he says, but on this point, I believe him. Knowing that at least some of what I experienced was real . . . it's a tiny beam of light through otherwise suffocating darkness.

A moment later the door opens and shuts. I'm numb all over again. Numbness. My familiar companion.

I feel like I've been torn apart then roughly stitched back together, as if somehow, I've gone full circle and find myself exactly where I started on my journey.

At least you'll never be lonely, my mother said once. But she was a liar too.

CHAPTER 37

I Can Play the Game, Too

I spend most of the morning and early afternoon surfing the internet on the computer in the library, still in my pajamas, still with my face a mess from crying. No, sobbing. Mostly, all I'm doing is torturing myself on purpose. I look up stuff about me, my brother, my old tennis team, our family, about my mom and her sterling reputation in New York and Greenwich's high society—the things I usually consciously avoid because I know how damaging and upsetting it will be. But I do it anyway. I comb over everything I can find.

When I feel I've reached the end of the internet on those topics, I check my email. I've completely forgotten about having reached out to my Wimbledon host family, too preoccupied the last few days. There's a response email waiting. A quick glance, and it's apparent that by telling Patrick my plan, it's made its way back to my mother, and she's swooped into action. The return email is missing all the usual warmth, and essentially says "no."

I close out of my email and stare at the blinking cursor in the Google search engine.

Don't.

But I do it anyway. I type "Patrick Evans + swimmer" and press enter. The results are aplenty, and I read one article after another about Patrick until I get to a few ambiguous pieces that allude to some unfortunate and abrupt end to his budding and promising swimming career.

I backtrack and change the search. I type "Patrick Evans + bodyguard" and press enter. His company page comes up, but there's no picture or bio, it just lists him as an employee.

"Fuck him."

I say it like it's going to make me feel better, but it doesn't. My emotions are torn in two. I feel so much betrayal, but I can't help that another part of me believes what was happening was real and genuine. His words from earlier repeat in my head. *Because I love you.* But also, that he wished he didn't.

"Fuck . . ." I say under my breath to no one except myself, but then the rational side of me pipes up.

He was a mistake. Stop feeling sorry for yourself.

Maybe it was destiny that Patrick and I met and everything unfolded the way it did. As shattered as this whole farce has left me, I also feel like I'm finally seeing reality for what it is. And if I can survive what I've been through so far, I can survive just about anything.

I check my flight. Still not canceled, which means I have a whole new life to begin in London, away from my parents, even if I am being watched, and if my mom wants to play games with my life. Well, guess what?

"I can play games, too."

The phone rings in the kitchen, and I imagine it is either my mother or my grandfather.

"Hello?" I say, sliding into one of the bar stools at the island, the scene of the crime earlier this morning.

"Hello, dear."

"Hey, Pop. How are you?" I'm positively bubbly, even if it is entirely feigned.

My mother has already used my grandfather against me once, and it's likely she's doing it again by getting him to call. The game never stops, and I have to be ready for anything at this point. Besides, the seed has been planted. No time like the present to let my plan hatch.

"You know why I'm calling. Have you reached out to your mother yet?" he asks, cutting to the chase in his usual way, though I'm convinced he already knows the answer to the question.

I imagine my mother is listening in. But I also start to wonder what Patrick's reported back at this point. No bother. *Game on.*

"Was just getting ready to call her," I reply, sticking with the sickly-sweet tenor, even though it kills me a little inside because it's my grandfather. It's her I'm mad at, not him.

"That's good, dear," he says and coughs, the same one he had the last time we talked.

"Have you gotten that cough checked out yet?"

"Yes, the doctor said it's nothing to be concerned about. Just related to seasonal allergies."

"Well, I guess that's good news."

Having played his apparent part, my grandfather moves to aimless chitchat. "Have you at least had a good time in Prague?"

I have and tell him about everything I've done, minus any details about Patrick. I don't know what he may or may not know about Patrick as my apparent bodyguard or fling or whatever. Either way, I'm not bringing him up.

We talk a little bit longer but before we hang up, I put back on the honeycomb voice. "Hey, Pop, ya know, I'm not sure what happened, but my debit card—the one with the account you helped me open?"

"Yes," he replies, and I catch an air of unease. He shot me down immediately the last time I brought it up but seems to be leaving an open opportunity for me to broach the subject this time. I take it.

"It seems something happened, like the account was put on hold. I have some shopping I'd like to do for my parents before I leave Prague tomorrow. There are these really beautiful one-of-a-kind matching tennis bracelets I was thinking I could get for me and Mom at Cartier. I thought it might be a nice way to patch things up, after everything that's happened. Can you check to make sure the card is working? Sooner the better. It's getting late, and I don't have much time left before the shops close. I want to use the debit card instead of my credit card so it's a surprise."

He's silent for a few seconds. My eyes shut, and I cross my fingers. "Sure, dear. That's very sweet of you to do for your mother. I'm sure she'll be touched by that. When we hang up, I'll call and make sure the card is working." *And probably report back to Mom, which is fine.*

My eyes spring open. I collect myself, even though I feel a surge of vindication. "Thanks a lot, Pop. I love you."

In response he repeats the thing he said during our last call. "I love you, too. You are more like your mother than you realize, dear."

I roll my eyes to myself, though I would never do that to my grandfather if he was standing in front of me.

At least I can say the call was a distraction and feels like it sucked me out of my self-brooding mood. In fact, I feel rejuvenated. Like I have just a touch of control over my life again.

I take a shower and get cleaned up. The hot, steamy water feels renewing, even though all I can think is what if I had gotten in the shower with Patrick earlier this morning. I would have stayed blissfully unaware. At least for a little while longer.

What was your plan, Patrick? Tell me and be my bodyguard-slash-lover?

I get out of the shower and get dressed in some comfy sweat

clothes, throw my wet hair up, and don't bother putting on any makeup—no need to look cute, no one to impress.

I grab the phone and sit on the couch in the living room. I take a deep breath and punch in a sequence of numbers I know by heart. The phone rings, and then I hear my mother's voice.

"Hello? Brooke?"

"Mom."

She doesn't say anything right away. I'm not sure if I should talk or if I should wait for her to lecture me.

"Brooke—"

"Mom—"

We both start to talk at the same time.

"Go ahead, Mom."

"No, I think I'd rather hear what you have to say," she says in her no-nonsense voice.

I exhale. It's going to take everything I can muster in myself to get this out *and* mean it.

"You know why I'm calling," I say, borrowing one of Pop's favorite lines. *I've learned from the best.* "I know about—" I break off and bite at my lip. Let her think I'm about to start crying.

"About what?"

"The security detail, and that they've been following me the entire time I've been traveling."

I let my words marinate for a minute. My mother doesn't say anything either.

"We got a call this morning, that you had attempted to dismiss the man assigned to you," she says curtly. "You can sever yourself from the family, Brooke, but we will not allow you to fall into undesirable hands." I interpret the true meaning behind her words: Cost the family financially, or God forbid, cause a scandal. "Unless you want to file a restraining order, it's non-negotiable. You will be protected."

A restraining order, huh? I can't admit I'm not tempted.

"I understand," I say, a little too quickly. I can tell my assent catches my mom off-guard. "Look, I remember when we were"—I say "we" to imply Liam, but I feel the need to correct— "when I was younger, and you said that we would always have some type of security following us whether we knew it or not. I know this is the reality for every Neville. I'm sorry for everything."

"I'm glad you understand, and it's good to hear you apologize."

Her voice is cold and calculating, with an air of self-satisfaction, but I can tell she doesn't yet trust this new obedient version of her daughter.

"I do. But—" Again I break off because it's going to take all my inner strength to get the next few words out.

"Yes?"

"I need to ask a favor." Big breath in. "I don't want that guy—Patrick Evans—to be assigned to me any longer. Can it be someone else on the security detail?"

She's quiet.

"Did something happen between you two?"

"No," I say, biting down on my lip, fighting back the water-works. I don't know how much she knows, but I can only hope she doesn't push this. "I don't want him punished or anything. I just don't want him around."

I can't stomach the thought of even looking at Patrick again, but I've also seen bad things happen to people who've been stupid enough to upset my family. As angry as I am, Patrick doesn't deserve that.

"He came highly recommended—prior Australian Special Forces, was head of security for a Saudi prince. As I understand, quite good at hand-to-hand combat and enforcement." I don't respond, and she doesn't linger further. "I'll see what I can do."

"Thank you."

"He may have to accompany you to London, however. Then we'll change him out."

The way she says it makes it sound like we're changing a blown-out tire on a vehicle that's going to get tossed in the dump.

"Mom?"

"Yes?"

"Can you also turn my credit card back on?"

My voice is sad and pathetic. I don't know if she really loves me. If she really wants to protect me, or if all this is about control. I also can't tell if she's smug that I've come crawling back or disappointed I didn't last longer on my own. In the end, I don't care.

Stay focused. Now it's your turn to play the game.

I add a little extra. The cherry on top. "I want to do some shopping for Pop before I leave tomorrow. I don't want to use my debit card because he'll see what I spend on that one. I want what I get him to be a surprise." Eyes shut, fingers crossed.

She draws out the eerie chill on the other side of the line then finally, she says, "Yes." But then adds. "Go to Chanel while you are out. I'll have some items set aside for you to pick up. You could use some . . . *sprucing* up." I'm confident she's referring to the last time she saw me. In Berlin. As the Goth Goddess.

Not quite the same feeling of justice I felt with my grandfather, but it'll do. My eyes ease open and my fingers untangle. "That sounds perfect, Mom."

We spend a few minutes talking about some random home stuff. The one thing we don't talk about is Liam or our confrontation in Berlin or her cutting me off. There's definitely no reciprocal apology.

"Brooke?"

"Yes, Mom?"

"I love you."

I breathe deep and exhale slowly.

What is love, anyway? I no longer know.

"Love you too."

There's a long pause. Then just as we're about to hang up, I remember I wanted to ask something. "Mom, I have a quick question." She doesn't reply but rather waits for me to get on with it. "The guy, Patrick, I spoke to him a little. He said he was instructed to get 'closer' to 'confirm a few things.' What did he mean by that?"

She clears her throat. "I wanted him to ensure you were taking your meds."

Do. Not. Lose. Your. Shit.

Our agreement—the bargain—thanks to my therapist, was that I could safely go on this voyage as long as I was taking the prescription meds for my diagnosis of anxiety and depression. That's right. Pain meds for my hand and other meds for the invisible hurt that no one could see; for all the tiny little pins and needles that puncture my thoughts behind a closed curtain in my mind.

The once-a-day handful of colorful pills—so small, big impact. For my mother, this made all the sense in the world. There had to be something seriously wrong with me for the *something* to have happened—nothing she did, of course. The meds helped excuse the truth, justified her friends consoling her with things like, "Poor Brooke, lost her brother and completely fell apart. It's totally understandable that she would need therapy and meds to help her cope." A perfect pretext to divorce my mother from any culpability.

I never stopped taking them, like a good girl, even though I desperately have wanted to because they perpetuate a different kind of numbness within me.

We hang up, and I stay seated on the couch for a little while longer in total disbelief. Long enough that I think my grandfather has switched back on my debit card and my mom has turned my credit card back on so I can use them.

The clump of paper with all of my angry words and thoughts for my mother is still sitting on the coffee table.

I grab the remote that controls everything in the room and switch on the fireplace. I pick up the papers, move purposefully to the fire, and toss them in, watching them burn and disintegrate into ashes.

It's drizzling outside. I'm dressed like a bum, and I don't care. I grab an umbrella from the closet and head out. I know exactly where I'm going, no travel diary needed.

I take the elevator downstairs and am about to walk out the front of the building when the guy at the front desk calls after me.

"Miss?"

"Yeah?"

"For you. The gentleman staying with you left it for you to pick up."

I stare at the front attendant's out-stretched hand with a sealed envelope in it. The envelope very clearly says: TO: BROOKE, FROM: PATRICK.

"You can throw it away. I don't want it." My voice is cool.

"Um," the front desk attendant sounds off, clearly unprepared for this response.

"I don't need it. I'm okay. Thanks anyway," I say and walk out into the rain, leaving the umbrella behind, after all.

CHAPTER 38

I Will, Promise

I wake up early on my own. I'm splayed out in bed with the sheets and cover disheveled. I had the recurring dream, only this time I didn't shrink into the ball and fetal position in front of the fireplace. In this version of the dream, I was beating and throwing whatever I could find against the windows and doors in my desperation to escape, and the thing is—I did it. I escaped. I left home, fighting on my own.

I lie in bed, staring at the ceiling for a moment, then slowly turn over into the pillow that Patrick had used. I inhale deeply through my nose. I can smell him. It hurts. Everything hurts. But I'm doing what is best for me, or at least what I think is best for me. The good news is, I won't have to do this part on my own. I have friends. At least that part of this whole experience was real, Lauren et al.

My bags are already packed. I'm taking a private jet back to London. There's not much for me to do except shower, get dressed, and leave. The end. Grand adventure—complete.

I throw Patrick's pillow off the bed and lie there a little longer, then force myself up.

Things end. You move on.

I get dressed, only this time I try. I put on one of the new outfits my mother had set aside for me at Chanel—thank goodness there was no weird experience with the sales associates. I fix my hair and makeup. Today, I look every bit the preppy-billionaire heiress. I'm playing the game. I'm playing my part.

Obscure tennis fact: No one knows for sure why we say "love" for zero in the game of tennis. One theory is that it comes from the French term *l'oeuf,* as in "egg," which means zero. Another theory is that it comes from the Dutch saying *iets voor lof doen,* which means "no stake in the game." I tend to lean toward the latter, and I know I have a stake in this game. In fact, everything is at stake.

I make some coffee for myself and go up to the rooftop to take in the view one last time. It's a beautiful morning. The grey is gone, and the sun is out. It's as if the sky is slowly yawning and awakening after its long somber slumber all day yesterday.

I settle into a seat, sipping at my coffee, with my knees pulled up to my chest. I avoid looking at the deck and pool where too many memories linger, waiting to upend the new, grounded resolve that's taking root.

My whole life is ahead of me, and I will show them what I'm capable of.

I know where I come from. But more than that, I know who I am and who I am meant to be. I spent all day yesterday brooding, coming to terms with the obstacles I have had to face. Our whole lives, Liam and I fought to change the rules of the game. To find a way to be free, within its hold. That fight killed Liam, but I won't let it destroy me. I might not be able to change the rules, but I can play the game.

I know one thing for sure: I'm done being the good girl. The compliant daughter who does what she's told, or pouts when she doesn't get her way.

This little puppet just grabbed ahold of her strings, and she's about to pull the whole damn stage down.

I sip down the rest of my coffee and head back inside to the kitchen, feeling better than I have in a long time.

I grab my bags and head downstairs. There's a car waiting for me to take me to the airport, and as I step outside, I slide my sunglasses on like the filthy rich heiress I am. *Paris Hilton, eat your heart out.*

Standing by the car is a tall, fit guy and for a second my heart skips a beat thinking it's Patrick. He turns to me, and I see a familiar face.

"Ms. Neville," Max says with a stoic expression.

He's dressed in a suit, and it's almost impossible to imagine that only a week or so ago we were lounging in a hostel, Patrick and I flirting while he shoved his tongue down Abby's throat. *Pig.*

Max opens the back door for me, and I leave my luggage for him to put in the back of the SUV. I don't say anything in return. I ignore him completely.

As I sit there waiting for him to get in the car, it occurs to me—I've seen Max. Not in Berlin but before. In Italy. The slick-looking James Bond guy with a weird accent. Every time I saw Max in Berlin, he had his stupid backward hat on, his long blond hair poking out underneath, and was unshaven. Basically, he looked like a college jock. *Mother fucker.*

He slides into the front passenger seat as the driver starts the SUV, and I have another epiphany.

I take my sunglasses off. "So Max, did you tell all the sales associates in Berlin I was a shoplifter? Or did you just buy them off and tell them to treat me like garbage? I'm betting if I had gone into Chanel, I wouldn't have had any issues, huh?"

"Just following orders."

I slide my sunglasses back on. Control. It's always, and forever will be, about control.

We get to the airport and drive to the hangar area where privately chartered jets fly out. Max is obviously escorting me back, so he'll be on the flight with me. I don't need to ask questions. I know the deal. I've come to terms with things. For real, come to terms. The good news is the plane we're flying in is big enough that he doesn't need to sit anywhere near me.

We drive up to the tarmac, where the jet is waiting. We're about thirty minutes early from when we're scheduled to leave. Max gets out of the front seat and walks around to open my car door. I get out and walk to the back of the vehicle to grab my day bag that's alongside my other luggage to keep with me during the flight. I think he might say something to me, but he might as well be a ghost. I don't see or hear him.

We board, and I take my seat. The flight attendants ask if I'd like any food or beverages and how they can make my flight comfortable. All I ask for is headphones. Just something to listen to music with so I can tune into one of my favorite Apple music stations, which I haven't done since leaving months ago.

It doesn't take long before some Bose headphones materialize. I connect to the onboard music system and zone out.

One of the flight attendants comes back, and I ask for a glass of champagne. Why not?

I'm sitting next to a window and slide the shade up so the sun is coming in. I can see a man below load my big Osprey bag into the belly of the plane and one of the pilots walking around, doing checks.

I take the glass the attendant has brought me and turn back to the window. As I stare outside and sip my drink, I'm struck by that same steeliness of my nerves that usually only comes when I'm staring down some poor soul on the tennis court.

I'm done begging for freedom.

My sight focuses from looking out at the tarmac to the reflection staring back at me in the three-inch thick window. My mind reaches back to the girl in the painting in Berlin.

Then my mind skips and dances from Banksy's irreverent art to Patrick's motto of living the big dream. I think of Alda, singing about freedom in the words of the legendary Hoff. Of Lauren dancing like the universe is hers for the taking, and Varun watching her, the center of his universe.

We are all free, if we choose to be.

The truth of it seems painfully obvious now. But sometimes you're just too close to see what's right in front of your face.

The pilots are finished with their outside and onboard checks. We're ready to take off. One of the flight attendants comes back through to check we're all fastened in. She takes my empty flute and walks past me to where I imagine Max is sitting in a lounge chair, farther back.

The plane plods along toward the runway, and we get ready to take off. As we do, I start to shuffle through my day bag for some lip balm.

I notice right away that something has been added to my bag, something that wasn't there when I packed my things. I pull it out and see that it's the same letter the receptionist tried to hand me the day before. *Nice work, Max.*

My mouth twists. I could tear it into tiny pieces and leave the detritus for Max to find as he's walking out. I could slip it under the magazine on the coffee table in front of me, where the cleaning staff would eventually find it. Instead, I stuff it into a pocket in the side of my bag and dig to get to a small compartment at the bottom. Inside is Silver Gilt Volume II and slipped between the back pages, a different letter. This one from Liam.

The plane starts to pick up speed as I open the worn folds of the envelope and pull out the paper inside. I'm careful. This is the most precious thing I own.

I haven't read the letter since I started my grand adventure, but it seems fitting to close out my journey by reminding myself why I did all of this, even if it didn't turn out exactly the way I had planned. Rather, it turned out better.

I unfold the letter and read the last words my brother ever shared with me.

Dear Brooke,

All I can say is that I love you and I'm sorry. Live your life and find your own happiness—for you and only you. I couldn't, but I know you can.

Love you always,
L.

I inconspicuously shake my wrist. My watch, plus the new diamond studded tennis bracelet, slide down my wrist, exposing some of the same words, in the same hand-writing, forever etched in my skin: "I know you can".

The plane is lifting into the air, and my body feels the weightlessness. For once, I feel everything there is to feel, but my eyes remain dry and clear. I watch everything below me: streets, lives, homes; a million different hopes, dreams, and realities melt into the clouds.

I will, Liam. Promise.

The End

Acknowledgments

There are so many thanks to give in finally getting to this point.

To my writing coach, Cate Hogan, thank you for your patience, nurturing, and belief in my "silly" little story that I couldn't quite give up on. You gave me the courage to scrap early, bad drafts and help me bring my girl and her story to life in a meaningful way. Thank you also to Erin McClary. Your editing, insight, and keen observance to the written word and publishing industry helped refine and propel Brooke's story to the finish line. I feel so honored to have worked with you both, Cate and Erin, and I can't wait to embark on the journey again and write the next book.

I also would like to thank Alan Dino Hebel and Ian Koviak with *the*BookDesigners for taking my middle school mock-up of a cover design and turning it into something that completely exceeded my expectations and imagination. The cover absolutely embodies the very essence and heart of this book—innocence, growth, and that winding road to freedom we all yearn for.

To my dear friends, Michael, Julia, Monica, Royce, Lizo, Katie, Lia, Ashley, Margie, Jason and Savannah Hoover (with Seekees Consulting—you badass!) thank you for your honesty and support, but also your willingness to read those early, bad drafts. Brooke's story wouldn't be the same without your feedback. To my friends (and law school professors) who haven't yet read the book (or the bad drafts) but encouraged me nonetheless—thank you.

Thanks to my tennis coaches—Jen, Bill, Andy, Tami, Andres, Ernie, Josh and Al. I wouldn't be who I am today without your influence. Each of you instilled in me the drive and dedication it takes to go after dreams. You helped mold me into a competitor, a hard worker, and opened my eyes to see that tennis is more than a sport. It is love.

To my parents, I love you both, madly. There are so many things you both have given me that I'm thankful for, like putting books and a tennis racket in my hands at such a young age. But most of all, it is your love and support that I am thankful for, and the unwavering belief you instilled in me that I could embark on this writing journey and create something special.

Mom, you are in my heart, always.

To my best friend—my hubby love—John. Thank you for everything. You are my champion, my biggest cheerleader, my rock, and the person who truly sees me. I love you. I could not have done this without you. I wouldn't want to do it without you.

Lastly, to all the female athletes I grew up watching play tennis and other sports—thank you. Your journey is our journey. Keep going.

About the Author

P.M. Vance is an attorney and an officer in the U.S. Coast Guard Reserve.

When P.M. Vance isn't immersed in her latest manuscript, she's enjoying life in New Mexico with her lovely husband and stepkids, and a growing menagerie of four-legged freeloaders. And, of course, she loves playing tennis.

"GAME" is the first installment in the coming-of-age Silver Gilt fiction trilogy.

Dear Reader,

First, and foremost, I want to thank you for reading my book! I hope you enjoyed it, and I certainly hope that you will read SET, the next in the SILVER GILT trilogy.

Okay, so I have a small favor to ask (it's a teensy-tiny favor, I promise!). Whether you liked the book or not, I would be greatly appreciative if you took a few minutes to write a review and post to Amazon, Goodreads and/or any social media platforms you might be on (feel free to recycle the same review and post on any and all of those forums you might be on). As an indie author, reviews are critical to our success and growth, as well as our sustainability. Thank you in advance!

For any of my tennis readers, I want to address two items you might take issue with. One, I purposely used the standard American spelling of "racket" instead of the British spelling "racquet." Two, I acknowledge that there is actually a very strict criterion to becoming a Wimbledon ball kid/person. I promise both were written as is with intention, and I hope you stay tuned for the next installment in the trilogy to learn why . . .

Thank you again for joining Brooke's journey.

Warm Regards,
P.M. Vance